GRI␣␣␣␣␣␣␣␣␣KET

ARCADIAN BEARS, BOOK THREE

BECCA JAMESON

PROLOGUE

"You mind if I sit here?" Alton asked, his fingers wrapped around the back of the chair across from Joselyn. The question was absurd. Speaking to her at all was absurd. Approaching her was absurd. Nothing about this situation was reasonable.

And she proved his point when she lifted her gaze—just her gaze, not her face—to meet his and said, "It's a free country." Just as quickly, she lowered her deep brown eyes with the gorgeous, long lashes back toward the huge book open in front of her and tapped her pencil on the table next to a notebook. Her thick dark hair was pulled back in a ponytail, but tendrils had escaped to hang across her tanned cheeks.

The only sign he had that she cared a bit that he was standing over her was the way her shoulders stiffened and she squirmed a bit in her seat. She wore a gray cardigan, but it hung open, doing nothing to hide the cleavage of her full breasts behind the edge of a navy silk camisole.

They were in the dining centre at the University of

Calgary. The overwhelming scent of fresh pizza filled the room. He often spotted her studying there after she ate. Joselyn had just started her freshman year. Alton was a sophomore. He'd been sort of stalking her but hadn't approached her until today. His balls were big, but it took more than big balls to attempt conversation with Joselyn Arthur.

He pulled out the chair anyway, manning up to the task, and slid onto the seat. After opening his backpack and removing a random textbook, he set his elbows on the table and stared at the top of her head.

She pretended to ignore him.

The room was crowded, noisy. It was a far cry from the library. For some people, the constant hum of excitement was welcome background noise. Apparently, this was true for Joselyn.

He slid his feet forward just enough to bump into hers casually under the table as if by accident.

She yanked her legs back and jerked her face up to glare at him, her head cocked to one side. "What do you want, Alton? I'm trying to study here. I have a bio test tomorrow."

"Bio? I'm good at bio. Took it last semester. Maybe I can help?"

She narrowed her gaze. "Didn't ask for your help. I have it under control."

He was certain she did. In fact, he was certain she had everything in her life under control. She'd graduated at the top of her class last year from the same high school he went to in Silvertip, about two hours west of Calgary. She could probably teach *him* more about biology than he could *her*, but that was beside the point.

He licked his lips. He'd made the decision to go all in this afternoon, and he didn't intend to back down now.

"You know, if you took a moment to drop the snarky routine and get to know me, you might find out I'm a nice guy. Perhaps we could even be friends."

She narrowed her gaze further, shooting daggers. "Has it ever occurred to you that maybe I don't want to be friends? Maybe the snarky routine is just who I am. Why don't you go bother someone else? It's a huge campus. Surely you can find some other coed to lure into your web, Alton. It's not going to be me."

He chuckled. At least she was interacting with him. Those were the most words she'd ever shared. "What if I don't have a web?" he retorted. "What if I'm just a genuinely nice guy making polite conversation with someone from the same hometown?"

She rolled her eyes. Her fingers gripped the pencil she held so tightly, he thought it might snap in half. Her spine was rigid, and if he wasn't mistaken, she squeezed her legs together under the table. "It doesn't matter if you're a nice guy or not, now does it?"

"Doesn't it?" he challenged.

She shook her head. "No. Your desire to befriend me didn't work in elementary or junior high or high school. And it still won't work now. So, again, please, find someone else to hit on. I've got work to do." She lowered her face back to the open book and turned the page, dropping the pencil, setting her chin on one palm, and staring intently at the paper.

Alton had no intention of giving up so easily. In all honesty, he didn't see it as a choice at all. It was reasonable and even expected that she would ignore him at school in Silvertip, but they were not at home now, and he intended to break through her thick exterior and get to know her now that they were at university.

Attending U of C had been a bit of a gamble for him.

He had hoped and prayed she would also choose the same university. For one thing, it was the largest university in the area. For another thing, both her older brothers had gone there. It was a safe bet.

And here she was.

He leaned closer, breathing in her scent. This was the closest he'd been to her in a long time, and it was both torturous and heavenly. "How about we make a deal?"

She groaned, shooting him another irritated look. "A deal? This isn't a game show, Alton. This is my life. I don't want to make a deal with you."

"Hear me out." He glanced around to make sure no one was listening to him and lowered his voice. "There aren't a lot of shifters here. It's nice to have a few friends who are of the same species."

She interrupted him. "We are not friends, Alton."

Damn, she was difficult. Why the hell was he putting himself through this again? He knew the answer. Maybe if he badgered her with the details… "That's true. We're far more than friends, and you know it. You're my—"

Her eyes widened. She cut him off with a hand out in front of her and the most furious glare he'd ever seen. "Stop. Don't say it." She then slapped her palm against the table with enough force for several people to turn their attention toward the two of them. She lowered her voice, gritting her perfect teeth and leaning across the table. "I swear to God, Alton. Enough is enough."

He grinned. "So you'll take my deal?"

She jerked back several inches, gripping the edge of the table with her fingers hard enough they turned white. "What the hell are you talking about?"

He smiled wider. Oh yeah. She was totally going to take his deal. "You stop acting like you can't stand the sight of

4

me and make nice to me on a regular basis, and I won't mention what we both know out loud."

She licked her lips. He had her. The trouble was he was making this shit up on the fly and had no idea how he was going to be able to uphold his end of the bargain. How long could she hold out?

Finally, she bit the corner of her lip and then spoke. "You want to be friends," she deadpanned, not wording it as a question.

"Yes." *For now.*

She leaned back farther, pondering the deal as she lifted her arms and crossed them. "Fine. Let's hear it. What do you propose?"

Shit. Now he had to make something up. He swallowed and laid down his terms. "You study with me two nights a week, and I take you to dinner twice a month."

She groaned, rolling her head back and looking at the ceiling. "I don't even like you."

Liar. He reached across the table, intending to grab her biceps so she would look at him.

As if lightning had struck the room, Joselyn jerked out of his reach so fast she nearly tipped the chair over backward. She unfolded her arms and held her hands out at her sides. "Don't."

"Jesus, Jos. What the hell?" Did she think he had leprosy or something?

She ignored the strange outburst and continued speaking. "Fine. Here are my terms." She stared at his outstretched hand until he pulled it back. "We study together *one* night a week for not more than two hours. You can take me to dinner *one* night a month—someplace nice—for not more than three hours. But," she narrowed her gaze again as if making sure he was paying close attention, "you don't ever mention anything beyond friendship, *and*," she added with extreme emphasis, "you never touch me."

Damn, she led a hard bargain. His cock stiffened to the point of pain, and he smiled. "Deal."

CHAPTER 1

Six years later...

Alton Tarben lifted his snout to the air and took a long whiff. Yep. She was nearby. Somewhere on the mountain. No denying it. He hesitated for a moment, wondering if it was a good idea to chase her down today. He shouldn't. He should turn around, tromp back down the mountain, and get as far away from her as possible.

Confronting her was never a good plan. Not six years ago or ten years ago or anytime in between. But damn if he could stop himself. And besides, what was she doing on his family's property? Curiosity got the better of him.

Had she scented him yet?

He blocked himself, hoping to catch her off guard, and turned to head her direction. Loping between the trees on the side of the mountain, he remained in his grizzly form. His paws crunched in the thin layer of frozen snow, broken branches, and fallen leaves.

He hadn't seen her in months. Four to be precise. His

body came to life as he tracked her, awakening from the permanent state of discomfort he lived in without her in his life. It pissed him off.

Joselyn Arthur.

His mate.

A fact they both denied, though Joselyn did so with an intensity that far surpassed *his* ability to shut her out.

He'd known she was his since third grade. Originally, he'd ignored the pull toward her with as much vehemence as she did him. And, truth be told, he should continue to do so until death.

She wasn't right for him. Nor was he right for her. Their families had a history that wasn't pleasant. Insurmountable history that made it impossible for them ever to be together. And who was to say she was truly his anyway? So what if he'd had a weird vibe indicating so for most of his life?

He didn't put much merit in Fate. Neither of them did. Grizzly shifters, in general, didn't. It happened. Sometimes Fate seemed to have a hand in who bound with whom. It had happened more lately than reasonable. But it was rare.

He told himself for the millionth time that Joselyn Arthur was nothing more than a sexy woman whose body called to him with enough force to make his dick stiffen just thinking about her. Didn't mean he had to bind to her for God's sake. But he sure would like to fuck her at some point just to see what would happen. Maybe work her out of his system so he could move on with his life.

He shuddered. The idea was preposterous. What he needed to do was find a lovely woman in town who wasn't a member of the Arthur pack and bind himself to *her*, essentially cutting off all possibility of ever knowing what could have been.

But he was a fool.

He inhaled deeply over and over as her scent grew stronger. His paws covered a lot of ground in a short time. She was alone. He hated the idea of her running alone in bear form in the mountains. It wasn't safe, but he had no say in her life—a fact she reminded him of every time he saw her.

For five minutes he knew she was in her grizzly form, but when he finally popped out of a copse of evergreens, yards away from her, he came to a grinding halt.

Joselyn was leaning against a tree, human, arms crossed, dark brown eyes narrowed, glaring at him. A light breeze blew her thick brown hair around her face. Her serious expression always made his heart ache. So rarely had he seen her smile that he couldn't remember the last time.

He slowly approached, still in his bear form, knowing it was easier to hide his reaction to seeing her if he did so. Damn, she was gorgeous. Every time he saw her, she was prettier than the last. Even angry, she made his heart race.

Her hair was pulled back in a ponytail—as it nearly always was. He'd seen it down only a handful of times in recent years, and it made him salivate with the desire to run his hands through it. He couldn't decide if she didn't care much about her appearance, if she intentionally chose to hide her beauty, or if she did it to keep him at bay in particular.

No matter which of those theories was correct, she failed miserably. She would look fantastic even in a sack. Pulling her hair back wet in a ponytail—as he knew she did most mornings—did nothing to hide her inner or her outer beauty, no matter what her intentions were.

Her eyes were melted chocolate that reached into his soul. Her round face was always a gorgeous tan color even in winter. Thick lashes that didn't need mascara were the envy of many women.

She rolled her eyes as he approached. "How long have you been tracking me?"

He chuckled into her head. *"How long have I failed to block you?"*

"You gonna circle me all day like I'm some sort of prey, or do you have the balls to shift and face me as a man?"

He stopped two feet in front of her and cocked his head to one side. She was feisty. He wanted to laugh, but he feared it would piss her off further. Instead, he summoned the change, closed his eyes, and allowed his body to make the shift from bear form to human.

As his fur receded and his bones reconfigured, he lifted up onto his hind legs. Fifteen seconds later he stood before her, fully human. Thank God he'd worn a winter coat and boots. It was damn cold out to be shifting into human form this high in the mountains.

Luckily, Joselyn had also ventured out prepared for the possibility of shifting. She wore fucking sexy tight jeans, boots, and a thick, navy down coat with her brewery's logo on the breast—a depiction of a glacier next to a lake. Apropos, since her pack owned Glacial Brewing Company.

As he met her gaze head on, he watched her breath, smoky in the air around her. Every exhale was closer together. He affected her as much as she affected him.

"How have you been?" he asked.

She sighed. "Small talk? Really, Alton?"

He shrugged. "It's the usual way people start a conversation when they greet each other after several months."

"I'm all right," she shot back. "The usual. Busy with work. Yourself?"

"The same." He hated this thing they did. This game they played. The same game they'd played for years.

Today things were markedly more strained between them. The lure to pull her into his arms was stronger than ever. Though he shouldn't be shocked. It had grown incrementally over the years.

He'd known for certain the pull would be stronger now than the last time he'd seen her several months ago. He should have turned around and fled instead of approaching. But she was like a giant magnet. He couldn't seem to stop himself.

For long moments, they stared at each other, neither blinking.

"You're on my parents' land." He tried to sound irritated.

She looked past him and shrugged, her gaze turning to take in the spectacular view of the distant, snow-covered mountains, the valleys between, and the perfect blue skyline. He didn't need to glance that way to know what she saw.

When she reached up to tuck an escaped curl behind her ear, he lifted his hand automatically. He needed to touch it, feel the strands between his fingers.

She jumped to the side to avoid his touch. "Don't," she mumbled.

He dropped his hand. "Sorry." It was a permanent rule of hers. No touching.

She lowered her gaze, toeing the thin layer of snow under her boot absentmindedly. "You shouldn't have followed me. It only makes things worse."

Is that what she believed? If she didn't want him to find her, why was she standing on his property?

He ignored the obvious. "What are you afraid of?" He stepped closer, goading her. And himself. "Perhaps, you should give in." How many times had they had this discussion? It was cryptic, but she knew what he meant. On occasion, over the years, he had forced her to discuss the attraction between them. Test it. Feel it out. Purge it. As if that were possible.

He watched her trembling, knowing he was getting to her. Again.

She lifted her head slowly. "There's no such thing as Fate. Stop acting like we're destined or something. It's nothing but a physical draw. It happens all the time. Even to humans. I'm sure if we threw in the towel and fucked, we'd realize all this posturing had been for nothing."

He flinched at the flippant way she used the word *fuck* when he knew full well it wasn't an everyday vocabulary word in her repertoire. He stared at her for several seconds, trying to decide how to respond to her absurd statement. After licking his lips, he spoke again. "First of all, you know that's crap. Even though not every single grizzly shifter is easily aware of their mate—and certainly not at such a young age—it does happen."

She pursed her lips.

He continued, leaning closer to her. "And don't even try to make light of the passion between us as if a one-night stand would put an end to the curiosity and mystery. If you truly believe we could walk away after having sex, then let's put it to the test." He lifted a brow, challenging her.

What the hell was wrong with him? Why was he pushing her to do something *he* agreed wasn't in their best interest?

She flinched. "Not a chance in hell, Alton. You've lost your mind."

"Afraid you might be wrong?" he continued to prod.

"What difference would it make? Our families would both flip their lids and explode if they ever caught wind of the fact that we'd been in communication at all, let alone slept together."

She wasn't wrong. And there was a good chance he had lost his mind. But some days he simply didn't care anymore.

At least she didn't refer to their joining as fucking again. That got on his nerves. He stepped closer, closing the gap between them to inches.

She retreated, shuffling backward farther than he'd approached. She held out a hand. "Stop. You promised."

He nodded. "I did. And I'll keep that promise for as long as you insist, but I'm growing weary, Jos."

"Then you shouldn't track me. You're the one who made things worse today by hunting me down."

He nodded again, slowly. "Perhaps you wanted to be found. After all, as I pointed out, you're on my land. I could turn you in for breaking the treaty," he added as if he would ever do such a thing.

She shot him a glare and pursed her lips for a moment before speaking again. "Accident. My bad. Wasn't paying attention. Don't read anything into it."

She was lying. He could sense it. "Fine. But come on. We used to at least be friends, civil toward each other. Now you won't even take my calls."

He'd stopped trying months ago when she stopped responding to even his texts. A man could only endure so much rejection.

She lowered her gaze again, her fingers reaching to tuck that same errant lock of hair behind her ear. It immediately bounced free again.

"Jos, it's simple. We have no choice but to explore this thing. You know it as well as I do." He'd never been this blunt with her before, and he had no idea why he was doing so now. It was a horrible idea. He knew it. She knew it.

She didn't acknowledge him.

"Been dating a lot lately?" he asked, knowing the answer. Silvertip, Alberta, wasn't large enough for anyone to keep their dating habits a secret.

She flinched. "Of course not," she told the ground. And then, as if realizing how odd she'd worded that statement, she rushed to cover it up, "I've been busy at work. A lot is going on."

He knew that was true. She worked hard. Always had. Even when they'd been away at the University of Calgary, she'd been a workaholic. He wasn't entirely sure her work ethic back then and still to this day had anything to do with an actual desire to be an overachiever so much as a deep-seated need to avoid the truth. About him. About them. About their future.

In all honesty, he too had ignored that truth for many years, and if he had any sense, he would continue to do so, but he was tired of fighting the pull. Fighting with her. He needed to know for sure. In his heart, he'd known she was his for many years, but was it only lust? Could it possibly be abated? And, more importantly, what would that entail? He knew the answer to that question without voicing it out loud.

Nothing could happen between them. He reminded himself of that often. And yet... He was hardheaded when it came to Joselyn. His loyalty lay with his pack, his family, his ancestors. The ties that bound him to his family were tight. As were the same ropes that tethered her to her pack. Strangling them.

The Arthurs did not mix with the Tarbens. Ever. It had been that way for over a century, and it would continue to be that way forever. Any attempt to defy that truth would only end in heartbreak for both of them. The attempt alone could alienate them from their town, their parents, their siblings, everyone.

And yet...

"I'm never going to give up, Jos," he whispered. "I can't. We've been back in Silvertip over a year. I miss seeing you. Talking to you."

"I know," she conceded. She licked her lips, staring intently at his before jerking her gaze back to his eyes. "It's hard."

"What's hard? Life in general, or denying your mate?"

She winced. "You can't know for sure we're meant to bind together."

He didn't answer. The only way he could respond would have been to contradict her, and doing so would infuriate her. Instead, he tried another tactic. "I miss you, Jos. We used to be friends at least. Please, take my calls. Answer my texts."

She swallowed hard. "Okay."

Finally. Headway.

He lifted a brow. Would she? Or was she simply saying what she knew he wanted to hear?

All through university, they'd been in contact. Like a forbidden fruit, they'd skirted the truth. Ignored the facts. Intentionally.

When they'd been younger, he'd agreed with her. His family would have wigged out if he'd made any overtures of intending to bind to a member of the Arthur pack. The feud between their families was over a century in the making and ran so deep that many of the older generation harbored a grudge so absurd it made Alton's skin crawl.

When they'd gotten away from Silvertip, they'd at least started speaking. Of course, this was due in large part to his bargaining skills—or what she preferred to refer to as blackmail.

Alton took things incredibly slow with her. For one thing, in theory, he agreed. They couldn't possibly end up together. However, he'd been drawn enough to ensure they saw each other often. He'd been a sophomore when she started at U of C. He'd moved into an apartment. Alone. Intentionally? Perhaps deep inside he'd always wanted the door to be open to the possibility she would one day be his. And he certainly didn't want to have to contend with a roommate if and when that day came.

But it didn't. Joselyn was serious about her convictions from the beginning. She insisted he never touch her, and she held on to that persistence the entire five years. Nothing about their relationship had ever been conventional.

He sighed. "Okay?" Hope.

She nodded. "I don't have many friends. I could use one. No one has to know." She narrowed her gaze. "But that's it, Alton. Friends. Stop badgering me for more. I won't give in. Besides, it would ruin our friendship."

Such as it was.

He missed her laughter. The way her hair fell around her face the few times she wore it down. The way she tucked her feet under her when she concentrated on her homework. He'd never had more than a strict friendship with her, taking what she would offer and not complaining. At least not often.

He hated that she didn't have friends, but who was he kidding? He didn't have many close relationships, either. His sibling and parents, but not many outside friends.

He knew the reason why too. His world was consumed with Joselyn. He had few other thoughts. If he couldn't share this thing with her, what else was there to discuss?

Besides, any close friend would wonder why he chose not to date or turned down offers to go out for a beer.

Alton Tarben spent his days in his own family's rival brewery, Mountain Peak Brewery. He worked long hours, and when he wasn't at the office, he filled his time running in the mountains in bear form or working out in human form. He did anything and everything to avoid thinking about Joselyn.

Her life mirrored his. He was sure of it. And she'd just admitted she didn't have close friends either.

"I'll call. You'll answer. We'll talk."

She nodded. Was she merely humoring him?

He fought the urge to reach out and touch her. It was stronger than ever. This futile attempt to deny him by avoiding skin-on-skin contact was driving him mad.

She stepped back, her hands shaking with nervousness. "I gotta go." Without another word, she shifted into her grizzly form and dashed off into the trees, leaving him standing there unable to move.

Hope. Was this a good thing? Or would renewed contact with her only drive him more insane than he already was?

CHAPTER 2

Joselyn stared at her phone one week later, flipping it around and around and then gripping it tighter to smooth her thumb over the text she'd received two minutes ago from Alton.

Can you talk?

He would text her like that first without calling. He wasn't insensitive to the fact that she lived with her parents and would need to ensure she was alone in her room to take a call.

At the moment, she was alone. It was nine thirty at night. She had retreated to her room as she did most nights to read or watch television.

She stared at the message again. She wanted to hear his voice. Desperately. But was it a good idea?

Discussing work would be totally off limits. They'd established that rule when they finished school and returned to Silvertip to join their respective family breweries. But the situation at her job was currently far more stressful than usual, and no way in hell could she bring it up.

Talking to Alton made her feel like a traitor to her pack. While her family was in the beginning stages of developing a fresh new competitive product, leaking even one detail would be devastating.

At the same time, any conversation with Alton in which she intentionally chose not to discuss her pack's business would also feel unfaithful to him as even a friend. It made her cringe.

She should not be speaking to a member of the competition for any reason. And she sure as shit should not be experiencing such a dry mouth, tight nipples, and wet panties at the prospect of hearing his voice while she lay in her bed under the covers. She moaned out loud as she rubbed her legs together. *Fuck.*

Thoughts of Alton always made her horny. She used him as her muse every time she masturbated. It was unavoidable. His image crept into her head against her will.

She'd never so much as touched the man, but the effort to avoid doing so took an immense amount of willpower.

What was the worst that could happen? She asked herself the question for the millionth time, knowing full well what the answer was. Sparks could fly, igniting a passion she was powerless to avoid. And Heaven only knew where one touch would lead. Undoubtedly in seconds, they would find themselves naked, their bodies pressed together at every possible point of contact.

Could they flush the need out of their systems and move on with life? She'd asked herself that question a million times also. And the answer was undoubtedly *no*. She feared he was right and they were meant to be together.

But why would Fate play such a cruel joke on them?

She came from a close-knit family. She loved them. As the youngest of three and the only daughter, she had spent her life doted on by her parents and brothers. Though she rarely heard them speak directly ill of the Tarbens, she couldn't be sure how they would respond to finding out she had befriended one of them.

The same was not true of the rest of her pack. Her father's two younger brothers held on to their feud with the Tarbens as if their life depended on it. She'd heard so many ridiculous stories in her lifetime that she had no idea which were valid and which were total fabrications.

The bottom line was that at some point more than one hundred years ago, the two families fought over land and water. Someone from one pack claimed someone from the other pack encroached on their property, and an all-out war began. Every time any member of one family ran into a member of the other pack in town, they would end up in a brawl.

Over time, tensions grew until blood was shed. Joselyn shuddered at the memory of the lore. She hated thinking about it. It gave her a sick feeling in her stomach every time. Until both packs were willing to come to a truce and let the past go, nothing would ever change.

And yet the animosity survived. Relationships between the packs were strictly forbidden. Even friendships. Who knew what would happen if something even more serious resulted from communicating with a Tarben?

Joselyn shuddered, still staring at her phone.

In her soul, she didn't believe any member of her immediate family would deny her whatever her heart desired, but the rest of her pack was another story. The feud ran deep. Fraternizing with the perceived enemy would cause a battle.

Sleeping with one of them would cause a war. And she couldn't imagine what would happen if she bound herself for life to a Tarben. Half the pack would probably self-combust.

She should not take his call. Pure torture. She should send him a snarky message and nip the idea of renewing her friendship with him in the bud.

It was one thing to hang out with him while they were at U of C. No one was around to discover them. But they were back in Silvertip now. Those days were over. So was that friendship. Why the hell had she agreed to renew communication with him last week?

She thought about her response. Spun the phone around in her hand for a few minutes. She should ignore the text. Tell him no. Tell him to stop stalking her. Tell him to find someone else to badger.

Instead...

Sure.

She hit Send on the text before she could chicken out.

Two seconds later, her phone rang. She took a deep breath and answered. "Hey," she whispered. Her voice came out unintentionally husky. It wasn't as if her parents could hear her conversation from the other side of the house. She cringed, not wanting to give him the wrong idea.

"Hey, yourself." He sounded winded. "How was your day?"

"Busy." She soaked in his voice as if she could store it for later. Every tone was memorized anyway. She had no trouble conjuring his words in her mind anytime she desired. And judging from the pulsing of her clit between her squeezed thighs, tonight would require a vibrator and memories of his soft voice filtering into her mind before she could relax enough to sleep.

"Me too. Why did I ever think two engineering degrees was a reasonable decision? Some days I'm pulled in two directions like a rubber band. It's possible I might snap."

She smiled.

For several moments, neither of them spoke. She heard his rapid breathing. It matched her own. Her stomach was in knots. She needed to shore up her libido and keep her feelings to herself. This friendship thing wasn't going to work. She could already tell. She should never have taken his call.

Work. Vague work conversation was a good thing.

"You think coming home to take the spot of marketing director right out of college has been a walk in the park?" she asked. "Seems like I spend more than half my time proving myself. I have to work twice as long and twice as hard to get my job done. At least half my family doesn't think I can do the job, nor do they trust me. It's infuriating."

"Damn. I'm sorry. At least I don't have to contend with that. My family respects me. Do you think it's because you're a woman?" he asked. She could hear the tentative tone of his voice. He didn't mean to insinuate they would be right. He was merely inquiring.

She sighed, pressing her thighs together as she closed her eyes. Why did he have to be so damn kind? "Probably. Plus there's some grumbling of nepotism."

He chuckled. "Nepotism? That's crazy. Everyone working in your brewery is a member of your pack. Same as mine. How could anyone accuse you of benefiting from nepotism?"

He was right, but he didn't understand the dynamics.

"Because my father's the CEO and pack leader. He gave me this job. Two of my uncles think I spend the day coloring."

"What?" Alton's voice rose in anger. "What ignorance. My father is also pack leader and CEO, but no one has accused me of being incompetent."

"Probably because your degree is in a respectable field with visible results," she pointed out.

"Marketing is respectable. And do they not realize you worked your ass off in school to also get a business degree?"

A flutter that started in her belly when she answered the phone crawled up to include her heart. Why did he have to be so reasonable and supportive? She needed to end this call before she said something she would regret.

"Jos?" The way he said her name made her breath catch. It always did.

"I'm still here." She sighed. "I should go."

"No. Please, Jos. Don't hang up."

She bit her lip, fighting a new emotion—sadness. His tone was desperate. This thing… This thing between them had to stop. Why did she keep torturing herself like this?

"Jos?" His pitch was higher this time.

"Yeah."

"Meet me somewhere."

"That's not a good idea. If someone caught us…" It was a bad idea for many reasons far more important than anyone seeing them.

"No one will catch us. I stumbled upon this old rundown cabin. It's just one room, hidden among the trees. No idea how long it's been there or who it belongs to, but whoever it is hasn't been to it for years."

Was he asking her to meet him in private in the mountains?

"I'm gonna clean it up a bit. I want you to meet me there."

She groaned. "Alton, that's a horrible plan, and you know it."

"What I know is that we're more than friends. What I know is that I need a bigger piece of you. What I know is that it's futile to deny the pull and ignore it forever. We've played that game. It's not working. Meet me."

"And do what, Alton?" She pushed herself to sitting on the bed, one arm going across her chest to squeeze her puckered nipples as she chased thoughts of being alone with Alton from her mind. "You think if we secretly start meeting somewhere, things will be all better between us?"

"I think we owe it to ourselves to explore the possibilities. Yes."

She shook her head, drawing her knees up to press more firmly against her breasts. "No." The cost of giving in to his demands was too high. Her pack. Her family. Her job. Her life. She couldn't do that to herself or her family.

"Jos." His voice was softer. Gentle. "I have so many questions."

"Alton." She mimicked him. "I don't want the answers. They won't change anything. In fact, they'll make things worse."

"Baby, please."

She jerked, her spine straightening at his use of such an intimate endearment. He'd never used that word before. It was too familiar, insinuating they had something much deeper than a passing secret friendship.

She couldn't breathe. She pulled the phone from her ear and stared at it as if it were personally responsible for contaminating her with an incurable disease. To avoid the possibility, she ended the call and dropped the phone on the bed next to her.

For long moments, she stared at the cell, holding her breath. Finally, she gasped. Tears ran down her face. Why?

Because that one word reached inside her and clutched her soul in its grip. She was lonely and probably depressed. For months she had ignored those facts, but speaking to Alton brought them to the surface.

She needed more out of life. She deserved more. And as long as she allowed herself to hold on to even the illusion of a friendship with Alton Tarben, she was holding herself back from happiness.

She had to stop talking to him. End this madness. After years of skirting the edge of something she couldn't deny happening between them, it was time to cut the strings and pull her life together.

She reached for the lamp next to her bed to turn it off and slid back under the covers. There was no way to ignore the voice in her head. *Baby…*

One word.

A plea. A breath. A sigh. Possessive. Endearing. Cherishing.

He had no right to claim her.

The pulsing between her legs grew as the word rang out over and over in her mind. She spread her knees apart and reached between her thighs to stroke herself over the thin barrier of her panties.

Oh, God.

Tipping her head back, she bit her lower lip to keep from making any noise. Her parents were nowhere near her room, but she didn't like to take chances with them.

Why was she still living at home? She made decent money. Could she get a place in town and have some privacy?

She knew the answer to the question. Answers, really. For one, Alton had talked her into returning to her parents' home when they'd left university. He said he didn't like the idea of her being alone somewhere. It wasn't safe. He insinuated he would feel the same about his sisters or any woman.

Or had he only wanted to know where she was and ensure it was harder for her to date?

She moaned as she dipped her fingers under the lace of her panties and tapped her clit. Squeezing her eyes shut, she admitted to herself that Alton's desires matched her own. She had no desire to date another man. Living with her parents made it that much more challenging.

She was twenty-four years old, a grown woman. She had a fantastic job and was banking every dollar she made. For what?

No way in hell was she going to answer that question.

Instead, she let her mind go, stroking her finger over her clit. Her thoughts went to Alton, as they always did. Visions of him touching her even though he'd never once touched her skin at all.

A part of her assumed she had blown up any contact with him to the point that actually having sex with him would be a disappointment.

Yep. She would continue to tell herself that. Keep him at arm's length. No. Push him further away.

When she dipped her finger into her channel, wetness ran out to coat her hand. She added a second finger, imagining the two of them being one of Alton's. What would it feel like to have him inside her, his mouth on her ear? *Baby...*

She dug her heels into the mattress and lifted her hips off the bed as she removed her fingers from her pussy and flicked them rapidly over her clit. Lately, she didn't even need a vibrator to get off quickly. The addition of that one word to her mental repertoire would have her coming easily for weeks. And it wasn't even imaginary. It was real.

When she reached the edge of sanity, tipping over, she flattened her fingers against her clit and pressed firmly against the pulsing. Slowly, she lowered her butt onto the bed, still gasping for air.

Baby…

She definitely could not meet Alton Tarben in a secluded cabin.

She removed her fingers from her panties, pulled the covers over her shoulders, and curled onto her side. Her body still shook from the intensity of the orgasm. Sweat coated her skin.

Concentrating on nothing but breathing, she finally slid into a deep sleep.

CHAPTER 3

Joselyn Arthur gasped as she was yanked awake by yet another nightmare. She bolted to sitting and twisted around as if looking for something…or someone.

She was alone, like always. The sun was streaming into her bedroom.

Sweat beaded on her forehead from the stress of the damn dream she'd had every night for the past week. The same dream she'd had with relative frequency the last few months she'd been at U of C. Something about her renewed contact with Alton brought it back to the surface.

She didn't even know what the dream was about. It always evaporated the moment she woke up. But it left her with an enormous sense of loss, as if someone she knew had died or was missing.

Dragging herself out of bed, she tried to calm her nerves by starting her morning routine. Shower. Dressing. Minimal primping. Coffee. It all happened in that order. It also happened in a rapid frenzy nearly every day because she was always late.

Mornings were not her friend. Never had been. One of many sticking points at the brewery. Some members of her pack would look for any reason to express their discontent about her. Never mind that she always stayed late and then took work home. They ignored those facts.

The truth was Joselyn kept her mind occupied for as many hours of the day as she could until she was ready to drop dead of exhaustion. When she finally did collapse into bed, she often had trouble shutting her mind down enough to fall asleep. It was little wonder she had trouble waking up.

By nine o'clock, she stepped into the front office attached to the brewery and nodded at the receptionist. "Morning, Liddie."

Liddie's smile was broad. "Morning, Joselyn." She didn't say a word about the hour or the fact that most of the rest of the office staff had been there since seven. Liddie knew Joselyn well. She also knew how late Joselyn stayed in the evenings.

As Joselyn headed down the hallway toward her office, muffled voices caught her attention. She stopped walking as the hair on the back of her neck stood on end. The door to her Uncle Carroll's office was ajar, and he was in an apparently heated discussion with her Uncle Jaren.

She should have kept moving, but something gave her pause.

"I don't like it," Carroll was saying. "Too many people know about the new product. Someone's going to leak information about it, and then we'll lose the upper hand."

Joselyn didn't move a muscle, hoping no one else stepped into the hall and found her eavesdropping. She knew what her uncles were discussing—the launch of Glacial Lemon and Glacial Orange. A huge company secret everyone hoped would give Glacial Brewing Company the upper hand over their main competition, Alton's family business, Mountain Peak Brewery.

The Arthur pack was tight. Always had been. Why would her uncles think someone would leak information to the competition?

And more importantly, how was this leak life or death? Sure, it would be nice to be the first to launch a new product and corner the market, but the way her uncles discussed the secret made it sound like it was a matter of national security.

Venom filled their words, making her shudder. Their deep ingrained hatred for the Tarbens made it difficult for Joselyn to swallow or breathe. The constant reminder that she was tiptoeing into forbidden territory even speaking to Alton made her light-headed.

Carroll continued, "Some of the younger generation are not as devoted to the pack. I don't trust them, especially Bernard's damn daughter," he hissed.

Joselyn winced. What the hell? What had she ever done to deserve their wrath? There was no way they knew anything about her relationship with Alton, such as it was.

Jaren spoke next. "You think she'd tell someone?"

"Of course. She's the one taking all the photographs and making her stupid marketing posters. It would be too easy for her to show them to someone."

"Seems a bit harsh to accuse her of something she hasn't done, Carroll." At least Jaren wasn't acting like a complete fool.

Carroll laughed sardonically. "I don't know why we need a marketing department in the first place. We've done fine without all this damn advertising for thirty years. Bernard's damn daughter graduates with her highfalutin degree, and suddenly we can't live without her sketches."

Sketches?

Joselyn's face heated to the point she might explode. Fuck both of them. *Sketches my ass.*

The orange and lemon malt beverages were still in the early stages of development. It had only been weeks since the first product had been taste-tested. Since that time, she'd been working her ass off to put together a marketing plan that would wow both Silvertip and the surrounding towns.

What Joselyn wanted was to be at the forefront of a product launch that would spread like wildfire to more than just Silvertip or even Alberta. To do that, they needed an amazing marketing plan.

Ignoring her uncles, she marched past Carroll's office, heading for her own. She would show them what good marketing could do for a product. The challenge was on.

No sooner had she dropped her briefcase on her chair and flipped on her computer than her mother entered the room. "You okay?"

Joselyn lifted her gaze, trying to school her face into something less angry. She wouldn't tell her mother or her father about the exchange she'd overheard. She was a grown woman and would prove her worth on her own. No sense adding to the problem by tattling to the CEO. Doing so would only piss her father off and send him slamming into his brother's office to demand respect.

Carroll would take out even more of his mistrust on Joselyn, and the strain among family members would grow incrementally.

Nope. She would prove her worth on her own merit. "I'm fine," she told her mother.

Rosanne tipped her head to one side, eyeing her daughter with doubt. "Okay, well, team meeting in the conference room in ten." She turned and left the room without further comment on Joselyn's bad mood.

Joselyn lowered herself onto her chair, taking deep breaths to rein in her aggravation. She would never become a company leak under any circumstances. She wouldn't even give anyone reason to suspect her. Easy. She was rarely in the presence of anyone in Silvertip at all. All of her hours were spent at the office or in her parents' home. Except for an occasional shift to her grizzly form to run free and blow off steam, she was the picture of a perfect team player.

Too bad she had to work so hard to prove her worth.

Was Alton right? Was her uncle's distrust based on the fact she was female? Or was he simply a crotchety old man who had nothing better to do than grumble and complain?

As if thinking about Alton could conjure him, her phone buzzed with an incoming text. Sure enough, she lifted the cell to see AT across the top, her way of knowing any incoming text or call was from the enemy and keep wandering eyes from knowing.

The slight method of hiding his name was probably futile since Alton's father and all four of his siblings also had the initials AT. Wouldn't take a rocket scientist to decipher her stupid code. Then again, no one ever touched her phone. She was the only person with the password, and she never left the cell unattended.

Hope you made it to work okay. Not sure why you hung up on me. I'll call you tonight.

In her mind, the three sentences were spoken in his gentle, caring tone, and they ended with *baby*.

She shuddered. There was no way she could take his

call later that night. This thing had to end before it started. Just seeing his words was a reminder of why nothing could happen between the two of them.

Two different worlds. Two different packs. Even though neither of them personally cared about the stupid rivalry between their families, Joselyn wasn't about to risk her pack's wrath by cavorting with the enemy at this crucial juncture in her brewery's standing.

The product launch was perfect. No other brewery in the area had a similar product. It would be a huge success, and Joselyn intended to be recognized for her efforts as a valuable team player. One who put her family first.

Nope. She wouldn't take Alton's call that night. And she sure as shit couldn't meet him in the woods at some secluded cabin where his pheromones would fill the room and tempt her to drop her inhibitions and make the biggest mistake of her life.

Alton was exhausted when he fell onto his couch that night. He didn't bother with the lights or turn on the television. He sat in silence, staring at the ceiling, looking for answers.

What was the matter with him? He knew better than to pursue Joselyn. He understood how worried she was about disrupting her pack by cavorting with the enemy, so to speak.

Hell, he knew firsthand. His pack was no different. His family was as divided as hers. Deep-seated anger toward the Arthur pack ran thick in their veins.

He'd known since he was about ten years old that the cute little dark-haired girl running around on the playground was off limits. He'd ignored the pull toward her for years before finally speaking to her in high school. Their initial conversations were stilted, both of them glancing around to make sure no one knew they were talking to each other.

At the University of Calgary, he'd thrown himself into his studies and then gotten his own apartment the second year so he could nurture this forbidden friendship with the gorgeous girl who was finally a woman.

He had no idea what he was getting himself into. It was stupid on his part to be so fixated on a woman he could not have. But she was never far from his mind, and truth be told, she was much stronger than him. It was Joselyn who set the rules. It was Joselyn who insisted he never touch her. It was Joselyn who made all the calls about when and where they met.

He let her because he had no other options. To admit to anyone that she controlled him so thoroughly would force him to hand in his man card. But she was stubborn and dug her heels in about taking things any further.

In his mind, when he'd initially propositioned her at U of C, he'd imagined wearing her down with his charm and wit. Every time he was near her, his feelings grew more intense. He prayed the same was true for Joselyn. But she never wavered.

Any time he pushed her, she retreated for weeks. The few times he mentioned she was his mate, she freaked out. Once she didn't speak to him for more than a month.

He couldn't live without whatever she would give him, so he accepted her conditions and kept his lips closed. In exchange, she studied with him, laughed with him, watched TV with him. He took it. He rarely pushed for more.

And he was dying a slow death inside.

It wasn't as if his situation was any different. He recognized it. His own family was a hot mess too. If he announced he was in a relationship with an Arthur, there was a chance he would lose his job and possibly his home in Silvertip.

But goddammit. He knew in his soul she was his. How long could this go on? And more importantly, what other option did he have? He would not force her to see reason. She would resent him for the rest of their lives if he tried to prove his point by touching her or hauling her into his arms.

He'd give anything to set his lips on hers and taste her essence. His confidence that there would be no denying the connection afterward was so high he'd bet his life on it. But it might be his very life he would have to exchange for the chance to find out. So he waited.

He stared at his phone. Should he text her? He'd said he would.

Not for the first time, he was angry. With her. With the situation. With their respective packs. With the universe.

Fuck it. He needed to stop pining over this woman and move on. Behaving like a lost puppy was making him look like a fool and getting him nowhere. If she wanted to be stubborn, let her.

He didn't need her. There were thousands of other women in the area who would be perfectly happy to date him. All he needed to do was pick one out, turn his way of thinking around, and choose a mate. The sooner he bound himself to someone, the sooner he would rid himself of this incessant need to have the one woman he would never have.

She'd made herself clear. Plenty of times. He was only friend material. Nothing more. And a secret friend at that.

He was done.

He lifted his phone and launched it across the room. It landed on the armchair with a slight bounce, doing no harm to the device. Fuck. He couldn't even perfect the simple destruction of property to feed his aggravation.

Enough was enough already.

CHAPTER 4

Two months later…

Alton paced the floor of the small abandoned cabin hidden between an overgrowth of trees and brush outside of town. It was a miracle he'd even found the place a second time. It was also obvious no one had been there in years.

However, it was sturdy, and nothing had been left inside it to attract bugs or mice. Not that unwanted critters weren't occupying the space when he first arrived, but they'd given up the habitat quickly enough.

Alton had no intentions of making the place livable by any stretch of the imagination. In fact, he'd shoved the couch back several feet to get it out of the way, and he'd brought a pile of blankets over the past few weeks and dropped them on the rug in the center of the room.

If he ever managed to get Joselyn to meet him at the cabin, his only goal was to protect them from the elements and keep them relatively warm so they wouldn't freeze their asses off and need to rush back down the mountain.

It wasn't the ideal location to woo a woman, but it was better than nothing.

Alton rubbed his forehead as he paced the few feet between the front door and the small table. The only other door in the one-room cabin led to a basement, or rather a cellar. The room below had nothing but a small cot in it and a narrow window high on the wall at ground level. It gave him the chills the one and only time he'd ventured down there.

The personal fight warring in his head to let her go had lasted about two weeks. In that time, he'd even gone to the town's one and only local bar—Tipsy's—in an attempt to mingle and put himself out there.

The effort had been futile and repulsive. No woman managed to turn his head, let alone awaken his dick. No matter how many beers he nursed, he couldn't shake Joselyn from his mind and replace her with another.

Meanwhile, his hand and his cock were well acquainted. He'd jerked himself off to visions of Joselyn at least once a day for weeks. Months.

Embarrassingly ridiculous was the fact that he'd never had sex with any woman. At twenty-five, he'd known Joselyn was his for over half his life. No other female had tempted him to cheat on her. It was absurd since he'd never so much as touched her, let alone dated her, but the touch of another woman had a tendency to make him cringe. So he hadn't fucked a single one of them.

He knew Joselyn wouldn't have, either. At least he hoped not. He had no claim to her other than what his mind knew to be true, so he couldn't very well be angry if she'd experimented with other men in her life, but it would be painful to find out.

As if he didn't have enough on his mind, his brewery was in the process of developing and launching a new product line that was sure to put an increased strain on the relationship he did not have with the competitor's daughter.

He sighed, closing his eyes while he rubbed his temples. "Fuck." It seemed like his entire world was a mix-up, like Fate played some sort of trick on him, placing him in the wrong family or the wrong providence, or the wrong century. Whatever it was, it wasn't funny anymore.

On top of everything going on in his real life, he spent at least two hours every Sunday night standing in this dilapidated old cabin hoping Joselyn would take him up on his offer and meet him.

She hadn't communicated with him a single time in two months. Not since the weird phone call that ended with her freaking out and hanging up on him for no apparent reason other than the possible fact that she didn't like him calling her *baby*.

Did he insult her in some way? He couldn't imagine how, but she still refused to respond to him since that night. And he refused to give up on her.

So he'd texted her the precise location of this godforsaken cabin six weeks ago and then reminded her every Sunday evening he was there if she would please join him.

How many weeks would he continue to put himself out there like this emotionally and physically?

As many as it takes.

Taking a deep breath, he froze in his spot, dropping his fingers from his temples and widening his gaze to the darkness of the room. Another breath confirmed the unmistakable scent of his mate. He inhaled slowly, his hands shaking as he wiped them on his thighs.

Holy shit. *She's here.*

Nerves ate a hole in him like a fifteen-year-old boy on

his first date. Except this was not a date. He had no idea what it was. There was every chance in the world she would show up yelling at him to stop texting her and leave her the fuck alone.

He would gladly face even her wrath if it put them in the same room. He was that whipped.

The door creaked slowly open as he stared at it, and he said nothing as she stepped into the small space and shut it behind her.

For several seconds, neither of them spoke. The room was lit only by the faint trace of moonlight streaming through the two small windows on opposite walls of the cabin, but the vision of a grizzly shifter was sharp enough for them to see fine.

Finally, Joselyn blew out a breath, leaning against the door.

"You came."

"I shouldn't have, but yes." She met his gaze. "You're persistent."

"I am. When it's important."

"How is it so important to maintain a relationship with me? I would describe it as dangerous and playing with fire."

"It's both of those things. No doubt. But it's also undeniable that I can't stop thinking about you." It was time to throw everything on the table and toss in his heart.

She reached behind the doorknob, making him lurch forward to stop her from leaving.

To avoid his touch, she jumped to one side out of the way and circled to the back of the dingy old couch, her arms wrapped around her middle.

He leaned against the door, blocking her exit, at least for a while.

"So I'm a hostage now?" she asked sarcastically.

He moaned. "Dammit, Jos. Don't do that. Don't act like this is all on me. Just...don't." Never once in all the years had he forced her to face the truth or prevented her from walking away from reality. It was time to put his foot down and insist she listen to reason for a change.

She hugged herself tighter, shutting herself off from him. "Fine. What do you need to say? I can't stay long."

"You know me, Jos. Better than anyone. You know I would never do a thing to hurt you. But I also won't let you hurt yourself. And unless I'm deranged, we're meant to be mates. I've known it for most of my life, and I know you have too."

She didn't speak, but she did cock out one hip and settled the corresponding foot at an angle.

He could smell the anxiety coming from her. In the tight space, he could sense her increased heart rate. Good.

"We have hurdles that seem insurmountable. I get that. You aren't the only one with family and pack obligations. Mine are the same. It's the reason why I let you walk away from me and return to Silvertip after university.

"I could have pressured you then. Maybe I should have. But I knew how much your family meant to you, and I didn't want to be the catalyst that upset your relationship with anyone, so I let you go. Maybe I shouldn't have. Maybe I should have insisted we run off together. Bind."

She flinched subtly, enough to let him know he was getting to her.

"I've given you years to find yourself. Grow into the woman you are today. I've waited patiently for you to realize on your own that we were meant to be together. I've never broken a single promise to you to keep my distance, keep my hands off you, hold my tongue."

She gave a sharp laugh.

"Okay, maybe I don't always hold my tongue, but far

more often than you can imagine." He took a tentative step away from the door. "Things are not improving within my pack. I had hoped to get a feel from my family that they would lighten up on their incessant need to feud with yours, giving us the opportunity to come clean. But if anything, it's been worse lately. Tempers are flaring."

"Same in my pack," she muttered.

He nodded. "I need more, Jos." There was no way he would force her, but he would give this one last-ditch effort to convince her to see things his way. "If I'm crazy and this entire thing we have is all in my head, I need to know that. I need to prove it so I can move on."

Did she give a subtle nod?

He swallowed and held his head higher. "Baby, let me touch you. Let me hold you. If the spark isn't there, we'll know. If it is, we'll deal with it." He watched her carefully as he used the endearment.

She dropped her hands to her sides and licked her lips. "I'm scared," she whispered.

"I know, Jos. So am I. Frightened out of my mind. But we have to know."

"What happens if we find out you're right? What if the spark is there and we can't deny it?" She took deep breaths. He didn't interrupt her, sensing she had something else to say. She continued. "What if I find out what I've suspected most of my life?"

Finally. Finally, she admitted she felt the same thing he did. Headway.

"We figure it out. We deal with it."

Pain covered her face. She lifted one hand to wipe a tear where it slid down her cheek. She turned her face to one side. Her voice trembled when she spoke again, tentatively, softly. "I don't need to touch you to know you're mine. I'm yours. I've always known."

His heart kicked up a beat. His cock also jumped to attention, stiffening further than it had already the moment he scented her outside the cabin.

Her hesitation was palpable. Taking this leap was huge. He knew it. He'd let her keep her distance for all these years because of it, but if he wasn't mistaken, she needed him to take charge now and press the issue further than he ever had.

"Jos."

She didn't move.

"Jos, look at me."

She slowly turned her face in his direction, wiping that damn tear again. It tore him up inside to see her in so much turmoil. Shaking. Frightened. Afraid to face the truth.

"Jos... Baby, take off your coat." He nodded toward his jacket where it was draped over one of the two ancient wooden kitchen chairs. "It's not that cold in here." The heat coming off their bodies from the intensity of this meeting was enough to light a fire.

She took small, tentative steps toward the table, slid her arms out of her thick winter coat, and draped it on top of his. When she turned to face him, she rubbed her arms. The long-sleeved, black shirt she wore was tight fitting and dipped low in the front, showing off her cleavage. Had she worn it on purpose?

He fought the urge to smile. "Come here, Jos." He wouldn't go to her, but he would insist she come to him.

She rounded the couch, arms crossed in a way that pushed her breasts up higher and made her nipples pucker. Beneath the V of her shirt, he could see the edge of a black lacy bra that made him groan inside. She never dressed provocatively. Ever. Not that this particular outfit was provocative by most people's standards, but for her it was huge.

For her, coming to meet him in a remote cabin in the woods was beyond huge.

He wondered how long she had pondered the decision to wear the particular bra and shirt combination and how many clothes were on her floor at home.

She stood two feet from him, facing the floor. Her usual ponytail fell around the sides of her head in thick gorgeous locks.

"Look at me, Jos."

She was pale when she lifted her face, tipping her head back to meet his gaze. She wasn't a short woman. She was six feet tall. Most grizzlies were taller than humans. But she was still five inches shorter than him. Her throat worked as he watched her swallow several times.

He could scent her arousal. Stronger than any time in the past.

Was he doing the right thing pressuring her like this?

Yes. He had to believe this was the right thing to do. Later they would sort out the complications. For now, what they both needed was confirmation. Assurance they were not mistaken. Not that he had doubts. Nor did she. But proof would tip the scale. Proof they would have as soon as they touched. Skin to skin.

"Jos... Touch me." The words slid easily from his mouth now, empowering him with every utterance.

She stiffened as more of her arousal filled the room. "It's a bad idea," she murmured.

He knew the war that raged inside her was fierce. He also knew she wouldn't have come to this cabin tonight— wearing that shirt—if she hadn't already decided to give an inch.

He lifted one hand between them and held it out, palm up. "Take my hand."

She stared into his eyes for several more moments before she lowered her gaze and lifted her hand. It was shaking hard. Her fingers looked so small and dainty next to his.

As she eased her reach forward, he knew this would be a monumental moment in both their lives they would never forget.

The second her fingertips hit his, a zing of excitement raced through him. Heat. Arousal. Electricity. Need. A consuming desire to strip her clothes off and devour every inch of her body from head to toe.

He didn't move a muscle, letting her smooth her hand over his until their palms touched. And then he wrapped his fingers around hers and brought her palm to his face, tipping his cheek into her hand.

She gasped but didn't pull away.

He grabbed onto and held her gaze.

Oh yeah. The last shred of doubt fled the cabin.

Joselyn Arthur was his.

Joselyn flattened her palm on Alton's smoothly shaved cheek and stared up into his chocolate eyes, opening her mind just enough to let him see how much he affected her.

She could see into his mind too. She so entranced him that it cost him a tremendous amount of effort to remain still and allow her to move at her pace. The deep feelings she'd had for him for several years grew even more intense at the realization of the level of his restraint. Restraint he'd carried with him all this time.

Not to diminish her own restraint. It had put stress on

her for the same number of years, but she knew now it didn't compare to his. Because he was male? Or because he was...dominant?

Not that every male member of her species was dominant. Not by a long shot. But for all these years, she had called the shots with a man she now saw through new eyes.

Alton Tarben had worked hard to hold back his natural alpha tendency to dominate her nearly their entire lives. It humbled her to see this in his mind. It also made her pussy cream.

How far would she let things go here tonight in this dingy cabin in the middle of nowhere? The test had been for her to touch him. Now she was touching him, and it wasn't nearly enough. She needed more.

She stuffed her ever-present doubts down deep and reached with her other hand to hold his face. A heady sense of power washed through her as she smoothed her palms down to his neck, thumbing the pulse point where she could easily close the distance and bind him to her for all time.

She stared at the spot where his shoulders and neck came together. In two seconds, she could close the distance, press her teeth into the tender flesh, and allow her personal serum to flow into his bloodstream, binding them together.

She wouldn't, but she had never been more aware of the power to bind that could consume a couple. It would drive them mad in no time. "Kiss me," she blurted, jerking her gaze back to his.

He licked his lips, his damn tongue stroking across first the full bottom lip and then the fuller top one. Lips she had fantasized about for years. She needed them on hers. She needed to feel them all over her body. She needed to do the same to him.

"You're sure?" he asked, his voice gravelly.

"Never been more sure of anything," she replied.

At the same time his lips captured hers, his hands landed on her waist. He gripped her firmly, angling his head to one side to lick the seam of her mouth, demanding entrance.

She opened for him, tasting him for the first time, an experience ten times stronger than touching him. Her knees threatened to buckle and might have if he hadn't been holding her up by the waist.

When he slid one hand around to her back to drag her against his body, she knew he would support her. His palm trailed up her back to tangle in her ponytail, tugging her head gently to one side so he could gain better access to her mouth.

He tasted exactly as she imagined, the scent of his pheromones that always filled a room warning her of his flavor.

He stroked the inside of her mouth forever, suckled her tongue, flattened his on her teeth. When he finally released her lips to trail kisses down her neck, she gasped for oxygen.

"Alton..." His name slid off her tongue like a balm. Her tone was new to her ears as well as his.

He slid his hand farther up into her hair and tugged the band restraining it until the thick locks fell around her shoulders and down her back. His other hand flattened on the small of her back, his pinky touching the sliver of bare skin between her shirt and her jeans.

She wanted more. She wanted him to strip her down and fuck her right there in the cabin. To hell with the consequences.

Her awareness of his power doubled when he flicked his tongue over the sensitive skin of her neck and scraped his teeth along the tendon. Part of her willed him to do it. Bite her. Put an end to this insanity.

But she had enough brain cells left to know better than to act so hastily. *"Alton,"* she warned into his mind. She had rarely spoken to him telepathically. For one thing, they never needed to. When they were together, they could speak their minds out loud. When they were apart, they were usually at a distance that didn't permit such intimate communication. Unbound couples could not communicate into each other's minds when they were separated by more than about fifty yards.

He slid his lips farther down to kiss her cleavage. *"Baby, I would never seal you to me without your permission. Relax."*

His words calmed her. Of course he wouldn't. Obviously, he was a man with far more restraint than she'd ever given him credit for.

When his lips hit the upper swell of her breasts, she shuddered, leaning back to give him more access.

Alton groaned, separating his mouth from her skin for the first time.

He met her gaze, his brow furrowed. His pinky was the only thing moving, drawing small circles on the small of her back. Did he have any idea what that did to her?

If so, he didn't care. He certainly didn't stop. "Well, that answers that question."

"Yes," she agreed breathily. "But—"

He shook his head, cutting her off. "Don't give this a *but* yet. Please. I just confirmed what I've known in my heart for most of my life. Give me a moment to enjoy holding my mate in my arms for the first time before you drag reality back into the equation."

She nodded. He was right. It felt so good.

Forever they stood there, drinking in each other's gazes. Her arousal increased by the second, as she knew his did at the same time.

Suddenly, she was falling backward. She grabbed his waist with both hands to keep from hitting the floor. But he had her firmly in his grip. He lowered her onto her back over a pile of blankets and settled himself on his side next to her.

He leaned his face in his palm, never breaking eye contact. His other hand smoothed down from her shoulder to flatten between her breasts and then lower. He then gripped her waist, fingers spread wide enough that his thumb rested against the underside of her breast and his pinky returned to torture that same inch of exposed skin at the small of her back.

She breathed deeply, each inhale drawing more of his essence into her system.

"We could walk away," he finally said.

Her eyes widened in confusion.

He gave her a wry smile. "I don't mean forever. I mean we could leave here now without having sex."

"Would it make a difference?" she asked, already knowing the answer.

"No. It would change nothing. Touching you for the first time changed nothing. Kissing you for the first time changed nothing. Making love to you won't, either. None of those things will alter the fact that you're mine."

"None of them will fix our problems, either," she pointed out.

"This is true." He lowered his face to lightly touch her lips with his again. "If we walk out the door right now, we will leave completely unsatisfied and unable to sleep."

She smiled against his mouth. "And if we have sex first,

you think you'll be fully satisfied and sleep like a baby?" she teased.

"No." He sighed. "It'll be worse. I'm sure."

She chewed on her lip for a moment, knowing already in her heart she would let him take her tonight. She'd known it before she left the house. It was the reason she wore her sexiest bra and panty set and told her mother she would be late. "What do we have to lose?"

He grinned again. "My virginity for one."

She gasped, swatting at his forearm. "You think I gave mine away to someone else?"

His smile widened. "I had hoped not. But I wouldn't blame you if you had."

She shook her head. "No. Of course not. It's always been yours to claim. Even when I was in total denial, it was yours."

His face lit up. "Good." A twinkle in his eyes teased her. "This will take about six seconds, then."

She giggled while her nipples puckered to stiff peaks and her pussy clenched tight. "Maybe if we get this out of our system, we can walk away."

A slow smile spread across his face. "Sure. We can go with that story if you want."

She shuddered, changing the subject. "It's freezing in here."

He nodded. "Yeah, but I don't think we'll feel it."

"You're right." They'd be glad the room was cold as soon as they touched skin to skin.

"I brought blankets."

"Several loads of them, it would appear." She patted the floor at her side.

"Yeah. I carried more every time I came. That couch makes me cringe. I'm sure it's a pullout, but I'm not willing to touch it to find out. And the only other surface in this cabin is a cot in the basement. Not going there, either."

"There's a basement?"

"Well, more of a cellar. Not someplace I would take a woman."

She nodded, shuddering at the idea. "Then I'm glad you amassed a stack of blankets." They were stalling.

Silence took over. He released her waist to thread his fingers in her hair. It was a mess of curls panned out around her. "Why do you always wear it pulled back like this?"

She shrugged. "I'm lazy and always late."

"It's so damn sexy when it's down."

His words reached deep, sending a chill down her spine.

He ran his fingers through the locks, staring at them. "So soft. I've wanted to run my hands through your hair for as long as I can remember."

Heat rushed up to her cheeks. She wiggled her free arm under his and flattened her palm on his chest. "I'm hoping there are other parts of me you've wanted to touch," she boldly stated.

He dropped her hair to cup her face. "You have no idea." And then his lips were on hers again.

She lost herself in the kiss and the sensation of his fingers running back down her body. He briefly gripped her waist, and then he cupped her breast for the first time.

She moaned and arched her chest toward him.

His thumb slid across her nipple, making her gasp into his mouth. *"Easy, baby. You're so damn hot."* His ability to communicate into her mind came in super handy all of a sudden. It also steamed up the cabin.

Seconds later, he slid his hand under her shirt, flattening his palm against her belly.

She gripped her knees together, imagining she might come the moment he touched her breast even through the lace of her bra.

He chuckled into her mind. *"Firecracker."*

She ignored him and wiggled to one side to slide out from under him and sit up. "Take your shirt off, Alton. Stop teasing." She whipped hers over her head with more courage than she'd ever exhibited in her life. She needed him. Now. Inside her. Tonight was not a night for foreplay.

He tugged his shirt off with one hand. She didn't even know what it looked like. He kicked off his boots next while she did the same. When he reached for the button on his jeans, she boldly rose onto her knees and undid hers as well.

Apparently, he drew the line at their separation with her fingers fumbling at the button on her jeans. Ignoring his, he grabbed her by the waist, lifted her to her feet, and released her button and zipper seconds later. He tugged the denim down her legs and tapped her feet to get her to step out.

She held on to his shoulders, touching his firm muscles for the first time.

When he drew her toward him, gripping her hips and setting his lips on her belly, she thought she might die. "Yes," she hissed.

He lowered his mouth to the lace of her panties and licked along the seam until her knees buckled.

Before she completely collapsed from the inability to concentrate on remaining upright, he swung her onto her back once again and leaned over her. His eyes met hers for only a second, the heat in them intense. And then they slowly swept down her body.

"Jesus, Jos. You're sexier than I imagined."

She couldn't speak out loud, but she did manage to

communicate into his mind. *"I could say the same about you."* She lifted a hand to plant it on his chest.

Alton set his fingertips on the upper swell of her breast and then danced them across to the other side and down lower. He swung a leg over her body, straddling her. As if he had hours of experience with bras, he popped the front clasp and then licked his lips again, the reverence in his gaze heating her skin and making her nipples jump to stiff peaks.

He finally cupped the swell of her breasts and stroked the skin so gently goose bumps rose in the wake of his fingertips. The moment he made contact with her nipples, she moaned.

A smile spread across his face. He glanced at her eyes and then back down, lightly pinching the tips of her breasts.

She grabbed his biceps, impressed by how firm the muscles were. "Alton…"

"Not gonna rush this, baby."

She swallowed. Rushing was exactly what she had in mind.

He scooted down her body, grabbed the lace of her panties, and dragged them off her. Before she had a chance to grasp her total nudity entirely, he nudged her legs apart with his knee and set it between her thighs. When he did the same with his other knee, she closed her eyes.

It was asking way too much for her to watch him looking at her so intimately.

He stroked his palms up and down her outer thighs next, his thumbs coming closer and closer to her sex.

She fought for every breath, struggling to focus on the need for oxygen while his fingers spread her lower lips and the cold air in the room made her hyper-aware of how wet she was.

"Gorgeous," he whispered. "So wet for me." He hadn't touched the moisture yet, so she had to assume he could see it. Smell it.

Her face heated further.

He reached between her folds and stroked upward until he flicked the tip of his finger over her clit.

She cried out, grabbing for his waist, fumbling in an attempt to touch more of him with fingers that weren't taking messages from her brain.

"So sexy. Come for me, Joselyn." He used her full name, making it super obvious he was acutely aware of who he was with and what this meant to him.

She squeezed her knees together against his thighs, her instinct to close her legs taking over.

"Uh-uh." He was shaking his head when she blinked. And then he set one hand on the floor next to her head, leaned over her, held her gaze, and swirled her wetness around her clit. He flicked it expertly.

"How do you know what you're doing?" she asked into his mind, unwilling and unable to voice her concerns. How many women had he done this to?

He smiled and responded out loud. "You're my first in all ways, baby. Don't freak out on me. I've done my research. I know how to take care of you."

She lifted her hips toward his touch, her eyes fluttering shut. She believed him.

"Watch me. Watch me while you come for me." His tone was both soft and demanding at the same time.

She stared into his eyes, her mouth falling open as the first orgasm she would ever have at his hands washed through her body. Most of her muscles clenched as she came against his fingers, hard. She dug her fingertips into his waist.

He eased his touch as she came down, and for the first

time in a while, she forced out a sentence. "Make love to me, Alton. Now."

He lifted up onto his knees and shrugged out of his jeans while she watched. When his cock popped free, she gulped. It was significantly larger than she'd imagined.

He chuckled into her head. *"Glad you approve."*

She flinched, realizing she hadn't blocked that thought. It was impossible to block him while she was this aroused. Even moments after coming, she was ready for him. More ready perhaps.

As he slid farther down her body, he reached between her legs and stroked through her lower lips again. His firm length rested against her thigh.

She grabbed his waist again, urging him with her hands.

He slid one finger into her, and her eyes rolled back. *Holy shit.*

Sure, she was a virgin, but she'd used toys on herself over the years. She shouldn't be that tight. Why did his touch elicit far more sensations than her vibrator?

He added another finger, and she moaned.

"You are the sexiest person on earth. I'll never tire of watching you come undone. I've never seen you so...open."

Under normal circumstances, she might have been mortified, but none of that was necessary. This was Alton. Her mate. The man she should be bound to and would if their stupid families weren't in a lifelong brawl.

So many years spent in turmoil. Fighting it now was futile.

She gripped at his two fingers with the walls of her channel, craving more. Craving him. Craving everything.

When he removed his fingers with a slight pop and lifted them to his mouth to lick them clean, she stopped breathing. Everything he did was more smolderingly hot than the last.

"Mmm." He moaned around her taste, and then he set his hand on the other side of her head, threaded both sets of fingers in her thick hair, and lodged his cock at her entrance. "You okay?"

"Jesus, Alton."

He held her gaze. "Baby," he groaned.

"Do it," she demanded.

With one sharp thrust, he entered her, taking her breath away, claiming her so quickly and so thoroughly, she lost all ability to think. Every brain cell focused on the stretch of her pussy around him. Too tight.

She dug her nails into his waist, trying to accommodate him.

He didn't move. She was fairly sure he didn't breathe, either. His arms shook beside her head.

And then she realized she too had not breathed. The shock of him filling her so fast and so full froze her in her spot. The initial pain fled just as quickly, leaving her needing more. She squirmed, sucking in a lungful of air. "Move. Alton, *move.*"

He misunderstood her, his eyes widening as he pulled out.

She shook her head, wrapping her legs around him and holding him lodged at her entrance. "No. I mean fuck me, Alton."

He hesitated a moment and then slid back inside. The second pass was so much better than the first, and she whimpered around the intensity of sensation bombarding her. Her lip quivered.

Alton groaned. "You okay?"

"Yes. Do it again."

He slid back out and thrust back in, his arms shaking.

He was holding back. He didn't pull out again yet. Instead, he lowered his face and kissed her. He licked the seam of her lips, entered, and tasted her all over again.

A starving man. Desperate.

She let him kiss her, but her mind was on her pussy and how badly she needed to come again. If he would just…

And then he released her lips, pulled almost out, and thrust back inside her tight warmth.

She bit her swollen bottom lip to keep from screaming. Why? No one was anywhere near them to hear her cry out.

She was going to come. He set a pace, thrusting in and out of her faster. She tilted her pelvis toward his cock so the base hit her clit with every pass. Tipping her head back, she concentrated on how incredible it felt to be filled by him. So much better than any toy she owned.

She was ruined.

On that last thought, she came, gripping his cock and causing him to scream her name as he came right behind her.

He lowered himself over her, propping his body up with his elbows to avoid crushing her, though she wished he wouldn't. It would be worth it for him to flatten himself over her so that as much of their skin made contact as possible.

Instead, when he finally caught his breath, he eased out of her and slid to his side next to her. One leg remained lodged between hers, and one hand flattened on her belly.

She stroked her fingers up and down his biceps.

He breathed heavily into her ear. "You're mine."

She smiled. *"I'm yours."*

She didn't realize she'd fallen asleep or notice when he covered their bodies with one of the blankets, but suddenly she was wide awake, bolting upright. Sweating.

The dream.

She twisted to one side to find Alton next to her, reaching for her. "Baby, you okay?" His hand landed on her arm, tugging her across his chest.

"Yeah. Nightmare." She sighed as she snuggled against his side and flattened her palm over his pecs. "Not the first one. I have the same one often. I don't even know what it's about. It evaporates the moment I wake up. But every time I'm left feeling like you're gone."

"Gone? I've never even been there before."

"I know. It makes no sense. But I reach for you. You're never there."

"I'm here now." He held her closer, chasing away the demons as he kissed the top of her head. His hand roamed up and down her back.

For how long? "What are we going to do?" she whispered to his chest.

"I don't know yet." He squeezed her tighter.

"What time is it?"

"Late. After midnight."

She drew circles on his chest absentmindedly. "I feel like I'm going to hyperventilate. I can't lose you."

He cupped her face, tilting her head back and searching her eyes with his deep brown penetrating ones. "You'll never lose me."

"You can't know that." She grabbed his forearm with her hand as if she could hold on to him and keep him from slipping away. "When I leave here, I won't even have any way to communicate with you."

He lifted a brow as if to insinuate she was to blame for not insisting they bind together immediately.

She rolled her eyes. "Come on. Don't make me the bad guy here. You know as well as I do we can't bind right now. Our families would freak out. Why do I have to be the voice of reason? You can't seriously tell me you'd enjoy starting World War III."

His shoulders fell. So did his expression. "No. You're right." He set his forehead against hers. "But I hate knowing how much you're hurting. And I can't stand the thought of not having constant contact with you." He kissed her lips softly, a feather's touch.

Joselyn climbed over his body, emboldened, straddling him. The blanket slid down to expose her chest. She went from sad and concerned to aroused in a heartbeat. As she slid her hands down to his waist, she deepened the kiss. "Need you again," she muttered against his lips. She had no idea what the future would hold, but she was here now, and she intended to have him again.

"Me too, baby." He released her face to run his palms down her body.

Wetness flooded her pussy at the way he looked at her. And the way he kept calling her *baby* in that soft, reverent tone of his.

"Don't move." When his gaze roamed down to her chest with a serious expression, she glanced down also. She gasped. Her full breasts were heavy, swaying between them. No wonder he licked his lips. The visual was sexy even to her.

"Alton…"

"Please, don't say anything. Let me have this. Let me memorize every inch of you. I'll need it to get me through long, lonely nights without you in my bed."

She swallowed, fighting the tears that wanted to leak from her eyes at the reverence in his voice.

With his free hand, he trailed one finger up her torso and between her breasts.

Her nipples jumped to attention, begging for more, and she bit her lip to keep from crying out.

She watched as he slowly spiraled her breast, circling around and around as he drew closer to her nipple. Willing him to touch it didn't affect him at all. And she knew he was inside her head listening to her every desire, or at least the thoughts she permitted him to see. She could allow him all the way inside her mind if she wanted, but she held something back, as if not entirely willing to give him complete access.

Instead of flicking his finger over the swollen bud, he switched to the other breast at the last second to give it the same treatment.

She shuddered. A tear fell.

He didn't glance up, but he knew anyway. "Don't cry, sweet Joselyn. Not now. Not while I make love to you. Happy thoughts." His gaze remained locked on her breast while he spoke.

She swallowed hard and arched into him. *"Please..."* she pleaded in her mind.

His response was barely audible. Deep. Sensual. "Do you know how much I love to hear you beg?"

As if on cue, his cock swelled against her sex. His finger left her breasts without making contact with the two points most craving his touch. It trailed down toward her sex, angling to one side at the last second to trace the crease between her thigh and her pussy. Again, not enough direct contact.

Joselyn lifted up slightly, needing him to reach between her legs and stroke her clit.

He ignored the movement, tracing a line back over her hip and around to her butt. "You smell so damn good." He inhaled deeply. "I want to memorize your scent too."

Another unnecessary statement. He would never forget her scent. As shifters, they knew the scent of dozens of their kind without seeing them. Whenever they met someone new, their brains remembered their scent even before their name.

It came naturally. But she knew what he meant. The bond between the two of them was different. They were meant to be together. The imminent separation they were about to endure wasn't natural. It would be painful.

Alton lifted his head and licked the seam of her lips, his tongue dipping inside to tease hers for a moment. "Your taste too. All of you." His eyes closed as he inhaled again and then kissed her with more urgency, his hand molding around her butt cheek to squeeze.

She melted under his touch. His kiss. He consumed her so easily. Was it like this for other bear shifters? What about humans? She would never know because she would never be with another man.

No matter what happened between them, she knew that to be true.

When he finally eased away from her mouth, he continued kissing her cheek, moving across her face until he reached her ear. He blew gently on the sensitive lobe, sending shivers down her spine before he bit down on the flesh playfully.

She squirmed.

Leaving her ear, he nibbled down her neck until he came to the sweet spot where her shoulder met her neck. She tipped her head to the side, giving him better access. Holding her breath, she willed him to claim her. Take her right then. Fuck their families. She wanted him to bind them together forever. All he had to do was break the soft skin with his teeth and let the binding serum flow from his mouth to mix with her blood stream.

She knew it wasn't good timing. But dammit, this aroused, her clit throbbing with need, her pussy grasping for him, she wanted to throw caution to the wind and let him bind them together.

She could do it too. It didn't have to be the man who claimed the woman. Or they could both do it at the same time. Separately even.

Instead of breaking her skin, however, Alton had enough of his sanity intact to merely lick the spot and nuzzle it with his nose. He moaned against her skin though, sending renewed shivers down her body.

"Alton…"

He hesitated, teasing her skin with his breath before licking a path toward her chest. When he flicked his tongue over her nipple, she thrust her chest closer to his mouth. She sucked in a sharp breath.

"Oh yeah. Feel my touch."

A heated flush raced across her face, but he wasn't looking.

Alton suddenly sucked her nipple into his mouth, drawing a soft cry from her lips. Damn, he was good. She closed her eyes, memorizing the feel of his lips on her skin much the same way he was doing.

The longer he suckled her—the more aroused she got. Unable to resist, she ground her open pussy over his cock.

Alton released her breast with a pop, his hand sliding to her back. One second she was straddling his lap, masturbating against him. The next second, she was falling backward until she landed on her back. Alton hovered over her, kneeling between her thighs, his palms on both sides of her head.

His gaze was intense, clouded, serious. So much serious.

She reached between their bodies and circled his cock with one hand. She set the other on his hip. "Need you."

"Such a hurry," he responded through gritted teeth.

She watched as she lifted and lowered her fist up and down his length. He was so damn sexy. The velvety feel of him in her hand undid her.

When he rocked forward into her touch, she knew he was losing the battle to take it slowly.

Slow might have its place. But not now. Not tonight. Not after their first coming together and one of her stupid nightmares.

She scooted her ass closer toward him, intent on pulling him down when she had them lined up perfectly. It was futile.

Joselyn wasn't a small woman. She was six feet tall and lithe. She worked out five days a week, priding herself on keeping her body in shape. But she was a pixie compared to Alton's six-foot-five stature with broad shoulders and a chest that went on forever. He'd always been taller than her, even when they were younger.

"Baby, you won't be able to control this." His arms were firm, elbows locked at his sides where he held himself aloft over her body. Several inches separated his cock from her pussy. No amount of desperate pleading from her tight warmth would entice him. Not until he was ready.

She lifted her hips, in no way closing the gap. Frustration mounted. She needed him again. Desperately. Now.

He didn't budge. When she felt a change in the air, she lifted her gaze to find him staring down at her. Still so serious. "Do you have any idea how I feel about you?"

She swallowed, relaxing onto the pile of blankets as she released his cock to slide her hands up his waist. "Yes." Her voice caught in her throat. Emotions took over.

"We'll get through this. Together. You understand that, right?"

"Yes." She totally did at that moment. She believed him.

His vehemence burrowed into her. Later, when she was no longer with him, her sanity would return, and she would realize his words were empty. But for now, she would take his promise and hold it tight. She would need to remember this feeling in the future when she found herself lonely and so very alone.

Slowly he lowered his body over her until his cock lodged at her entrance, and he rested on his elbows, his face inches from hers. "You're the most important thing in my life, and you always will be, no matter what distance or time separates us. It's just a bump in the road. We'll get to the other side."

She nodded, unable to form words. And then her mouth fell open as he entered her with a thrust that took her breath away.

As if he needed to drive home his point, he pounded into her. He lowered his face to one side of hers and set his lips on that sweet spot at the base of her neck again. In contrast to the way he thrust in and out of her pussy, he gently kissed her throat, nuzzling the spot as a reminder of what they would be someday in the future.

Bound together.

For life.

CHAPTER 5

Four months later…

"Mom, have you seen my blue sweater?" Joselyn raced into the kitchen as she did nearly every morning. She pulled her hair up into a ponytail as she looked every direction for the stupid sweater that wasn't where she'd left it.

Rosanne Arthur glanced over her shoulder from where she was loading the dishwasher. "Seriously, Jos, you're a grown woman. Almost twenty-four years old. A professional with marketing talents I can't even wrap my mind around. And yet you can't seem to get out the door on time or find your shoes. Sometimes I think you're more like a toddler than an adult."

Joselyn rolled her eyes as she lifted a foot. "I have my shoes on, Mom."

Rosanne glared at her.

Joselyn shot her a mischievous grin, closed the few feet between her and her mother, and kissed her on the cheek. "You coming in today?"

"Yep. I'll be there by noon. Would you take that stack of papers on the table to your father? He's as forgetful as you most days."

"Sure." Joselyn raced toward the kitchen table, scooped up the pile of paper, and spotted her sweater balled up in the chair. "Ah ha." She lifted it victoriously and dashed from the house while she managed to shrug into it. If she was lucky and traffic was light, she would be in her office sitting at her desk by nine. Eight thirty was her goal, but she never met that goal and long ago gave it up.

It wasn't as though anyone would fire her. After all, her family owned Glacial Brewing Company. Nearly every employee was a brother or cousin or aunt or uncle. The Arthur pack was strong and united.

She slid into the front seat of her adored silver Honda Accord and started the engine just as her phone rang. A smile split her face, and her heart raced as she connected the call through her Bluetooth. "Hey," she casually stated in total contrast to how she felt inside.

"Hey, yourself." Alton's voice was low and sultry.

"Are you already at work?" He usually beat her since mornings didn't seem to pose nearly as much drama in his world. He'd always been a morning person.

Alton answered her question, shaking her out of her thoughts. "Been at my desk an hour, babe." He chuckled. "Did you comb your hair before you left the house this morning, or is it pulled back in that silly ponytail?"

She smiled in spite of how frustrating it was that he knew her so well. "Ran out of time. It's clean, though. Do I get credit for that?"

"Ah. So in addition to pulling it back, it's wet." He laughed.

It wasn't as though she'd changed. All through high school and then university she'd found it difficult to be bothered with fixing her hair. And the truth was she had been blessed with thick, perfect, wavy, light brown locks that fell around her face in a way most women would kill for.

Alton loved her hair. The few times they managed to see each other in the last several months, he ran his fingers through it for hours, from her scalp to the ends. Over and over. Staring at it. Mesmerized. He also teased her about how late she was for everything. Mercilessly.

"Yeah. It's wet. It's not like I had an extra twenty minutes to dry it. I meant to wash it last night, but... I do not want to talk about my damn hair this morning, Alton." She took the next right turn, driving slower than necessary to drag out the conversation. "When am I going to see you?"

It had been a week since the last time she saw him, and that had been a fleeting fifteen minutes stolen late in the evening. Arranging to meet was difficult. And then doing so without getting caught was worse.

"Friday? I have a meeting that might run late, but I'll try to get there by seven?"

She sighed. "Okay. The cave? It's going to be so cold." The biggest problem was the weather. Alberta in the evening was cold nearly every day of the year. It was February, which meant the temperature could be in the low teens at seven in the evening. And dark.

The only way to avoid detection and keep from outing themselves as a couple was to shift into their grizzly forms and head for their favorite meeting spot in the mountains. The trouble with that was when they shifted to human form—they were left standing in the cold, chatting for as long as they could tolerate. At least he held her. But it had been more than a month since they'd had sex.

"I can't fix the cold. But I'll wear my thickest coat, and

you can get inside it with me. I don't trust that little cabin anymore. Ever since Nuria was held hostage there, the place gives me the creeps. Besides, half the damn family knows where it is now. Yours too."

She shuddered. Truth be told, the tiny, run-down cabin had made her skin crawl a bit in the first place. And ever since Alton's brother Austin rescued his mate from there, she feared it was no longer a safe place to hide. She blew out a breath. "I guess we don't have a choice."

"Oh, we have choices, baby." His voice held an edge to it that made her stiffen. He was right. He was also wrong.

In recent months some members of their families had reconciled. In fact, their two sets of parents were even bumping heads for the first time in decades. But that was the extent of the reuniting families. She wasn't sure what her parents would say if she told them she had secretly been in love with Alton for her entire life and planned to bind herself to him.

"I need another night with you. It's been weeks."

"Thirty-two days," he deadpanned. "But who's counting?" His voice wasn't filled with laughter. He was a little pissed. Even without the mental connection they lacked, she could read him well most of the time.

If—when—they bound together, they would be able to communicate telepathically for the rest of their lives, even at a distance. Until then, as regular shifters, the only time they could delve into each other's minds was when they were nearby. Which wasn't often enough.

"I know. I'm sorry. Let's figure it out. I'm going through batteries like they're beer," she teased, trying to lighten the mood.

Alton groaned. "Baby, don't say things like that."

"What? You don't like my simile?"

"I don't like the visual of you doing to yourself what I

should be doing to you with my mouth." His voice dipped lower, the sexy growl reaching through the connection.

Shit. She should never have mentioned her vibrator. Now she was wet and squirming in her seat. She gripped the steering wheel harder and forced herself to pay attention to the road.

"I gotta go, baby. Someone's waiting outside my office. Friday, okay? And please be careful. I don't like you alone in the mountains, especially at night."

"I'll be fine, Alton."

"Seven."

"I'll be there." She drove the rest of the way in silence, a tear sliding down her face. She swiped at it several times, not wanting to arrive at the brewery with bloodshot puffy eyes, but it persisted. Dammit.

When she pulled into her usual parking spot, she took deep breaths and composed herself before exiting the car. A gust of wind hit her as she reached behind the front seat to grab her bag. It was fucking cold. Even in the middle of the morning with the sun out. There was every possibility it would be too cold to keep their teeth from chattering Friday night higher up in the mountains.

This shit had to change.

It was time to figure things out and come up with a game plan.

Alton Tarben leaned back in his chair and tapped his desk absentmindedly with a pen. Luckily his cousin Vinson had only stuck his head in the door to ask a quick question and then left.

Four months.

A damn long time to maintain a long-distance

relationship with a woman who lived four miles away. And that was just counting the time since they'd first had sex. If he was honest, he'd maintained this secret relationship with her for most of his life. He was frustrated to the point of breaking, and he knew she was no better off. He forced himself not to snap at her over their predicament, particularly as it wasn't her fault. But he knew his aggravation leaked out more often than he would like.

He also was unfairly placing too much of the blame on her shoulders, as if he were willing to tell everyone they knew and loved to go to hell and complete the binding as soon as she agreed. The truth was much more complicated. There were details he needed to iron out before they could mate, details he kept from Joselyn to avoid conflict.

Alton managed to speak to her by phone at least every other day. And they tried to meet in the mountains once a week. But it was no way to maintain a relationship. And it was pure torture on his cock.

The reality was that Jos was his mate. He knew in his soul they belonged together. Destiny or some shit had put them on the same path. It wasn't a concept most shifters believed in, but they apparently hadn't walked in his shoes because he'd known that cute, brown-haired girl with the lopsided ponytail was his since grade school.

The years had taken their toll. The past four months had been brutal. He was totally done with this farce. Too bad the pile of shit he needed to deal with first was growing instead of shrinking. The end was in sight, but would she still be as eager to bind to him after she found out what company secrets he was hiding?

And then there was the issue of their damn family feud. Some days he considered skipping town and taking her to the other side of the country. To hell with family loyalty.

He'd done some digging lately into the history of the

feud, and what he found out didn't make him feel warm and fuzzy. If there was any merit to the lore, no way in hell would the two families reconcile in the near future. Even though recent incidents had brought at least a temporary truce to his immediate family and hers, he doubted it was enough to sustain lasting peace.

His mind wandered back to Joselyn. He blew out a long breath and adjusted his cock. The sound of her voice alone had made him hard. He was going to get carpal tunnel from masturbating.

It was so hard to find the time and place to spend the night. He wasn't kidding about the thirty-two days. That shit was no joke. They had gone to great lengths to lie to everyone they knew and meet up two hours away for a stolen night at a hotel on the outskirts of Calgary.

Not wanting to waste a moment of their time, they'd practically slammed each other into the back of the door to get their clothes off while keeping their lips pressed together. The first fuck had been just that—a fuck. Pent-up need forced them to get the first one out of the way because neither of them could think straight until they'd had at least one orgasm.

Thirty-two days ago... Seemed like longer. After fucking her probably too hard against the door—which she never complained about and even appeared to crave—he'd lifted her into his arms and carried her to the bed. Their second round was slower than the first. Slower being six minutes instead of sixty seconds with a sixteen-second rest in between.

It wasn't until they'd come together three times that they finally spoke out loud. Not that it was necessary. They were so in tune with each other that every thought leaked into the other's head as they made love. As Nature intended. He shuddered, considering how much more powerful that connection would be after they bound themselves together.

Alton smiled, leaning his forehead against the palm of his hand.

Damn, she was hot. He knew she worked out several times a week. And it showed. She had the finest body he'd ever set eyes on. All lean muscles, long legs, and strong biceps.

His mouth watered. He gripped the pen so hard it snapped out of his hand and went flying across his office.

Of course, when he wasn't at work, he also spent most of his time working out. What else was there to do when the person you wanted to be with was off limits?

And the number of hours the two of them worked was equally ridiculous. Jos was totally not a morning person, but he knew she stayed later than nearly everyone. She accomplished more in the dark. Always had. Even at U of C, she would stay up late doing homework or a project.

The desire to bind together was constantly at the surface. It was an inexplicable pull that no shifter could deny. And yet, they had. For far too long.

And it was time to figure out his shit and claim his woman before they both needed to be institutionalized for insanity.

CHAPTER 6

Joselyn burst into the clearing high in the mountains at a pace that would put most grizzlies to shame. When she spotted Alton in his bear form next to the entrance to their small cave, she stopped moving.

His natural unshifted form was gorgeous. Thick dark fur. Huge brown eyes. He cocked his head, making her smile inside.

She inched closer, trying not to appear too eager, though she had no idea why she bothered. When they were nose to nose, in silent agreement, without having exchanged thoughts, they leaned back and shifted to their human form. It took only seconds to stretch out their bodies, elongate, rise onto two legs, and will themselves to take the shape of humans.

"Fuck it's cold out here," Alton said as he tugged his coat open and reached to pull Joselyn against the warmth of his chest.

Immediately she calmed. It soothed her to be in his arms. The stress and insanity of the rest of her life evaporated the moment he wrapped his arms around her.

When his lips landed on the top of her head as he inhaled her scent entirely into his lungs, she lifted her face. She needed those lips on hers in a kiss. He claimed her mouth instantly while backing them up into the small cave. She may have put up a fight against this joining for many years, but now that she'd been with him intimately, she couldn't help the total surrender.

How high was the cost? She didn't know yet, but it was time she made a decision about what she was willing to pay for a future that included Alton.

They had accidentally found this spot one day a few months ago. It wasn't a deep cave, but it was enough to keep them out of the rain or snow and break the wind.

They kept a weather-proof plastic box in the corner, and as soon as they reached it, Alton broke the kiss to reach down and pull it open. Two seconds later he had a thick blanket in his hands and was wrapping it around their bodies.

She shivered from the cold and the excitement of having him in her space.

He shrugged out of his coat and dropped it to the ground before dragging her closer.

"You're gonna freeze," she said as she tucked herself in the perfect circle of his arms, the blanket wrapped around them both.

"I'm going to do a lot worse than freeze if we don't have sex tonight, baby."

She sucked in a sharp breath, her nipples tingling at the suggestion. Sex had not been on her radar in this weather. But he had a point. If they didn't at least come together for a quickie, she might lose her mind. As it was, her sanity was holding itself together by a thin tether that threatened to snap most days.

She set her hands on his chest and nodded. "You're

right." There was no way they could even hold a conversation until they'd fucked. As usual. A thrill ran through her body at the idea of literally fucking fast and hard against the cold stone of the cave.

Alton spun them around until her back was against the wall. His hands shook against her as he reached for the hem of her sweater. She batted him away. "You do you. I'll do me." The urgency, always present in their couplings, was right on the surface. There was no time for foreplay.

As soon as she had her clothes off, leaving nothing but her socks, Alton wrapped the blanket around them both, pressed her back to the stone wall again, and cupped her face. "You know what I can't wait to do some day?"

"What?" she breathed.

"Peel your clothes off slowly, layer by layer. I want to watch you unravel while I take my time bringing you to a slow orgasm before entering you."

She shivered as his words hit her hard. His breath was warm against her face, but his words cut like ice. Pursing her lips, she set her forehead against his chest and wrapped her arms around his middle. For a moment, they stood there. One being. Combined. Not noticing the cold.

Alton broke the fleeting, precious union when his cock throbbed against her torso. He moaned as he reached down to cup her sex and stroke his fingers through her folds. "Jesus, baby. You're so wet."

"Mmm," was all she could respond with as she wrapped her fingers around his cock and stroked it from base to tip.

That was all the foreplay they had time for before Alton hoisted her off the ground and lowered her onto his length.

She screamed when he filled her. Tight. So tight. She gritted her teeth to avoid coming before he had a chance to thrust at least twice.

"Wrap your legs around me."

She did as he told her, grabbing his shoulders while he pressed her into the cold stone behind her. The cold didn't matter. Not for the next few minutes. She couldn't even feel it.

Alton held her up under her butt and bent his knees slightly to pull out and then thrust back into her.

She gasped, releasing the breath she'd been holding as her first orgasm washed through her body, shaking her to the core. Every jolt made her flinch in his grasp. The most amazing feeling in the world washed over her. And still, she wanted more.

Again he thrust. His face was strained. She knew he was close. He'd been close before she arrived. When they went this long without having sex, he couldn't stop his orgasm from ramming through him like a tidal wave.

With a sharp intake of breath, he came, and when he did, she followed right behind him, her second orgasm drawn from her body from the pressure of the base of his cock against her clit.

They remained in that position, breathing heavily, for as long as they could stand until the cold got to them. She wanted to tell him how much she enjoyed what they'd just done. She wanted him to know how aroused she'd gotten when she realized he intended to fuck her standing up in the cave. She wanted to say so many things, but her mouth wouldn't move. Would he think she was weird or something for finding this situation so hot?

Alton met her gaze. His expression was more serious than usual as he lifted her off his cock and set her feet on the ground. He didn't mention the steaming hot way he'd just taken her hard and fast. "Get dressed, Jos, before we both freeze."

She scrambled to put her clothes back on while he did

the same. Something wasn't right. Something was most assuredly wrong. As if she had a sixth sense, she knew her world was about to tip a little on its axis. Was he feeling remorse for taking her so roughly? God, she hoped not.

As soon as she was tucked back into her coat, Alton hauled her into his embrace, wrapping them in the blanket once again. This time he leaned against the wall, his feet spread, giving her the space to burrow against his warmth. At least he wasn't pulling away.

He didn't meet her gaze. Instead, he threaded his fingers through her hair and tucked her head against his chest. He inhaled her scent audibly for several breaths before he spoke. "I can't do this anymore, Jos." They had this conversation often. Tonight he sounded more serious than usual.

She stiffened. "I know. You're right. We need to figure something else out."

He said nothing. Was he telling her they needed to break up?

She panicked for a moment before he flattened his palm against her back and soothed her through the layers. "Shhh, baby. Don't freak out. I just mean we need to end this insanity. I want you in my bed. Every night. Where it's warm and cozy. I don't want to hide anymore."

She nodded against him. *Thank God.* "I'd love that. You have a plan?"

"Nope. Just stating the obvious." He glanced away, his brows furrowed, lips pursed. Nervous tension crawled up her spine again.

She had to be imagining it. Why did he seem to be hiding something from her?

She held him tighter, those ever-present pesky tears leaking. Shaking her weird doubts from her mind, she held her tongue. Silent as usual. She spent most of her life suffering in a silent prison of her choosing. Locked away in a world that had played a horrific joke on them by drawing them together like magnets when they both knew what sort of damage it would do to their respective families if anyone ever found out. So they fought against nature with all they had.

Except it was time to do something. *Now.* Was it possible? After all, their parents were in communication now. And a few siblings. Crazy events of the last few months had drawn their immediate families together. Why not her and Alton too?

If only she didn't have pack obligations pulling her in a different direction. No matter how many times she tried to convince herself that her mom and dad and even her siblings would support her, the same could not be said of the rest of the pack.

She knew for a fact most of her cousins were not on board with the idea of reconciliation yet and certainly none of the older generation. Most of them were hell-bent on maintaining that the entire Tarben pack was a bunch of conniving idiots.

She knew World War III would break out the moment anyone found out about her relationship with the enemy. The same was true of his pack. Making the conscious choice to start that war was difficult. Accepting the repercussions might be even worse.

There was a possibility one or both of them could lose their jobs and their families. They could be forced to leave Silvertip. They both knew it. They were on a challenging path toward that fate, but shit was happening at work she felt obligated to see through to completion before she lowered the boom.

It would seem, based on the stilted conversations she had with Alton about their respective breweries, that he was in a similar predicament even though she couldn't imagine how that was possible. Her brewery was about to launch a product that would set them apart from the competition. What the hell was he working on?

The reality was her job was stressful, and working for the competitor of your life partner was even more stressful. As long as they met briefly, snatching stolen moments in the night, they had no time or reason to discuss work. But if they completed the binding and outed themselves, everything would change.

Alton rubbed his hands up and down Joselyn's arms. "You're thinking so hard." He kissed the top of her head again. The weirdness that had surrounded him for a moment was gone. Maybe she'd imagined it.

"Mmm. Always."

He chuckled as he grabbed her biceps to lean back far enough to meet her gaze. "What should I expect? It's dark. Nighttime is your friend. As soon as the sun goes down, Joselyn Arthur's brain goes into hyperdrive."

She smiled back. He was right. No denying the truth. She might struggle to get up in the morning, but thank God the days were short in Alberta, Canada, at this time of year because her best work was often accomplished spread over the kitchen table at her parents' home when most people were sleeping.

He closed his eyes and squeezed her closer. "I've been doing some digging. Do you know what the original disagreement was between our families?"

She winced. "Yeah. Originally, land and water, but I've heard a child died somehow. And then something worse happened in retaliation."

"Yeah. That's what I found out. It seems both families were claiming homesteads along the river and then diverting the water to their own land. Before there were any national ordinances against this activity, the river would at times run lower. At some point, I think my pack claimed a homestead on the west side of the river and your pack went ballistic, insisting we stay on the east."

She nodded, tipping her face up and setting her chin on his chest to watch him as he spoke. He knew more about the history than she did.

"I imagine every household spent lots of time pissing and moaning about the other pack so often that their children grew up in this hatred."

"Do you know what the last straw was? Did a child really die?"

He nodded. "Yeah. At least that's the legend passed down from one generation to the next. It was over a hundred years ago, but apparently after the land dispute, two fathers were out hunting with their young sons. They encountered each other and began arguing.

"The seven-year-old boys had been raised to hate each other and imitated the standoff, pulling their knives out. The problem is they were too young to understand the consequences, and one of them stabbed the other fatally."

She gasped. Her heart ached for that boy's family. "Let me guess. An Arthur stabbed a Tarben."

He rubbed her biceps. "That's the lore. Later that night the father of the dead child—one of my ancestors—went to the Arthur home and rained bullets on the one-room cabin. The mother was shot and killed. The feud was solidified and remains today, in some ways stronger than ever."

"God that's awful."

"Not as awful as still holding on to that grudge to this day and forcing friends and lovers to remain in hiding." He set his forehead against hers, his voice serious.

She swallowed. For long seconds they stared at each other.

Finally, Alton frowned. "You look tired, babe. Are you sleeping?"

She tipped her head to one side. "Are you?"

He sighed. "Good point."

She slept only a few hours a night, and most nights she woke up before the sun, gasping for breath. That same damn nightmare that began to plague her years ago would not let go of her.

Never once did she remember what the dream was about. Not a single detail. She just knew that it yanked her awake every time, sweating and scared out of her mind. She also found herself momentarily disoriented, thrashing about in search of something.

That part wasn't a mystery. She was searching for Alton, needing to assure herself he was still there. Alive. Breathing. Warm. Hers.

Except he never was. She had woken up in his arms only a handful of times in the last four months.

The universe was cruel.

"I should move out of my parents' house," she stated for the hundredth time.

"Why? You have the perfect set up. All of your siblings have moved out. You have your own wing of the house with more rooms than you need, and your rent is free." He grinned.

She rolled her eyes. "You just like knowing where I am."

He tapped her nose. "I like knowing you're *safe*. There's a difference."

"I'm twenty-four years old. Billions of women my age live on their own without fearing for their lives every day, Alton."

"None of those women are my woman, baby." He kissed her lips gently, reverently. "I worry about you."

She licked her lips, tasting him, craving more.

"And if you don't start sleeping, I'm going to worry even more. Why don't you change your schedule so you aren't rushing around in the morning? Sleep later. Go in at noon. Work second shift hours or at least half of first and then second." He smiled broadly. "I know you work fifteen hours a day."

"Pot meet kettle."

Now he laughed. "Okay, you have me there. But I'm just trying to keep my mind off you. What else would I do with my time? It's easier to pretend I'm a workaholic who can't leave the office than confront my family members about getting a life. I'm pretty sure most of them think I'm gay."

She giggled. "Good. Let them think that."

"You know the world is seriously fucked up if a man has to pretend to be gay to keep his true relationship a secret."

"There's nothing wrong with being gay," she teased, biting her lip.

"I didn't say there was. But I happen to be heterosexual, which makes it comical when my cousins give me a weird double glance all the time. One of them even confronted me last month when he pointed out a hot chick he was ogling and noticed I never even glanced."

Her entire body warmed. "You didn't glance?"

He frowned. "Why would I? The sexiest woman alive is already mine."

Yeah, she loved this man more than life itself. Which made it that much harder to be without him on a regular basis. Stolen moments and quick fucks were not going to cut it any longer.

But her job... And her family... *Fuck.*

Alton flinched when that word stabbed through her brain. He kissed her forehead again and held her closer. "We *will* figure this out. We have no other options."

They stood there, holding each other close, swaying together for a long time. Words weren't necessary. They could talk on the phone later if they had something to say. For now, Joselyn needed to be in his arms, feeling his heartbeat next to hers, his breath wafting across her face, his cock—hard again—pressing into her belly. She gripped the back of his shirt in her fists, trying desperately to ignore the cold.

It was time to go. Her nose was stiff. Her breath came out in cloudy puffs. And her parents would wonder why she was gone so long. They were already suspicious and concerned about these evening runs she took.

She couldn't blame them. There had been a few incidents in recent months that warranted some diligence. For one thing, her brother Isaiah's mate, Heather, was attacked on a hiking path by one of Alton's cousins. And then, to make matters worse, Alton's older brother Antoine tried to kidnap Heather.

As if that weren't enough drama for the quiet town of Silvertip, Alton's other brother, Austin, recently bound to his childhood sweetheart, Nuria, after years of separation. She too was threatened by several locals and eventually kidnapped by a hired man. The fact that he'd held her hostage in the small cabin where Joselyn used to meet up with Alton was the reason Joselyn was now standing in the cold tonight.

Every shifter involved in each incidence was in the custody of the Arcadian Council in the Northwest Territories, but the insanity put people on edge and forced them to be more careful.

Most grizzly shifters weren't running around outside

alone anymore, not even in their bear form in the mountains. And certainly not females.

Alton blew out a long breath. "I can hear your thoughts, and your mother's right. It's not safe. I don't like this arrangement."

"We've talked about this, Alton. I'm not worried about someone grabbing me while I wander up the side of the mountain in bear form. What are the chances? Just because a few bad guys messed with our town doesn't mean anyone is in any more danger than we ever were. They're all in custody. The Arcadian Council is handling it."

"One of those *bad* guys was my brother, Jos. My *own* brother." His voice rose as he stiffened against her. "I knew he was an oddball, but I would never have suspected he was capable of rape or forced binding or worse. So, forgive me if I trust no one these days."

She nodded, but her insides were in knots. He trusted her, and she was about to royally piss him off in the professional world. "I should go."

"Yeah."

Neither of them moved.

Alton sucked in a breath as if he had something else to say, but no words came out. She couldn't see inside his head well. Emotions, yes. How he felt about her, yes. But he was blocking other thoughts.

And who was she to react to the sting of his secrets when she had so many of her own?

CHAPTER 7

On Sunday afternoon, Alton went to his parents' house for dinner, something he did nearly every Sunday. The entire family did. At least the immediate family. Antoine, the oldest, was no longer around, of course. He would probably never see the light of day again in his lifetime. But the rest of Alton's siblings came every Sunday unless something dire got in the way.

Austin was there with Nuria as were both of Alton's sisters, one older and one younger, Abigail and Adriana. Neither of them had found the right man to bind to yet. Until a few weeks ago, none of the Tarben kids had completed a binding. Austin was the first to fall, and he was thirty.

Although, if Alton were honest with himself, he'd known who his mate would be for longer than the average shifter. Granted Nuria and Austin had met in the fourth grade also, so who knew? Maybe his sisters also knew their mates and kept it secret.

Dinner wasn't ready yet, and Alton had a pounding headache, so he excused himself and wandered toward the tree line on the other side of the barn. His family had always kept a variety of animals, but when his parents opened the brewery twenty-nine years ago, they hired a foreman to maintain the barn and whatever creatures inhabited it. Currently, Alton thought there were two horses, a cow, and a few goats.

Beth Tarben, his mother, thought it was important for her kids to grow up around animals, which was comical since they could shift at any time and lope through the mountains at one with nature.

Spying his favorite rock inside the tree line, Alton perched on the edge of it, taking a deep breath as he glanced at the back of the barn. It had been repainted a few times over the years, but it still sported the dark brown siding it had always had. The same siding as the two-story house situated in front of it. And the matching brown paint also coated the log fencing that stretched across the clearing behind the barn where the animals could roam.

The two acres were surrounded by evergreen trees that cocooned the property, hiding it. Protecting it from unnecessary detection.

For most of his childhood, the barn had represented a place of solace. So many good memories happened in that barn. He'd learned to take care of horses in there, saddle them, brush them down, feed them. At one time or another, he'd enjoyed a wide range of cats and dogs.

He never had time for anything like that anymore. Life always got in the way. And besides, he often did not permit himself to enjoy life too much while his mate wasn't at his side. It seemed wrong in a way.

He pulled his phone from his pocket, inhaling the air around him to make sure he was alone before he sent a quick empty text. Nothing reached his nose except a few animals and the ever-present scent of pine.

Seconds later, his phone vibrated, indicating an incoming call and bringing a smile to his face. "Hey," he whispered, his usual greeting.

"Hey, yourself," she responded in kind.

"You busy?"

"Nope. I'm in my room curled up by the window staring at the pages of a book."

"Are there words?" he teased.

"I have no idea." She sounded sad.

"Baby…"

"I miss you." Now he could hear the tears in her voice.

"I know."

"We can't keep this up."

"I know that too." It was a broken record with them.

She sighed. "You at your parents'?"

"Yep. Everyone's here. It makes my chest hurt to watch Austin with his new mate Nuria. They're so damn happy. I had to escape for a few minutes."

"So you're sitting on your rock behind the barn."

"Yep." She knew him well. "Your knees are pulled to your chest, and you have a ponytail?"

"Yep." She giggled, the sound going straight to his cock.

"Wish I could tug that band free and run my fingers through the waves of hair."

She sighed again. "Alton…" Her voice was filled with emotion.

He rubbed his forehead, inhaling deeply, which caused him to sit up straighter and glance around. "Gotta call you back. Someone's coming." He ended the call without waiting for a response and stuffed his phone in his pocket. If anyone ever stole his phone and went through his records, he'd be toast.

At least he had his own apartment and lived alone. Joselyn lived with her parents. Even though she had her own cell phone in her name, not connected to anyone else in her family, he worried one day someone else would pick it up, or she might inadvertently leave it lying around, and they would be found out.

Seconds after ending the call, he realized who was approaching. It wasn't one of his immediate family members. It was Austin's mate, Nuria. Alton hadn't had much time to get to know her yet. He remembered her from when they were kids, but she was five years older than him and moved away when he was ten.

She stepped into his line of sight with her hands tucked into the pockets of her jeans. Her long brown curls hung in ringlets around her face, curtaining her from the world. Timid was the best way to describe her. She'd had a hard life before returning to town two weeks ago and binding to his brother. Theirs was a love story that rivaled Alton's. In fact, he might have to concede defeat to Austin seeing as his brother went fifteen years not knowing where his mate was or if she was alive even though he'd known at a young age she was his.

The concept of being so certain two people belonged together was foreign to a lot of grizzly shifters. Other species operated under a fated premise, but not the bears. At least until recently. There seemed to be more and more locals coming out of the woodwork with long stories of destined romances.

Alton winced at the thought. He was one of those statistics. If many others like him were keeping their relationships secret, perhaps there was some merit to the idea of Fate stepping in.

"Hi," Nuria said as she got closer. "Sorry. I didn't mean to interrupt you." She tucked a curl behind her ear and lifted her deep green eyes to meet his gaze.

"You didn't."

She smiled warmly but held his gaze. "You were on the phone."

He winced. Had she heard him? How the hell had she gotten close enough to know that without him scenting her? He rubbed his forehead with two fingers. Apparently, he was getting sloppy.

She didn't press the issue further. When she spoke again, she changed the subject. "I just wanted to uh…" She dropped her gaze to the ground and used one toe to shuffle the dirt around. "Well, I mean we haven't had a chance to get to know each other yet."

He relaxed his shoulders but wondered what she was trying to say. It wasn't like they hadn't spoken at all. She'd been at the house the previous two Sundays for dinner with Austin. Alton wasn't sure why she would specifically single him out for a chat.

And then she dropped the bomb. "Look," she lifted her face again, tucking another loose curl behind her ear, "I know."

"You know what?" He gulped and then held his breath. *Fuck*. Did she know about Jos? How?

"Don't freak out or anything. I don't think anyone else knows. But it was obvious to me. And I wanted you to know that I know. And also…" She stopped moving, holding his gaze. "I can't keep this from Austin. It's not fair. We don't have secrets. It's been two weeks, and we've been so busy that it totally slipped my mind until today, but seeing you… I have to tell your brother."

Alton stared at her, not completely sure they were even on the same page, let alone the same book. And he sure didn't want to out his relationship with Joselyn unnecessarily if she was speaking of some totally unrelated topic. He opted for a one-word, vague answer. "How?"

"Two weeks ago. The day I was kidnapped, and then

that crowd of people was here at your parents' home. The Arthurs were here, several of them. I saw you. I saw her too. I think your family and hers were so preoccupied with dealing with the Arcadian Council and worrying over me that no one noticed."

Alton couldn't breathe. If Nuria noticed, surely others had. But no one had said a single word.

"It was the last thing on their minds that day, Alton. And I assume the two of you don't often find yourselves in the same crowded room."

"No. We don't." Though neither of them had said Joselyn's name, it was evident Nuria knew about them. *Fuck.*

"I just happened to catch a look you exchanged, and then I watched you skirt around each other in a sort of dance. Broke my heart." Her voice hitched, and she reached up to wipe a tear from her face.

Alton choked, but he didn't move.

"Alton, I spent fifteen years living on the opposite side of this country missing your brother so badly it caused physical pain. Take my word for it. You don't want to do that. You actually can't. Denying the pull to bind isn't possible. Not even with time or space. I've proven that the hard way."

He swallowed the lump in his throat. His voice was low and gravelly when he spoke. "I know. Believe me, I know."

"It's like a piece of your soul won't be whole until you bind yourself to the one you love. I thought I could walk away. I thought I could do it fifteen years ago, and I thought I could do it fifteen days ago. But it's not a choice. It will eat you alive."

He knew that much better than she could imagine.

"How long have you known?" she asked, tipping her face to one side while she tried to corral another curl behind her ear. The air was brisk, but still too cold to stay out there very long.

Alton stared at her for a moment, considering his options. He didn't have to tell her anything. He could blow her off. He didn't even know her well enough to confide these secrets.

On the other hand, he had no one else, and he now needed to deal with the fact that his brother was about to find out. "Longer than you and Austin," he breathed out, relief over the admission racing through his body.

"Oh, Alton." She pressed her hand to her mouth and sobbed.

He took a deep breath. Why did it feel so good to share this with someone? A practical stranger? "Third grade. I guess you've known about Austin longer, but I was even younger. I was nine. I remember the day perfectly."

Tears rolled down her face. "Why?" she choked out.

Good question. *Why?* He tipped his face toward the ground as though looking for the answers in the dirt while at the same time avoiding the emotion on her face. "It's complicated."

"It's never that complicated."

"Yes. It is. This time it is. You know how our families feel about each other."

"But that's changing. You were all together just two weeks ago right here in the same house. Don't you think you can come out of that closet now?"

He shook his head. "That was a fraction of our families. Just because my parents made nice with her parents for a while under dire circumstances doesn't mean Jos and I can step forward and declare our love. Most of my aunts and uncles would freak out."

"Who cares?" Her voice rose. "Surely you'd rather be

happy with your mate than appease all those people? Family or not."

She was right to a certain extent. But there was a lot more to it she didn't know. She couldn't possibly fully understand the dynamic between the two packs. Binding himself to Joselyn could be the end of their lives in Silvertip. Yes, the pull on his soul to claim her was strong, but pack ties were also strong, and severing those ties was an enormous step. For both of them. "I know. And I wish it were that simple. It just isn't. For either of us. I'm heartened that our immediate families are on speaking terms. It also gives me hope that Austin is such good friends with Joselyn's brother Isaiah." Was it enough, though?

"They've been friends for fifteen years too, you know. Hiding. It makes me so sad to think two teenagers had to conceal their friendship and meet in the mountains for all these years so they wouldn't piss off their parents."

He nodded.

"But you know what? No one even cared in the end. Not your parents nor Isaiah's. Those are the same people who will be open and understanding of your situation, Alton."

"Maybe."

"I'm sure of it." She stood straighter, forcing a smile. "Or you can continue to torture yourself year after year, meeting secretly in odd places until you realize you'd rather die than not have her with you."

"I'm past that point," he admitted, holding her gaze.

She pursed her lips, obviously trying not to let her tears start up again.

"And I'm working on it. It's only been two weeks since all hell broke loose, bringing the families closer together."

"It's been building longer than that. Your two fathers

came together a few months ago too when Antoine went all stupid and tried to bind himself to Heather."

Alton chuckled at her word choice. "Stupid? Nuria, my asshole brother tried to rape you fifteen years ago. Who knows if he meant to bind Heather to him or kill her that day? Or both. He's a fucking bastard. We don't even know how many other women he's accosted over the years. Stupid is too kind of a word."

"Okay, but he's your brother. I didn't want to be disrespectful."

Austin chuckled again. "He's not my brother. He's a fucking idiot. I hope I never see him again. If he ever surfaced again and Austin didn't kill him with his bare hands, I would do so for him on your behalf."

Nuria nodded. "Nevertheless, I feel horrible for Heather. That poor woman has us all beat after what she's been through. She wasn't even a shifter until a few days before that when…"

Austin held out a hand to stop her from continuing. He didn't want to verbalize the atrocities of any other member of his family at the moment. He was embarrassed enough as it was. It didn't matter that everyone he ran into insisted he was not his brother or his cousin Jack, who attacked Heather in the woods in the first place, causing her to transition.

"Well, that's all. I didn't mean to interrupt your call. I'm sorry about that. I'm sure finding the time to speak to each other is hard enough as it is. But finding a time to speak to you privately was also a challenge. And I wanted to give you the heads up before telling your brother."

Alton nodded. "I appreciate that. Would you do me a favor and let me tell him?"

She chewed on her bottom lip again. "When?"

He shrugged. "Doesn't matter. Tonight is fine. After dinner? Your place?"

She glanced over her shoulder. Someone else was approaching. They both sensed it at the same time. Austin. "That will work," she hurried to add. "When we get home after dinner, stop by."

"Okay."

Austin stepped into their line of sight two seconds later. His face lit up as he spotted Nuria, and he came toward her. "There you are."

She smiled as he wrapped his arms around her middle. "Ran into Alton. We were getting to know each other."

"Good." He rubbed a thumb over her face. "You're freezing. Let's get back inside." He turned them both around, glancing over his shoulder. "You coming?"

"Be there in a sec." Alton stayed right where he was, watching his brother and Nuria disappear. A tight knot formed in his stomach that wouldn't release. Watching the two of them fawn over each other made him physically ill. Not because he wasn't happy for them, but because he was so miserable with himself.

CHAPTER 8

Joselyn leaned over the marketing plan she had spread out on the kitchen table, tapping her lips with a pen. Her brain was mush from too many numbers—market shares, focus groups, demographics. The lists were endless, but she wanted to be sure she wasn't overlooking anything that might thwart her brewery's launch. She had been working for two hours on a Sunday afternoon to keep her mind off the abrupt end to her phone call with Alton.

She spoke to him most days. They rarely went more than two days without finding the time, but she didn't have the liberty to call him back when she knew he was at his parents. Occasionally they had to end a call quickly when someone approached. It happened. It hurt.

When the back door opened, a whoosh of cold air filled the room. Her parents had been up in the mountains for an hour roaming around in their bear form. They did that most Sundays. Their cheeks were red from the short walk in human form from the tree line to the house. Her mother was laughing at something her father had said as they entered.

When Rosanne spotted Joselyn at the table, her smile fell. "You're working?"

Her father, Bernard Arthur, leaned over the copy on the table and peered at it. "That's amazing, honey. You do such good work. Thank God we have you. No one else in the family has an eye for this stuff."

Joselyn's gut clenched. She hated feeling indispensable. Especially under the circumstances. There was every chance in the world that she and Alton would have to leave town after they outed themselves. Then her father would have to find a new marketing director. "Don't be so dramatic, Dad. I have a marketing degree. Anyone can get one."

He smiled as he righted himself, taking her chin in his hand. "You have talent, my sweet, humble daughter. No degree can make someone talented. It comes from the heart."

She swallowed. She did have talent and an eye for marketing, but she hoped like hell someone else in the family had gotten the gene too because she was at the breaking point. "Thanks, Dad."

He dropped her chin and faced the papers again while her mother bustled around in the kitchen putting a kettle on to boil water. It was her daily routine. Afternoon tea. Allister spoke again. "You think we're ready to launch?"

"I believe so." She bit her lip hard. She did that a lot lately. The stinging pain took away some of the guilt.

"Good. Because it's next Monday, hon. Eight days. All this last minute tweaking is unnecessary. You've nailed it."

She nodded. If he only knew where her nerves were coming from. They had nothing to do with the launch.

As if her father read her mind—and if she didn't pay attention to blocking better, he probably could—his next words made her jump. "The Tarbens are going to piss themselves when they find out about this."

She nodded again, unable to utter a word. That was her primary concern. The most important person in her life was one of those Tarbens, and she had no idea how he was going to react when he found out she'd been secretly involved in this scheme to get ahead of the game and bolster her family's sales, leaving the Tarben brewery number two in the area.

It scared the daylight out of her. It kept her up at night. It even got in the way of her phone calls with Alton. Damn family secrets. For years she'd hoped their families would reconcile eventually and she could be with Alton in peace. But she hadn't counted on something like this. The entire Arthur pack was banking on making a lot of money off this new campaign at the expense of the Tarben pack.

Joselyn was stuck in the middle. She hated herself for her role. She hated herself even more for not mentioning it to her mate. But how could she? This was a family business. It wouldn't be fair to her extended pack if she leaked confidential information to the competitor that could ruin their marketing plans.

Besides, they didn't have a single clue she was sleeping with the enemy.

When Joselyn was at work, which was nearly all the time she was awake, she threw herself into the task and gave it her all. She forced her mind to ignore the niggling feeling she was about to destroy the tentative hold she had on her personal relationship and did the job she was assigned to.

It sucked. It made her sick most days. But she did it.

It wasn't as though she had knowledge of some giant merger that was going to eat Alton's family business and spit them out. It was simply a new product, one that had been carefully guarded from the Tarben pack to get an edge in the industry.

Even though there was renewed communication between the two sets of parents and a set of their sons, it wasn't as if they played bridge together on Friday nights and sang Kumbaya around a campfire.

They'd bonded twice, once over Heather and then again over Nuria. Joselyn wasn't convinced the relationship was strong enough to survive an actual binding between the two families yet. And that didn't even take into consideration what her extended family would say. She shuddered.

"You okay, honey?" her mother asked, handing her a cup of tea. "You look tired. You work too hard. There are bags under your eyes."

Joselyn rolled those eyes. "Mom, stop worrying about me. I'm a grown woman." She blew on the tea and took her first tentative sip.

Rosanne leaned over the ad lying on the table and ran her fingers over the bubbles erupting from the top of the two-dimensional bottle. "Every time I see this, I get chills. It looks so real I have to touch it to prove it's not."

Joselyn smiled. "That's the idea. Glad it's working for you. I love what the graphic artist came up with. Now, let's hope everyone else in Silvertip, Alberta, and North America agrees and rushes to the store to wipe the shelves clean of Glacial Citrus."

Personally, Joselyn thought the lemon- and orange-flavored malt beverages were going to be a huge hit, and not just among the target audience of women, but even with men. There were dozens of microbreweries in the area, but none of them were producing a product geared toward women.

Only the big breweries usually took on such a risky

venture. But this had been in the works secretly with Glacial Brewing Company even before Joselyn returned from U of C and took over the marketing department.

When she'd first arrived back in town two years ago, young and naïve and silently freaking out over the total separation from Alton, she'd worried the older members of her family who all worked in the brewery would resent her expertise or the position the board had given her.

The reality was no one else in the family was qualified for the job. That was the reason she went to U of C to get her marketing degree in the first place—to fill a need in the family business.

The first months back in Silvertip had been challenging. She found it difficult to sleep at night. Work was stressful. She doubted her decision to return to Silvertip every day.

Although she had kept Alton at arm's length the entire time they'd been at U of C, she considered him a friend. And she missed him.

Every time he tried to discuss the possibility of there being more to their relationship than mere friendship, she shut him down. She'd been too young to handle the idea. Scared. So many concerns riddled her, it was difficult to acknowledge which one was the most gut-wrenching.

Fear of being banished from her pack, her immediate family, and her hometown was top on the list of anxieties. The truth was they both came from a long line of deeply loyal packs who worked together and played together. Grizzly packs were tight. Severing from one was not easy. She'd heard stories of other shifters leaving their packs only to spend their lives feeling incredible desolation. Suicide wasn't uncommon for a banished pack member. The solitude could be astronomical. Would it lessen if the reason for leaving the pack was to bind to a member of another pack?

Besides her concerns regarding banishment, she had other apprehensions. Her parents had paid a lot of money for her to get her university degree. She felt awful enough that she'd lied to them for all these years by omission. Heck, she'd lied to herself too. It would have killed her to turn her back on her family so abruptly and hurt everyone who loved her. After two years, she didn't want to let them down by separating from the pack to enjoy the fruits of her education somewhere else.

Alton had the same problems. At least they had that in common. It wasn't difficult to understand how the other felt about the subject. Family loyalty. A sense of debt from the bills of their education. And a huge fear of the unknown if they simply took off and didn't glance back.

At first, they had no contact with each other, and then he'd called. Denying the pull toward him was difficult.

Now what would happen? Just when they were about to snap and go insane with the need to be together, this explosion of a secret could forge a divide between them that would be insurmountable.

Joselyn honestly had no idea how Alton would react. Maybe it wouldn't be as bad as she expected. Maybe it would be worse. In the two years since they'd returned and taken positions in their respective family breweries, they had intentionally agreed never to discuss business.

The plan had served them well. But this was different. This wasn't about spreadsheets, the ups and downs of beer sales, bottom line sales, or even differing tastes. This launch could be damaging to Alton's family.

Where did that leave Alton and Joselyn?

She shuddered, reminding herself that her fleeting conversation with him earlier had been cut far too short.

She missed him so terribly. Making it worse was this secrecy. He was her life mate, the man she should have bound herself to long ago. She wanted to share everything with him. *Everything*. Her thoughts and dreams and even her rotten day at the office.

Instead, she found herself knee-deep in what could very well be the biggest mistake of her life.

When Joselyn's dad popped the lid off a beer behind her, the sound jolted her back to the present. "I don't know what you're so worried about, honey. No one else is concerned. Your work is amazing. Everyone agrees. Even my father would have been proud, and that's saying something." He tipped his head back and took a long swig.

Joselyn smiled. "Grandpa Arthur did have good taste." He had died five years ago, but she remembered him as a surly old man who was the primary antagonist in maintaining a century-old feud with the Tarben pack. Nevertheless, he had an eye for art.

The house phone rang on the kitchen counter while Joselyn continued to stare at the colorful depictions of orange and yellow malt beverages spread over the table. She paid no attention to her mother taking the call until she stepped up to Joselyn's side and held the phone out. "It's Nuria Orson," she mouthed while shrugging and lifting her eyebrows.

Joselyn took the phone from her mother and wandered toward the living room area to plop down on the couch. "Hello?"

"Hey, Joselyn. It's Nuria Orson. Not sure if you remember me, but I just moved back to Silvertip a few weeks ago."

"Yes. Of course." Joselyn leaned back, wondering what Nuria might want to speak to her about.

Nuria giggled. "I'm sure the entire town knows who I

am. If they didn't remember my family fleeing in the middle of the night fifteen years ago, they were reminded in a big way when I returned."

"Yes. I'm so sorry for all you've been through. I've heard."

Nuria was six years older than Joselyn. Joselyn didn't specifically remember her from childhood, but she'd seen her a few weeks ago at the Tarben home after she'd been abducted and rescued. Joselyn hadn't spoken directly to Nuria that day, but she'd at least had her memory jogged when she saw her big green eyes and gorgeous dark curls.

The visit to the Tarben home had been the first and only time Joselyn had ever been in Alton's family home. It had also been strained and stressful. Besides finding herself swept into Alton's world with dozens of other people that day, it was also the first and only time she and Alton had been in the same space while surrounded by everyone they loved.

And they'd done so without acknowledging they knew each other.

Joselyn closed her eyes, remembering the day well. It was etched in her mind. She'd gone there with her parents to show support for the Tarbens as they dealt with a local kidnapper. In spite of their long-standing family feud, the two packs had at least bonded—if only temporarily—over a mutual need to ensure the entire community's safety.

Joselyn had spent the whole time worrying that her relationship with Alton would be found out. If so many people from both families hadn't been in the house with far more pressing matters to concern themselves with, things would have gone differently. There was no reason someone shouldn't have noticed the connection between Alton and Joselyn.

Grizzly shifters didn't put off a distinct scent indicating

they were bound to another bear until after they completed the binding. However, often their immediate families could sense a connection, especially their parents.

"Thanks," Nuria responded, dragging Joselyn back to the present. "The reason I'm calling is because I heard you got your marketing degree from the University of Calgary, and I was wondering if you might not mind speaking to me about it. I'm going to enroll in classes soon."

"Sure. Anytime." Joselyn was a little shocked by the request. After all, she didn't know Nuria at all. But maybe she had an interest in marketing.

"Are you free tonight? I mean, I don't want to bother you if you're busy or anything, but I thought since it's a Sunday, maybe you had some time? Perhaps you could come to the house?"

Wow. That was even more shocking. Joselyn worried her lip. She had no reason to turn Nuria down. In fact, it might be helpful to her sanity if she got out of the house for a while to take her mind off the upcoming launch and her stress over what it would do to her relationship. "Sure. I could do that. What time?"

"How about eight? I'm at the Tarbens this afternoon, but we'll be home by then."

Joselyn took a deep breath. Lucky Nuria. She was able to reconnect with her childhood sweetheart, Alton's brother, and now she was all nestled into the Tarben family fold—welcomed with open arms—while Joselyn remained the permanently hidden, secret girlfriend of the younger brother.

She'd give anything to be at that damn family dinner with her mate. That's how it should be. Instead, the only thing she'd gotten from Alton so far that day was a quick call that ended too soon.

Would it be weird to spend time at Austin's home while

knowing she belonged to his younger brother in her soul? Probably, but on the other hand, maybe it was a step in the right direction. A connection with Alton's brother couldn't be a bad thing.

She decided to accept the weird invitation. "Sounds good. I'll be there."

"I guess you know where we live."

Joselyn smiled. Silvertip wasn't that big. She knew where nearly everyone lived, friend or not. "I do."

"Okay, perfect. See you then." The call ended before Joselyn could respond. She found herself staring down at the phone in her hand wondering what sort of bizarre relationship she might forge with Nuria Orson.

CHAPTER 9

Alton forced himself to sink into the plush loveseat in his brother's living room. Austin was five years older than him, but the two of them had always been close, especially since their older brother Antoine had been a strange guy for as long as Alton could remember.

Strange wasn't a very realistic term anymore after everything they now knew about Antoine, but hindsight was doing no one any good.

Alton was not looking forward to this chat with Austin. Not even close. But he totally understood Nuria's position. He couldn't expect her to keep this secret from her mate.

Alton shuddered when he considered how many secrets he was keeping from *his* mate. A permanent headache had formed behind his right eye as a result. If he didn't make some serious life changes soon, he would lose his mind.

On the plus side of outing his secret relationship to Austin, perhaps his brother would have some advice. It wasn't like Alton had anyone else to talk to. He'd been living in a very lonely world for four months. Or, if he was honest, most of his life.

Austin stepped into the room from behind Alton and tapped his shoulder with a cold beer. "You look like you could use a drink."

Alton took the bottle and glanced at the label. It was a light ale from one of the newer lines. "I *feel* like I could use a keg."

Austin lowered himself onto the couch and set his elbows on his knees. "I've noticed you've been stressed lately. More so than usual, I mean. Is something going on with you?"

Alton glanced at his brother as Nuria joined her mate on the couch. Instead of getting right to the point, he dodged the real question with a plausible answer. "This shit with the new launch is probably getting to me. It seems like every ten minutes Vinson barges into my office to double-check something with me."

Vinson was their cousin. The man was thirty-six, but most days he seemed significantly younger than Alton, who was twenty-five. He was an uptight sort of guy.

Austin sighed, rubbing his neck and then leaning back. "I hear ya. It's overwhelming. I'm exhausted."

Nuria set her hand on her mate's thigh, but her gaze was on Alton, her wide eyes imploring him to speak.

Austin continued, not noticing his mate's gesture. "The worst part is keeping this shit from Isaiah. We've been friends for fifteen years. Granted, no one knew that until recently, but we've never fought. We're like brothers in some ways."

Alton stared at his brother. There was no comparison between the relationship Austin had with his friend and the one Alton had with his own mate. For the millionth time, Alton wanted to fall into a crack in the floor and escape.

"Not that I mean to diminish the relationship I have with you, of course, but Isaiah and I are the same age, and he's always been there for me when I needed him most."

"Yeah. I get that." Alton sighed. It shouldn't bother him that Austin had such a great friend in Isaiah Arthur. After all, the two of them had indirectly and unknowingly bonded over the actions of Antoine fifteen years ago.

What bothered Alton most was that Austin and Isaiah had managed to out themselves as friends recently and now enjoyed the ability to see each other freely in public without enduring too much ridicule.

If it weren't for the damn family feud, Alton himself would not be sitting in his brother's home about to spill his inner secrets on a Sunday evening. He'd be in his *own* home snuggled up on the couch with his *own* mate watching reruns or old movies on television. A home he had yet to build because he didn't want to do it without Joselyn's input.

Alton had declined the offer of moving back in with his parents when he returned from U of C. Instead, he'd gotten an apartment in Silvertip and had lived there alone for the past two years. There was no way he could ever have a roommate. His disposition was often not the best, a product of sexual frustration above all else.

"Tell him," Nuria urged into Alton's mind. *"It can't be that bad. Like he just said, his best friend in the world is her brother. He's not going to judge you."*

She had a point. It wasn't so much that Alton was afraid to tell Austin about Joselyn. It was deeper than that. This would be the first time he admitted the relationship existed to *anyone*. Earlier in the afternoon with Nuria had been the first time anyone in the world had noticed and approached him.

He was still a little freaked out by her sixth sense. If she, a near stranger, could pick up on his feelings, how many other people had or would in the future?

None. Because he was never with Joselyn in public. The first time in two years they had seen each other when anyone else was in the vicinity had been that day two weeks ago. And neither of them would have chosen to be in the same room that day. It had happened out of their control.

Before Alton had a chance to bare his soul, Austin spoke again. "I'm so worried about what this is going to do to Isaiah tomorrow that it's affecting my sleep. My hands are shaking." He held one out to demonstrate.

Nuria wrapped her fingers around his in a sweet attempt to soothe her mate.

Alton couldn't help but smile at how happy he was for his brother, in spite of his jealousy. Besides, Austin had inadvertently given him the perfect opportunity to segue this conversation into the reason Alton was sitting in Austin's living room in the first place.

Nuria knew it too because she shot Alton a wide-eyed look.

With a deep breath, Alton jumped right in. "Hey, at least Isaiah is just a close friend. Imagine if your *mate* was a member of the Arthur pack."

Austin laughed. "That would totally suck. I don't think any relationship could survive the catastrophe tomorrow will bring to the Arthurs. Not even one that was already bound together." He glanced at Nuria, who stared at him with a solemn expression.

Alton held his breath while he waited for his brother to realize what he'd just heard.

Austin furrowed his brow, still staring at Nuria. "What? Did I say something wrong?" He slid his gaze to Alton and then froze, his mouth hanging open.

Alton didn't move a muscle. He didn't even blink. He couldn't have spoken out loud if he wanted to anyway. He was choked up, emotions bubbling to the surface. The last thing he wanted to do was break down in his brother's living room.

He hadn't cried since he'd broken his arm in first grade. Not that he didn't feel emotions. He felt them deeply, especially when it came to Joselyn, but he always managed to hold them intact. Hide from those around him. Divert his thoughts.

This was huge, though. Revealing a lifelong secret for the first time made the entire thing so real it hurt deeply. An indescribable pain caused a tight knot in his stomach and a lump in his throat. The beer he held precariously in his hand threatened to slip through his grasp and slide to the floor.

Time stood still. Interminable seconds.

Austin finally closed his mouth and licked his lips. "Please tell me I'm misunderstanding."

"I wish I could." Alton had no idea how he managed to form those words. They were gravelly, but he spoke them.

"Who?" Austin frowned as Alton imagined him searching his mind for the possibilities.

"Joselyn." Alton let out a long breath as soon as her name left his lips. Like a huge weight had somehow been halfway lifted from his chest, he felt a new pressure behind his eyes. He set his bottle on the floor with shaky hands and closed his eyes while he rubbed his temples, trying to rein in the need to start crying.

"Oh, God. Alton…" His brother's voice was strained. Filled with sorrow.

Nuria spoke into Alton's head. *"It's going to be okay. I promise. You're doing fine."*

Alton blinked his eyes open to look at her. *"Why don't I believe you?"*

"Because you're scared. It's like a raw wound. But you'll get through this."

Alton tipped his face toward the floor. God, he hoped she was right. It didn't seem possible at the moment, but he prayed there was merit to her kind words.

"How long?" Austin cleared his throat. "I mean, how long have you known? Oh, shit. We were all at Mom and Dad's two weeks ago. She was there. Is that when you met?"

The sardonic, horrified noise that escaped Alton's mouth shocked even himself. "I wish. Things would be so simple if that were the case." He lifted his face to find Austin's concerned expression, his brows drawn tight together.

Austin groaned. "Oh, God. I'm so sorry." He glanced at Nuria. "I'm such an ass. How did I not know this?"

"Wasn't your fault. Don't be ridiculous," Alton added. "I kept it from everyone. The only reason I'm coming clean with you now is because your mate sensed it and didn't want to keep a secret from you."

Austin wrapped his arm around Nuria and pulled her closer to his side. At least he didn't appear to be mad. That was the last thing Alton wanted. "So, it's been a while? Did you run into her somewhere after you moved back here?"

Alton shook his head. "I've known since I was about nine. So has she." He smiled before adding, "And we both went to U of C together. We enjoyed a friendship of sorts. That's why I took so long to finish my degree. I was dragging my feet to draw out the time we had."

Austin's eyes widened farther. "Holy fuck. You spent all

that time with her? And didn't bind her to you? And then moved back here? How the hell is that even possible? You've been back two years."

Alton sighed. "I didn't say it was easy. It's a giant mess. We're miserable."

"When do you even see her?"

"Not often. We sneak away. There's a spot where we meet. Except this time of year, it's fucking cold, and we can't stay long. We speak on the phone several days a week..." He let his voice trail off. It was too painful to paint that picture.

Austin's expression turned to one of sheer horror. He absentmindedly threaded his fingers in his mate's hair and pressed her head against his chest. Understandable. "That cabin..." His voice trailed off a moment. "That's why you knew where to find Nuria. You meet Joselyn at that cabin, don't you?"

Alton nodded. "We used to sometimes. But not since that day. Can't risk it now that so many people are aware of the place. We have another spot. A small cave higher up the mountain."

Austin's eyes were wide as he nodded slowly, obviously stunned. He had to be imagining himself in Alton's shoes.

Crazy, since he hadn't lived a life true to himself, either. Alton decided to point this out. "You do realize that you spent fifteen years separated from Nuria only to get her back a few weeks ago. I can't imagine that kind of pain and daily torture any more than you can picture mine. Fate dealt us both a rotten hand."

Austin shook his head. "Not the same thing at all. I hadn't *slept* with Nuria. That's inconceivable, Alton."

"You're right. Even though it is my life, I find it unimaginable most days."

"Why the hell did you do this? You could have bound

together and told the world to go fuck themselves years ago." In a different situation, it might have been almost comical the way Austin reached across his body with his other hand and wrapped Nuria even tighter against him.

Nuria permitted the odd treatment, probably realizing her mate had no idea he was reacting so violently to the news and expressing it by holding what was most dear to him closer. Her lips were pursed. Her eyes held a slight twinkle.

Alton jerked his gaze back to his brother. "Trust me, I considered it multiple times. It's complicated, but you have to understand, until recently we never acted on the pull between us. We rarely spoke of it. Joselyn refused. To keep the peace between us, I kept my lips shut most of the time."

"You weren't together while you were at U of C? I mean *together* together?"

Alton shook his head. "Nope. Never touched her. Literally."

Austin shook his head again. "That's fucked up. That's no way to live."

Alton shrugged. "In the end, we discussed the possibilities. Our parents paid a lot of money for us to go to U of C. We felt we owed them the respect of returning and helping with our respective family businesses. Besides, you also have to realize this decision was made two years ago when neither of our parents was even on speaking terms with the other.

"Since we both felt a strong sense of family loyalty, it would have been painful to lose everyone we loved. We had no way of knowing if we would be entirely banished or not. You know how tight the bond to the pack is. It smothers me most days. Knowing in my heart how hard it would be for me, a grown man, to have Mom and Dad turn their backs on me, I couldn't begin to imagine what that would do to Joselyn.

"We just didn't know. We never tested the waters. All we had to go on was instinct. So we made this choice. We moved back here. We rarely spoke of it. Joselyn preferred to pretend we weren't meant to be together. And now…"

"And now shit is about to hit the fan, and holy fuck, you must be close to pulling all your hair out."

"Yes."

"Shit. Does she know about tomorrow's launch?"

Alton shook his head. "Of course not." He wiped his hands on his jeans, cringing for the millionth time at the giant secret he kept from her.

So many times he'd wanted to tell her about the plans his brewery had. He'd been working on it for months now, and it would have been nice to share his excitement with his mate, but that was never an option. For one, Joselyn was not bound to him. For two, sharing company plans with the competitor was pure stupidity. But what if that competitor was the most important person in your life?

His loyalty was so conflicted lately that he couldn't sleep well. It wasn't as if he was involved in something illegal, but most days he felt like he was strangling himself with the guilt. So what if his brewery was launching an innovative new product? Of course, they wouldn't share that information with anyone. Of course, the entire plan would be tightly guarded.

But Joselyn was his mate. And this launch would undoubtedly hurt her.

Austin groaned. "I wouldn't want to be you tomorrow."

"I don't even want to be me tomorrow." Alton picked up his beer and took another long drink. He leaned back in the cushions. That pretty much summed up the entire saga. There was little else to say. It wasn't as though Austin could solve this problem, and certainly not in the next twelve hours before all hell broke loose.

The sound of an approaching car made everyone sit taller.

"Are we expecting someone else?" Austin asked his mate.

Nuria chewed on her bottom lip. "I might have invited Joselyn to stop by and help me choose what classes to take at university."

Alton jumped to his feet as the car door opened, confirming what Nuria just admitted. Joselyn's scent was right outside.

Austin twisted to stare at his mate. "You did what? Why?" His voice rose.

She winced. "Well, I was only thinking of the star-crossed lovers and getting them together and fixing this wrong. I didn't consider the implications of what your stupid launch tomorrow would mean to the two of them."

Austin groaned as he too stood.

Alton's heart pounded. His hands started sweating, and he felt a flush race up his face. Joselyn was getting closer. He could feel her presence outside. He even knew when she hesitated, the moment she undoubtedly realized he was inside the house.

She didn't communicate with him though, which made him nervous. Although to be fair, he didn't reach out to her, either.

When her knock sounded too softly on the front door, Austin rushed to answer.

Alton couldn't move. He remained standing right where he was as the door opened to reveal the reason for his existence standing on the porch.

She looked shell-shocked but somehow managed to keep her gaze on Austin as she spoke in a choked voice.

"Hi. Uh, Nuria asked me to come by. She said she needed help making university choices?" Obviously, Joselyn hardly understood the reason for her visit.

Even though Alton couldn't see his brother's face, he still knew he rolled his eyes as he opened the door wider. "Come in."

Nuria stood. "Hey," she said.

Joselyn looked like she might faint. He couldn't blame her. She'd been ambushed, and so far she didn't even know it, so she was trying to pretend she didn't know Alton as anyone more than a passing relative of Austin's.

Alton needed to fix the imbalance of knowledge first and foremost. "Baby, we've been tricked." He swallowed to clear his throat before continuing. "I think Nuria believed an intervention was needed to get us together."

Joselyn's face turned a darker shade of red than what Alton felt his own skin must look like. She stood two feet inside the house without moving while Austin closed the door.

Alton found his feet and raced across the room to pull her into his arms.

She slumped against him. He tugged her coat off her arms and dropped it on the floor at their feet before cupping her face and holding her a few inches back.

She blinked huge, questioning eyes.

"They know."

"How...?" She cleared her throat. "How did they find out?"

"Nuria must have some sort of mate radar or something," he teased, trying to lighten the mood in the room. "She saw us looking at each other two weeks ago at my parents' house. She was the one who confronted me earlier today when I had to hang up on you."

Joselyn still looked shocked. She didn't speak. Finally,

her hands wrapped around his middle and squeezed as a tear slid down her face. "I'm sorry."

Nuria interrupted the moment. "Oh, God. Please don't apologize. You misunderstand. I was only trying to help. Nothing leaves this room."

Austin spoke next. "She's right. You two obviously need a safe place to meet, and you need to figure out a way to move forward. This has to stop. It's unnatural. It hurts me just hearing about it. Nuria and I will go out for a while, shift and go for a hike, and give you a chance to talk...or, uh, whatever."

Without taking his gaze off Joselyn, Alton sensed his brother and Nuria shuffling around the room until the sliding door off the kitchen opened and closed quickly.

Austin reached out to Alton. *"Guest room. First door on the right."*

Alton wanted to smile at the implication, but the moment was too serious for that yet.

"Are you mad?" Joselyn finally asked, tentatively.

He flinched. "God no. Baby, no." He held her head tighter and kissed her lips, forcing himself not to devour her just yet. They needed to talk first. Fuck after. "First of all, this isn't your fault. Secondly, I trust my brother and his mate to keep this under wraps until we're ready to tell everyone. And thirdly, he's right. We can't live like this."

"Okay, that last part isn't news." She lowered her hands down his back and slid them under his shirt. When her palms flattened on his skin, he sucked in a breath. Even though her hands were cold, her touch was welcoming. It never failed to calm him.

"So Nuria isn't going to university?" she asked out of left field as if the reason for her being there hadn't fully sunk in.

Alton chuckled. "I'm sure she is, but I don't think she needs your help."

Joselyn nodded. "It's not like she would move to Calgary and leave Austin here working in Silvertip. I should have realized how stupid that sounded."

Alton's cock stiffened more by the second. He wished he could keep the little head from taking over. It wasn't reasonable for Alton to continually fuck the living daylights out of Joselyn the moment they got together as if she meant nothing more to him than a good lay.

But that was usually what happened. They had so few precious hours together, and they wasted none of them. This unexpected bonus union had Alton bursting with the need to be inside her.

And God bless his brother for thoroughly understanding and getting out of the house so Alton could have sex with his mate.

He tried to tamp down the arousal by gritting his teeth. So many things needed to be said. He didn't even know where to start.

Joselyn tipped her head to one side, a renewed flush creeping up her cheeks. "Do you think you're the only one who feels the need to fuck first and talk after?"

"What?" Her words shocked him.

She rolled her eyes. "Alton, I'm as horny as you are when we get in the same space. You don't need to hold back on my account out of some misplaced desire to be chivalrous. Before I can concentrate, I need your hands on me. Everywhere. Now." She gripped his back with her fingertips to emphasize her words.

Relieved, Alton swung her up into his arms and plodded toward the guest room without taking his gaze off her. She was here. In his arms. In real life. He could enjoy at least a few hours with her before he had to let her go again.

He stuffed his concerns for what the future held for them to the back of his mind. Their problems could wait. Although he knew the fork in the road was wide and dismal, all that mattered at the moment was making love to Joselyn.

CHAPTER 10

Joselyn felt like she was in a dream. Totally surreal. Maybe she'd gone to sleep and conjured up the completely illogical call from Nuria in her mind to replace her usual nightmare with a sweet dream about Alton.

But this was not a dream. He held her in his arms, his gaze never leaving hers as he moved through the house. She didn't care where he was taking her as long as, when they arrived, clothes would be removed and naked skin would touch.

Suddenly she was falling, and he was falling with her until they bounced together on a soft surface. A bed. *So much better than the cold stone wall of a cave.*

His lips landed on hers, taking, giving, sucking, licking. Desperate. More than usual. She felt that same level of desperation, but hers stemmed mostly from carrying around a pack burden. Why did he happen to exude a similar vibe?

Perhaps they were both just tired, past the breaking point. The clock was ticking, and they needed to crawl out of this mess that had become their secret lives before it ate them up inside.

Suddenly, his hands were everywhere, searching her body as though she'd been shot and he was frantic to find the exit wound.

She lifted her ass off the bed so he could wiggle his palms under her sweater, and then he hauled it over her head. The second the material was out of the way, she landed again with a thump, and his mouth was consuming her.

He moaned into her as his hand trailed to her breast, molding it, squeezing almost too hard. Perfectly. Like he was crazed. He didn't usually handle her so roughly, but she craved this. It was driving her wild. Her panties were soaked inside her jeans, and her clit was pleading for release from the confines.

She spread her hands over his lower back and then tucked them into his jeans to squeeze his butt cheeks. He clenched them and bit down on her lower lip, not enough to break the skin, but enough to make her wish he would.

Joselyn had never felt this level of urgency to complete the binding. Something external seemed to be controlling her like a drug. It seemed crucial to bind together. Now.

She broke the kiss and tipped her head to the side so she could think better, gasping for air as Alton licked a line down her neck and nuzzled the sweet spot.

"Do it," she pleaded into his head.

"Do not tempt me, baby."

"Do it," she insisted again. *"Just fucking do it."*

He growled into her mind and then pressed his lips firmly to the spot before continuing down her body. Mumbling against her skin, he said, "Not... Gonna... Bind... You... To... Me... Today..."

"Why?" She shoved at his shoulders to get him to lift his

face. "Alton, why? I don't want to go on like this. I don't care what anyone thinks or says anymore. Please." She'd never begged before, never felt this strong compulsion.

She couldn't even ponder the implications of her request. Her job. The upcoming launch he knew nothing about. The fact that it would be horribly wrong of her to bind to him without sharing that detail. A detail she wasn't at liberty to share with him.

She needed to wait until after the launch. After he realized what she'd kept from him for six months. After he'd had a chance to process what her pack had done to bend more of the competition to their favor.

The right thing to do was wait to bind to him. Pulling this bait and switch was more unethical than the secret itself. But dammit, she wanted him to be hers.

He met her gaze, his hands once again cupping the sides of her breasts while he rested on his elbows. "Not today, baby. Not in the heat of the moment in my brother's house. I want it to be special. Drawn out. Sexy. I want you to be pampered for hours until you know that you belong to no one but me."

She lifted a brow. "Do you think there's a doubt?" At least he was providing the voice of reason at a time when she felt more pressure than ever to ignore reason and embrace selfishness.

He smiled but didn't respond. His hands grabbed the front closure of her bra and popped it open.

Her eyes rolled back as her breasts spilled free, and he latched onto one with his mouth. The other one found itself pinched between two fingers.

She moaned until he twisted the offended bud and gave it a slight tug. The sharp sting of pain was welcome, and she screamed out, hoping that indeed no one was in the near vicinity to hear her. She couldn't sense another shifter or human, but under the circumstances, she hardly detected anything at all. Her mind was completely consumed with ensuring Alton was inside her sooner rather than later.

When he switched his mouth to the other nipple, she grasped for his shirt. "Need your skin," she muttered.

Not releasing the suction he had on her breast, he reached over his shoulder with one hand and tugged the shirt over his head. He whipped it past her breast so quickly she barely noticed the momentary lack of contact.

As her arousal grew, she worried she would come in her jeans, and she wanted him inside her, touching her. She grabbed his shoulders again and pushed. "Alton, stop."

He released her nipple, lifting his confused gaze to meet hers. "What's the matter? Did I hurt you?"

"No." She shoved him harder, scrambling out from under him. "But I'm gonna hurt you if you don't get naked right this second." She pushed herself to her knees and unbuttoned her jeans with trembling fingers.

Alton smirked as he shoved off the bed and divested himself of his shoes, jeans, and underwear before she could even shrug her jeans down her body.

She yelped when he grabbed her legs and yanked her forward so fast she lost her balance and fell onto her back. Without breaking eye contact, he jerked off her shoes and tugged the denim and her panties down her legs.

"Finally," she whispered. "Now fuck me. Please. I'm seriously not in the mood for gentle. Save gentle for some time in our forties or fifties. Right now I want to feel alive. I'm not a flower bud, Alton. I need you to fuck me hard."

Even though she'd begun to realize months ago that she liked a bit of kink and some aspects of rougher sex, she had never had the balls to verbalize her desire. Until now.

His eyes widened slightly, and he licked his lips. As he

climbed over her, hovering above her body, his knees straddling her, he furrowed his brow. For a second she feared he might not like her request. Was it possible he didn't want the same thing as her?

"You want it rough, baby?" He lifted one eyebrow.

"Yes," she stated before she could lose her nerve. "Don't hold back."

He cocked his head, a slow smile forming. "How long have you felt that way?"

She flushed. This awkward pause in the middle of their frenzied dance embarrassed her. Besides, she was wet and needy, her clit throbbing while he wanted to have a discussion about her sexual preferences. "A while." She bit her lip.

"Why didn't you say anything?"

"I wasn't sure how you'd feel about it."

Seconds passed. The only sound was them breathing in sync with each other and her heartbeat in her ears, if that was even a thing. His hesitation freaked her out.

Finally, he smiled broader. "That's so fucking hot."

She let out a breath.

"I can do rough."

"Please." *Any day now would also be good.*

He chuckled, making her realize she hadn't blocked the thought. After leaning forward to give her lips a quick peck, he spoke again. "One of these days, you're going to let your walls down and let me totally in while we're having sex. If you didn't expend so much energy blocking me when we're in bed, I would know these naughty thoughts of yours."

She licked her lips. She knew what he meant. It's like she was holding a piece of herself back when they had sex. Saving her deep, innermost thoughts. For what? It wasn't a conscious decision. It just happened. Like humans might save sex for marriage or not want to orgasm with a partner until they felt safe. That's kind of how she felt about opening her mind to him and letting him see inside her soul. He could have that piece of her—after they bound themselves together.

Besides, she wasn't sure she was ready for him to fully know the sorts of thoughts she had in her mind when they were having sex. She blushed every time she contemplated her kinky side, even when she was alone in her bedroom in her parents' home. Masturbating to the idea of him more fully dominating her.

He reached for her face with one hand and cupped her jaw, his thumb dragging across her bottom lip until he pulled it down. "I think I understand."

She nuzzled his palm.

"You're sure?"

"Yes." She squirmed, reaching for him.

He hesitated again, seemingly reading her face since she wouldn't let him into her head. Satisfied, he nodded.

And then the fireworks started.

One second she was lying beneath him staring up at his perfect handsome face, and the next second, he grabbed her waist and flipped her onto her belly. Before she oriented to the new position, he lifted her hips off the mattress. "Knees. Elbows," he demanded.

The two sharp words made her pussy pulse and her nipples tingle.

Yes. God, yes.

She didn't care if he heard her silent thought or not, as long as he kept the bossy act and added some more rough handling.

Should she be embarrassed by this request? Maybe. But at the moment, she didn't give a shit.

"Spread your knees farther," he demanded.

She creamed, wetness leaking down her thighs. Her body trembled, a tight ball in her belly growing larger. It wasn't the words he used. He'd said the same thing in the past. It was the tone. Demanding. Nothing soft. Nothing gentle. No endearment tacked on.

Perfect.

When she apparently didn't comply fast enough, he nudged her legs open roughly with one thigh between them. He reached around with both hands to grasp her chest, pinching the nipples firmly and then gripping her breasts tighter than he'd ever held them before.

The slight sting of her nipples and dull pain of his grip drove her arousal higher.

When he released her tender flesh and grabbed her hips, she set her forehead on the mattress, fighting for oxygen. Her breasts hung in front of her, swaying with every movement, her nipples low enough to graze across the sheet. When had he pulled the comforter off the bed?

A fire burned inside her, demanding release.

Alton thrust two fingers into her pussy without warning. He gripped her hip with his other hand as he fucked her rapidly. "Is this what you want, Jos?"

She moaned. "Yes." The word came out as more of a hiss. This was what she wanted.

He yanked his sopping fingers from her pussy and pinched her clit hard enough to make her scream out at the unexpected.

"Yes," she shouted.

"Oh, baby, that's so hot. You have no idea…"

She begged to differ. She'd never been this turned on. Was she demented for craving this from him? She didn't think so. Enough research assured her lots of women liked rough sex now and then. It wasn't like she didn't also like it sweet and slow and gentle. But there were times when hard and rough and demanding were necessary.

He grabbed her shoulder, holding her so she couldn't rock forward out of the reach of his fingers as he thrust them into her again.

His cock bobbed against her butt cheek.

When she reared back to press more firmly against his length and entice him to put it inside her, he pulled his fingers from her channel and landed a firm spank on her butt cheek.

Her breath caught in her throat. Heart pounding, she tried desperately to inhale another breath.

Alton smoothed his hand over the burn where he'd spanked her and leaned forward to kiss her spine. "Too much?"

How could she answer that without sounding like a total deviant?

"Jos? Talk to me."

"I'm so turned on right now—I could come on demand."

She could hear the smile in his voice when he said, "Do it. Come."

She'd been half kidding, but when he said those words in a deep, commanding voice, she came. Hard. It was the most unusual orgasm she'd ever experienced with nothing touching her clit or her pussy, but the pulsing rolled through her body anyway, shaking her to the core.

"Fuck. Jos, you…" He didn't say another word. Instead, he set his other knee between her thighs, grabbed her hips, and thrust into her to the hilt. He screamed out, an indefinite noise that echoed in the room.

He gripped her butt cheeks with both hands, spreading them, molding them, undoubtedly leaving small bruises in the wake of each finger.

She would see those bruises in the mirror later, and her pussy would clench at the memory.

He fucked her harder, thrusting in and out so fast that the first unfinished orgasm morphed into a second, leaving her unable to breathe until it subsided enough to allow her to concentrate on his actions again.

He held her cheeks wider apart, which should have sent a warning signal to her brain. Instead, she willed him to touch her *there*. They'd never had anal sex before. They hadn't even discussed it. But suddenly she knew she wanted to try it someday. For now... *Yessss*.

She moaned at the sensation as he stroked the sensitive skin of her forbidden hole with his thumbs. Pressure built inside her, threatening to explode. Insane after two incredible orgasms.

He released her butt with one hand and reached around to stroke her clit with his fingers while continuing to fuck her. A second later, without warning, he removed his hand from her clit and pressed a finger—wet from her arousal— into her rear.

"Oh. God. That...feels so amazing." She was thankful she'd been able to speak at all to let him know what she felt because, after those words, her world spun out of control. It seemed like she was floating. Gravity had no effect on her.

Every conscious thought focused on the feel of his cock thrusting in and out of her pussy in conjunction with his finger inside her tighter hole. The membrane was thin. She could feel his finger against his cock through the barrier. It was unusual. It was amazing.

Another orgasm built. She needed to come again. *"Rub my clit,"* she pleaded into his head.

He reached around her body with his free hand and stroked the swollen nub, overwhelming her with sensations. "That's it, baby. Come again for me. Come again, and then I'll follow you."

Her breath caught as her clit started to pulse again. The throbbing built in intensity as her pussy and her tight rear hole both convulsed around their intrusions, gripping, squeezing, milking him. A flood of wetness burst around his cock as the internal orgasm took over.

He followed right behind her as promised, his length deep and steady, his fingers still strumming her clit lightly and massaging the inside of her ass.

As she came down, he pulled his finger out first and then his cock.

Her arms were shaking so badly, she would have collapsed if he hadn't grabbed her hips and eased her to her side. "Don't move, baby."

She couldn't even blink. How did he think she was going to move?

He padded naked from the bedroom only to return moments later with a wet cloth in his hand. This time he shut the door before he gently rolled her onto her back, spread her limp legs, and wiped their lovemaking from her pussy.

After setting the washcloth aside, he climbed beside her and hauled her weak frame against his body. He kissed her forehead. "I love you so much."

"I love you, too," she managed to say out loud.

He stroked his fingers through her hair soothingly for a long time. "What brought that on?" he finally asked.

"I don't know. It was bubbling under the surface for a while." She drew circles around one of his nipples, watching it stiffen.

"And? Did it meet your expectations?"

"And then some." She tipped her head back to meet his gaze. "Were you okay with it?"

"Okay?" He chuckled. "Hottest sex I've ever had."

"You say that as though you've had sex with hundreds of women and I'm just here for comparison," she teased, tweaking his nipple to emphasize her words.

He grasped her hand away from his offended nipple and kissed her knuckles. "When would I have slept with someone else, woman? Before I met you when we were nine? Because don't even think of insulting me by insinuating I would have cheated on you at any point. You know my heart, soul, and body belong to only you no matter how much time or distance may separate us. I've always belonged to only you. No way would I have touched another woman, not even while you spent years keeping me at arm's length. Never."

She swallowed around the emotion that threatened to upend her emotional stability. When a tear ran down her face, he kissed it away.

"You're mine, baby. Forever."

"Yes."

In the ensuing silence, Joselyn's mind wandered, making her wish she could erase the world and run off with her man to someplace where no one knew who they were. At this point, she didn't even care if they never saw another shifter.

"You're worrying again." He tapped her temple. "You might block me, but you can't keep your emotions from me."

She sighed. What she wanted to do was tell him what was about to happen at work in eight days. She wanted to let all the words tumble out of her mouth so she could free herself of the burden of secrets. But she wouldn't do that to her family. Her parents. Her aunts and uncles and siblings and cousins. They were counting on this launch to boost the brewery into a new playing field.

A lot was riding on the success of the new product launch. If she leaked the details to Alton, all hell would break loose.

She gave him a truthful statement, though. "Work is stressful."

He groaned. "Tell me about it. I'm in over my head too. Why did we make the decision to come back to Silvertip again? Some days I struggle to remember."

"Every day. Every hour lately." She snuggled closer to him. How long could they enjoy this interlude before her parents wondered what the hell happened to her?

At least another half an hour. An hour if she came up with a plausible excuse.

She closed her eyes and inhaled his scent deeply, yearning for the day when this would be commonplace. Not the exception.

CHAPTER 11

Alton pursed his lips. He was such an ass. What he should do was tell her about his family's launch tomorrow. It was insane that he had such huge news and couldn't share it with the one person who meant the world to him.

It seemed absurd in a way. It wasn't as if she could do anything to stop it at this hour. The new product was going to launch first thing in the morning. What would it matter?

But he bit his tongue and held his thoughts.

Family loyalty. He was beginning to lose sight of what that meant. Family loyalty? When was he going to be permitted to extend that loyalty to his mate? The woman he should be living with.

When was he going to break away from what was expected of him and permit *himself* to switch his loyalty to his mate?

He couldn't put the blame for this fucked-up situation on anyone else. He did this to himself. He agreed with her to return home to join their respective family businesses two years ago, thinking it would destroy them if they ran off and left their families high and dry.

He'd feared exile from the people he loved most. He'd worried himself to death that Joselyn would never be happy if she hurt her parents and brothers and they never spoke to her again.

But would that have happened? And more importantly, would it happen if they came out as a couple today?

He winced. Today was gone. And tomorrow would change everything. His fear was real. She might be pissed enough at his familial allegiance to turn him away. After all, what asshole did this to his other half?

Or maybe he was over-thinking things, and she wouldn't see it as a big deal? So what? So his brewery was launching a new product?

He prayed his nerves were unwarranted and he was turning a rain shower into a hurricane unnecessarily.

"You're thinking hard too, hon." She patted his chest.

"Yeah." He made a decision. Perhaps if he talked to her, made a plan for the future, something definitive, it would soften the blow tomorrow. Maybe knowing his intentions toward her would keep her mind from thinking the worst of him when the news broke.

He gently peeled her from his chest and scooted back to sit up against the headboard. When he was situated, he lifted her onto his lap. She wiggled around, tossing one leg over his until she straddled him, her warm pussy resting against his already once-again hard cock.

He stared down at the vision of her gorgeous breasts in front of him as she arched forward. Unable to do anything else, he slid his hands around to her chest and cupped the soft flesh of her globes. He tapped a spot on the inside of one breast. "You're going to bruise." Her skin was delicate. He winced. On the other hand, as a shifter, her healing power would eliminate the bruising quickly.

She looked down. "Yeah. And I'll get aroused tomorrow every time I think of your fingers grasping me so firmly. When I touch the spot, the slight pain will remind me how it felt to have your cock buried deep while you fingered me...in some interesting places." She flushed.

"Well, I'm not going to complain." His cock pulsed against her. "Not saying I want to treat you like that every time. There's a time and a place for gentle lovemaking, but if you enjoy it rough sometimes too, I'll never deny you that, baby."

She sighed. "What are we going to do?" she implored.

He took a deep breath. "I don't know, but I say we start planning."

"I don't think there's much to plan. I mean, we don't know a single variable. The only thing we can do is call a family meeting, tell everyone, and see what they say."

He nodded. "It's not like their reactions will influence us one way or the other. We won't be asking for permission. We'll be asking for acceptance."

"Exactly."

"So we do this with all of them together? Or smaller groups? Your parents at one time and mine at another? Do we invite siblings?"

"I don't know. Can you think of a plausible way we could convince all those people to come to the same place at the same time? I mean, it's going to take us about a half a second to tell them the news, and then our part will be done. All we can do is sit back and see how they react."

He ran a hand through his hair. "And there's no way to predict the reaction from either side, so our plans kind of end with the big reveal. When put that way, it seems so simple. What have we been waiting for?" he joked. "All I have to do is say, 'Hey, everyone, Joselyn and I are in love. We're going to bind together, and we want your blessing.'"

She grinned. "You make it sound so easy."

"Oh, that part's the easy part."

"Yeah." Her shoulders slumped. "Given what we've seen lately with our fathers working together, especially helping Austin and Nuria a few weeks ago, I can't imagine any of them freaking out and going ballistic on us."

"Me neither. Too bad our family trees fork in about nineteen other directions. Even if we did have the support of our immediate families, there's no way my extended family is going to buy this. I can list at least a dozen bigoted aunts, uncles, and cousins off the top of my head who will tell me to go to hell and not return."

"Yeah. Me too. But we can't continue to live like this to appease distant relatives. We can't even continue on this path if we don't have the support of our parents. It's tearing me up."

"I know, baby. I totally agree." He slid his hands up her body again until he could cup her face. He watched her get emotional again, and he couldn't blame her.

The truth was he was doing her an injustice by allowing and even encouraging this charade for so long. She deserved better. She deserved to bind to a man who could grow a damn spine and stand up to his parents and hers, challenging them all to consider the implications of disowning their own flesh and blood.

"How about we discuss some possible outcomes and what responses we intend to have," she suggested.

"Okay. Best case scenario first."

She nodded. "We tell our parents, they cry for what we've been through, hug us both, and welcome each of us into the fold of the other family. We sing Kumbaya, and everyone enjoys a beer."

He laughed. "Kumbaya?"

She shrugged. "I keep thinking of that song for some reason. It's stuck in my mind. Every time I picture this coming out of ours, I pray everyone will sway in song and rejoice in our union."

He laughed harder. "I'm pretty sure that's going a bit far. That's way beyond best-case scenario."

She giggled, the sound once again going straight to his cock, as it always did. Her lithe body vibrated as she squirmed in his lap, her pussy grinding down on his cock. If she wasn't completely aware of what she was doing to him, he would be shocked.

He grabbed her ass to hold her still.

She sobered instantly, her gaze locking to his for a long time before he smoothed one hand up her back and pressed her forward until their lips touched. "There's another route we could take," she murmured against his lips.

"What's that?" He watched as a slow teasing smile made her eyes sparkle with mischief.

"We could bind first and announce after."

He returned her smile. "Wouldn't even have to explain ourselves in that scenario."

"Nope. Think of all the words we would save."

For a long time, he simply looked at her while they both sobered. If he had his way, the world would freeze, leaving him stuck permanently in this moment, her loving gaze meeting his.

"We should let your brother come back inside," she whispered. "It's damn cold out there, even for bears."

He nodded. "Already told him to come back whenever he wants. They'll leave us alone in here as long as we'd like."

"I need to get home."

"I know."

She blew out a long breath. "When should we plan to do this thing?"

"Soon. I mean days. Not weeks. I'll figure something out. Maybe next weekend?"

She nodded, a smile forming on the edges of her mouth, but her brow was furrowed with worry.

He couldn't wait for the day when she looked happy and carefree all the time. That day would come, wouldn't it? He hoped so. Even in the worst-case scenario, which they hadn't discussed, he prayed she would be happy. If they found themselves moving out of town and living in a new place with no contact at all with their relatives, could she sincerely smile one day without the permanent cloud that always lurked in the back of her eyes?

Please, God.

When Joselyn got home, her brother Isaiah's truck was in the driveway.

For a minute, she sat in the silence of her silver Honda Accord and watched the gentle fall of snowflakes out the window. The world appeared so peaceful and serene when there were giant flakes of snow falling lazily toward the ground.

Snowflakes didn't have a care in the world. They weren't concerned with where they landed or how cold the earth was. They just meandered through the sky until they found a resting place.

If only her life were that tranquil.

When she finally trudged her way to the front door and opened it, she was surprised to find the house dark. Not a single light was on. Isaiah's scent was strong, however.

At the same second she confirmed his presence as she shut the front door, he spoke, nearly giving her a heart attack. "How long?" he asked, his voice dead.

Shaking, she stepped farther into the living room, shrugged out of her coat, and draped it over the back of the couch. She cleared her throat, meeting her brother's gaze where he sat across the room in an armchair. In the dark. The only person in the house. "Pardon?"

He leaned forward, setting his elbows on his knees casually. "How long have you been in a relationship with Alton Tarben?"

She flinched. How did he know? She glanced around. "Where're Mom and Dad?"

"They had dinner plans. Said they'd be back later. Answer my question."

She tried to judge his tone. It didn't have an accusatory lilt to it, and she wouldn't expect such a thing from her older brother, but it did hold a quality she couldn't put her thumb on. Sadness?

She opted to go for the entire truth. "About fifteen years." It felt good to spit it out.

He groaned. And then he surprised her by pushing to his feet and coming across the room. As soon as he rounded the couch, he grabbed her by the forearms and pulled her into his embrace. He held her tight while he spoke to the top of her head. "Sis, God. I'm so sorry. Why?"

She couldn't stop the tears from falling. Would it be like this every time she told someone new? This...this stabbing pain that came with admitting the horror that was her life?

How had this happened twice in one night? She was raw. The world was unraveling at a rapid pace around her. There was no way she could keep this enormous secret much longer. It felt like it was leaking out of her pores.

For a long time, he held her, rocking her back and

forth. She couldn't remember a time in her life when her brother had hugged her so hard for so long. They were a close family, affectionate. But this was above and beyond. He was six years older than her. She had always been the kid sister.

Finally, he grabbed her biceps and held her away from him. "Why?" he repeated.

"You have a better plan?" she asked.

He licked his lips, his gaze landing over her shoulder on nothing. "I've been sitting here for over an hour trying to come up with one."

"So you can see my plight." She shrugged free of him and rounded the couch to sit in the corner, pulling her knees up to her chest in a tight ball.

He followed, sitting next to her but giving her about a foot of space between them.

"How did you find out?" *How many people know?* She left that question unspoken.

"I drove by Austin's place earlier without calling first. I was shocked to see your car there, but when I got to the door, before I even knocked, I realized you and Alton were the only two people in the house."

She nodded. At least he was the only person who knew. Right? "Did you tell anyone else?" How had she not sensed his presence? She knew the answer immediately. She and Alton had been so preoccupied with each other and not expecting anyone besides his brother and Nuria to return to the house that Joselyn hadn't kept even one corner of her mind open to the outside world. A dangerous move that could easily get her into trouble one day.

He shook his head. "No. Not my place."

"But you did feel the need to confront me."

He smiled, his perfect teeth showing even in the darkness of the room. "I felt it *was* my place to give you some advice. I just wasn't going to out you to Mom and Dad. That's your gig."

She sighed. "You think I need advice? You think there's a single thing you could say that would change anything?"

He leaned back, setting his head on the cushion and staring at the ceiling. "Remember when I met Heather?"

She nodded. Words weren't necessary, and he didn't need to see her. The question was rhetorical. It had only been a few months. Half the continent knew about it.

He continued, "I know most of our species believes we aren't fated to mate a specific person in this life. That we have free will. That we can control our destinies, but I learned something the day I met Heather, and it jolted me to the bone."

"What was that?" she whispered.

"Most people are wrong. Maybe it doesn't happen to everyone. Maybe it doesn't even happen often, but it does occur, and it was that way for me. The moment I inhaled her scent, I knew she was mine."

"I know." She did. He'd told them all. This wasn't new information. But he must have had a point.

The day he'd met Heather was clear in her mind. She would never forget meeting the frightened, injured human woman who'd been attacked on the hiking trail by one of Alton's estranged cousins.

The scratches that ripped her skin open from Jack Tarben's claws forced her to transition into a species she'd known nothing about. But the important thing was that Isaiah already knew she was meant to be his before she was transformed.

It was huge. It was unheard of. But it worked out. And now they were together.

"It took me two days to convince Heather she was mine. Two of the longest days of my life." He hesitated, and then he turned to face Joselyn. "I can't imagine waiting even one more minute to bind myself to her. My soul was in turmoil. Breaking. My heart stalled. My world did not spin."

She hitched a breath. "Are you questioning my affection for Alton?"

He didn't respond.

She dropped her knees and sat up straighter, leaning toward her brother. "You take those two days of torture and multiply them by about seven years, and then we'll talk again."

He nodded, his face scrunched. "Why only seven years?"

"It wasn't nearly as painful to live with until I became an adult and left for U of C."

"Wait. Alton went to the University of Calgary too."

"You're sharp."

"You spent five years there."

"He's catching on." She smiled.

"Shit, Jos. That's fucked up."

"Yes, it is. I'm clear on that. We felt a sense of family obligation. Then we both got caught up in our jobs, and that duty kept getting harder to denounce. But we're reaching our limit."

"And then some. What's your plan?"

"Alton wants to make an announcement next weekend. Maybe get both families together or something."

"Next weekend? So before the launch?" he asked.

"Yeah. I'm not sure how wise that is. It would make me feel like I've trapped him without full disclosure if we completed the binding before he found out my family had a new product releasing that could be damaging to his family."

"You think?"

She moaned. "It's not like I can tell him."

"Oh, believe me, that part I understand. I can hardly stand to be in the same room with Austin. We've been friends for fifteen years. We don't have many secrets. I feel like a fraud every time I'm with him."

"Yeah. Lucky for you, you're not sleeping with him." She flinched after those words left her mouth.

"Okay, TMI." He chuckled. "Don't need that sort of visual of my little sister." He stood and turned to face her. "I gotta go. Heather's waiting for me." He headed for the front door and grabbed his coat from the back of a chair. "I just want you to know I understand. I would never judge you. You have my support. But fix this thing. Sooner rather than later. Before it eats you alive."

She nodded into the darkness. "I will."

The sound of the door shutting behind him made her flinch. Left in silence, she shoved off the couch and made her way to her end of the house. She didn't want to face her parents again that night. She just wanted to be alone.

As soon as she locked the door to her bedroom, she headed to the adjoining bath and flipped on the lights. She needed a long hot soak. For one thing, there was no way she would be able to sleep with the scent of Alton on her skin. For another thing, the warm water might help calm her racing mind.

Next weekend. Shit. She hadn't wanted to argue with Alton about the timing. In fact, she couldn't. What would she have given as an excuse for not wanting to make the announcement at that time?

It wasn't as if they had to bind that moment simply because they outed themselves. It was nothing more than a public statement. Telling people they were a couple wouldn't be a lie. Binding together without discussing her family's launch the following Monday would be deliberately deceptive. She couldn't do that.

As she peeled her sweater over her head and then removed her bra, she glanced at her reflection in the mirror. The faint marks from his fingers lingered on her breasts. His grip had felt firm enough to leave a reminder on her chest for at least a day, but apparently, even in human form, her body was healing rapidly.

If she shifted into her grizzly form, the bruises would disappear quickly, but she had no intention of doing so tonight. For one, she didn't have a reason to. She wasn't in the habit of shifting in the house unless it was necessary. For another thing, she had hoped to see his marks in the morning—a reminder of their time together.

Already she missed him.

As she removed her jeans and panties next, she twisted around to see her butt in the mirror. Same thing. Fading indications of where his fingers had gripped her hard enough to make her come.

Was it weird that she liked sex a little rough? Alton hadn't seemed to think so. He'd been turned on by her admission. And the truth was she'd always fantasized about him taking her with a bit of force.

She turned on the water to fill the tub and then stared at the mirror again while she waited for it to heat and fill. The woman looking back at her was tired and pale. Her natural vibrancy was tamped down by stress. Her hair, usually lush and shiny, had even protested to hang limply around her face.

As she turned to lower herself into the tub, she closed her eyes and took a deep breath. Changes were imminent. Was she ready?

She had to be.

CHAPTER 12

Joselyn was running late, as usual. When she pulled into her spot at the brewery, reaching for her briefcase, she sensed something odd in the air. Something wasn't right.

She turned around, shut the car door, and faced the building.

Shit. Something was definitely not okay. No one was outside, and the world appeared perfectly normal from where she stood, but the stressful vibe she had from inside the front offices was palpable in the air.

She hurried forward, wondering what the hell was going on.

When she pushed through the front doors of the building, she found the lobby jammed with at least two dozen of her relatives. They were all shouting over one another, huddled around the big-screen television on the far wall. The news was on. Had there been a storm somewhere? Or a national disaster?

Before Joselyn could get anyone's attention to ask what the commotion was all about, someone whistled loudly, and a hush fell over the room. All eyes turned to the TV as the news broadcaster said a few words Joselyn couldn't hear. And then the camera panned to the left to show Allister Tarben standing next to his brother Riddell. They were beaming with pride as they pointed out a giant advertisement between them.

"What the hell?" Joselyn mumbled as she inched closer. She dropped her briefcase next to the front desk and peeled her coat off to set it on top of her bag. Liddie, their receptionist, stood like a statue next to the desk, so Joselyn stepped around her to get a better view of the television. And then the world spun out of control.

The hush lasted only moments, and before Allister and Riddell finished speaking, the volume in the room rose to a new decibel. Shouting. Cussing. Even screaming.

Joselyn couldn't move. She blinked at the television, trying to make sense of what she was seeing. The unveiled artwork was eerily similar to the campaign she had planned for her own brewery for over six months.

The problem was this announcement was coming from Mountain Peak Brewery. Not from her own family's office.

As if drawn by a magnet, she crept forward, ignoring the bodies between her and the TV and not taking her eyes off the screen. When she was close enough that she had to tip her head back to see better, she finally fully absorbed what was happening.

Mountain Peak Brewery, the very place where her mate worked, had beaten them to the punch and launched nearly the same product one week before the scheduled launch Jocelyn had worked so hard on.

The same product.

The same, or at least similar, advertisement.

She rubbed her temples with both hands. This could not be happening.

Unable to breathe, she turned and walked away from

the cacophony of noise, headed down the hall toward her office, and slumped into the chair behind her desk. She set her forehead against her fingers and inhaled slowly.

She was dizzy. Confused. A headache was already forming behind her temples. Her brain stopped functioning.

She had no idea how long she sat like that before her mother stepped into the room. "Joselyn?"

She lifted her face, still too shocked to speak.

Rosanne's brow was furrowed. "I didn't see you come in. I guess you heard?"

She nodded.

Rosanne sighed and came more fully into the room to slump into a chair across from Joselyn. "Your father's about to have a heart attack."

"I'm sure."

"The board is scrambling to figure out what to do. How to respond."

Joselyn nodded again. What could they do?

Reality slammed into her. The Tarbens had to have known. They knew about the planned launch from their competitor, and they stole the idea and arranged their own launch to beat the competition.

Alton knew. *Fuck.* Alton *knew.* A flush raced over Joselyn's body, making her feel like she might faint after all.

The Tarbens stole this idea, pretended it was their own, and sandbagged the Arthurs. There was no other explanation. There was also no way Alton hadn't known this was going to happen this morning.

She'd had sex with him last night. She'd been naked in his arms twelve hours ago. They'd discussed the future. And all that time he knew his family was about to attempt to ruin hers in the morning.

The flush was replaced with a complete draining of blood from her face. She would be white now.

Someone else leaned into her office, but she didn't hear what they said. Her mother got up and rushed from the room, leaving her blissfully alone.

She had no idea how much time passed before Isaiah slid into her office, shut the door, and took the same seat her mother had occupied.

She sat with her hands flat on the desk, her gaze on her computer screen, seeing nothing. Feeling like she'd been punched.

"Did you know about this?" he asked softly.

She flinched before jerking her gaze to his. "What?" Her voice squeaked.

He lifted a brow.

"You think I knew about this? Are you fucking kidding me?" Her voice was high-pitched. Shrill.

"I'll take that as a *no*."

She shook her head. "No, Isaiah. No, I did not."

"Have you spoken to Alton?"

She winced. "No. And I have no intention of doing so."

He hesitated. "Ever?"

"Right now I'd like to burn him alive. So, no. At the moment my intention is to never speak to him again."

Isaiah looked pained.

She narrowed her gaze. "Did *you* know about this? You could have just as easily found out from Austin," she pointed out.

He blew out a long breath. "I didn't know, either. Maybe the two of *them* didn't even know."

"That their brewery was launching a new product this morning?" She lifted a brow. "We don't have a single employee who's unaware of our ruined launch for next week. How could two employees and pack members as high up as Austin and Alton in the management of Mountain Peak Brewery not know about a launch?"

Isaiah shook his head. "Of course they knew about the launch. Maybe they didn't know it was stolen."

She leaned forward, bracing herself on the desk, feeling every bit as wild as she assumed she was behaving. "How the hell could they not know? The entire concept had to come from somewhere. Do they think it came out of thin air?" She thought back to his behavior last night and over the past few weeks. He'd been shifty and worried. More so than usual. Concerned. Oh, he knew. He totally fucking knew.

Like her own pack and brewery, there wouldn't have been a single person working in his brewery who didn't know what was planned for that morning and the devastating effect it would have on their competition. Essentially the Tarbens had pulled the rug out from under the Arthurs. Any effort to go forward with their own launch next Monday would make them look like fools. A day late and several hundred thousand dollars short.

Joselyn shuddered as she remembered so totally giving herself to Alton last night. They'd shared a new experience together. She'd given him another piece of her. No, she still hadn't opened her mind up to allow him full access to her thoughts, but it hadn't been easy for her to admit she wanted to add a bit of kink to their relationship. And she'd loved it.

What was he thinking now? What had he been thinking last night when he so thoroughly debauched her hours before his brewery intended to make hers the laughing stock of the entire region?

She set her forehead on her palms again and groaned. Nothing made sense. She knew he loved her. She knew he wanted to be with her. Right? They had a spark, a something between them that insisted they bind together for life. They'd felt that spark for most of their lives.

Right?

Isaiah stood. "I don't have the answers, but try not to jump to conclusions. If you call Alton and start tossing around accusations, you could do serious damage to your relationship for no reason." He paused a moment and then continued. "I'll leave you alone, but think about what I'm saying." He left the room, shutting the door with a quiet snick.

Joselyn pushed to standing and paced across the floor to stare out the window. Snow was falling again. Giant flakes meandering toward the ground with no care or knowledge of the storm building inside the brewery.

Leaning her forehead against the window pane, she welcomed the cool glass against her skin. How did his family find out about this launch? Because one thing was for certain, someone intentionally stole secret information and sabotaged the Arthurs.

There was no way to deny the Tarbens had orchestrated this launch. Every detail of their promo emulated hers. Mountain Peak Brewery had intentionally set out to attack Glacial Brewing Company where it would most hurt.

She almost laughed when she considered how stressed she'd been worrying about how Alton would react to finding out her family had secretly planned and launched a new product. That stress had eaten her alive for months.

She felt like a complete fool. While she had needlessly worried about *her* launch, Alton had known all along that his family had stolen the entire concept and planned to beat their competitor to the punch.

Isaiah's words rang in her head. *Maybe Alton hadn't known...* But that possibility seemed preposterous.

She shuddered. Did she even know him at all? What sort of person would do this to another? And their own mate. When had their relationship ceased being what she'd once thought it was?

How had he managed to sleep at night?

Thoughts raced through her head, flying around, crashing into each other, piling up until she couldn't follow any one line of thinking for longer than a second before she had another thought.

There had to be a mole, someone inside her brewery who fed information to someone inside his.

She stiffened further. Was it possible *she* was the connection? Had she inadvertently leaked information to Alton?

She shook the idea away as fast as it consumed her. She refused to believe he would use her like that. She *knew* him. She'd known him for most of their lives.

Surely Alton hadn't planned to fuck her up the ass since they'd been nine. That made no sense. She refused to believe the time they'd spent together had been a fraud. He'd stayed in school for six years just to be near her. No one would pretend to love another for that many years while secretly waiting to sabotage their family's business. Not a chance. The entire concept for next week's launch had been conceived six months ago, not years.

He'd never asked a single question about her work. He would make an awfully inept spy if he'd been waiting all these years to undermine her brewery only to then never attempt to pry details from her.

She'd also never told him a thing about the launch. Not one word. She'd never had anything work related on her person when she'd seen him. She wanted to spend every second of their time together either having sex or curled up together. He'd never been to her house. She'd never been to his apartment. They met most often in the mountains carrying nothing.

Joselyn simply didn't believe she was so naïve that she could spend most of her life mistakenly thinking Alton was her intended mate. No way. They were lovers. Her heart beat out of her chest when she was with him—a chemical reaction to his pheromones. Nature intended for them to be together. She wouldn't play this sort of joke on a living, breathing being.

Think. Let's assume he didn't have any ulterior motives until more recently. Was it possible someone else in his family knew about his relationship with Joselyn and put him up to this? Maybe even blackmailed him?

She shuddered. Would he do that to her? Even under duress?

No way. She couldn't believe it. But the evidence suggested otherwise.

There was no telling what he would do after what she'd learned this morning. At the very least, he failed to inform her his family had planned to sabotage hers for months. That was above and beyond the pale all by itself.

Oh, she knew she'd skirted the edge of what would be considered acceptable by not informing him about her launch in the first place. But that was business. Her obligation to her family ran deep. It hadn't been nefarious or deceitful. It had been a strategic plan to gain a new section of the market. Businesses were constantly developing new products. Hers was no different. And no matter what her relationship status was with Alton Tarben, she never would have spilled company secrets.

She went back in time in her mind, trying to figure out when Alton knew. If he didn't find out from her, who did he learn of the launch from?

Joselyn wrapped her arms around her middle.

Obviously, she wasn't the leak. There had to be another explanation. And yet, the moment anyone found out about her connection to Alton, they would assume the worst. No one would ever believe she hadn't shared the details.

Her head pounded harder. This was insane. She started shaking. Her legs wouldn't hold her up any longer. She turned around and slid to the floor, her back against the wall and her head between her knees.

Maybe some other member of her family also had a clandestine relationship with a member of the Tarben pack. She wasn't the only person who could have a connection.

The door to her office opened slowly. She glanced up to find Liddie easing into the room. "You left this in the lobby." She held up Joselyn's purse, briefcase, and coat and then set them on a chair next to the conference table. "I'll just, uh," she glanced over her shoulder, "leave you alone." On her way out the door, she ran into Joselyn's mom. "Oh, sorry."

Rosanne bustled in as Liddie left, shutting the door behind her. "Joselyn? What the heck are you doing?" She crouched down in front of Joselyn and took her daughter into her arms, stroking her hair. "Honey, I know this is bad, but why are you hiding in here alone on the floor in a fetal position?"

Joselyn lifted her face, not bothering to stop the tears.

"Honey, what is it?"

"Tell Dad to come. You should hear this together." She could have communicated with her father herself, but she didn't have the energy, and she didn't want to give away her stress telepathically.

Her mother nodded. "He's on his way. Why don't you get off the floor and sit on a chair?"

Joselyn shook her head. "I'm good here." She drew her

knees up, thankful she'd worn khaki pants instead of a dress or skirt that day.

When her father came into the room, he silently shut the door. "What's going on? Jos?"

Joselyn lifted her gaze to her parents. Where to begin? She decided to spit it all out. "I've been in a relationship with Alton Tarben for four months. I've known we were meant to be together my entire adult life." The words flooded out. Why had she always thought it would be so hard to tell them?

Bernard gasped, taking a chair. "Alton? He's the one that's your age, right?"

"A year older. Yes."

Her mother kneeled down next to her and wrapped an arm around her shoulders. "Why are you telling us this now?"

Joselyn turned her gaze toward her mother. "People are going to think I'm the leak."

Her mother frowned. "Why would you say that?"

Joselyn rolled her eyes, but her father spoke. "Did you tell him about the launch?"

She shook her head vehemently. "No. Never. I wouldn't do that. But obviously it leaked somehow, and I'm probably the only person in the family who has a close relationship with one of the Tarbens."

Her father hesitated, his brow furrowing. "Let's not get ahead of ourselves here. You might be making more out of this than necessary. For one thing, you aren't the only person with a connection to the Tarbens. Hell, Isaiah's best friend is Alton's brother."

"Come on, Dad. You know Isaiah didn't tell company secrets to Austin Tarben. I wouldn't believe that in a million years."

"I'm merely pointing out that you wouldn't be the only

possible suspect. Besides, I find it highly unlikely either of you had anything to do with the leak. I'm not buying it. Isaiah has been close friends with Austin for too many years. No way would he have undermined our business by discussing it with his friend. And even if he did inadvertently tell Austin something, I don't believe it would have gone further. I trust Austin.

"And I can't imagine in a million years that Alton would ever do anything to hurt you. It's inconceivable, honey." He crouched down next to her mother and set a hand on Rosanne's shoulder. "I'd sooner cut off my right arm than ever do anything to upset your mother. That's how it works when you meet the right person. And after binding to them, it's even stronger. Mates don't have the capacity to hurt each other intentionally."

Would everyone else in the pack see it the same way?

"Honey," her mother began, "why have you been hiding this?"

Joselyn couldn't stop the tears from falling. "I don't even know anymore." She choked on a sob and then continued. "At first I thought it was necessary not to upset the family dynamics. Cause a rift in the pack. At some point along the way, it was just normal for us. There's always been something that caused us to put off telling anyone. Or maybe we were just cowards."

"Honey…"

"Are you sure he's…the *one*?" Bernard asked.

Joselyn nodded.

"Then there's no way he would undermine your relationship like this."

She thought back on all the times she'd asked him to bind them together. Fuck the world and just do it. Hadn't he also made similar suggestions? They had tossed the ball of responsibility back and forth between them. When one of them was weak and wanted to throw in the towel and tell the world to fuck off, the other took the reins of reason.

Her father spoke again. "I think you're overreacting right now, honey. We all are. Everyone's pointing fingers at everyone else this morning. It's natural. The blame game has got to stop, starting with you. Sit on this for a few days." He sounded just like her brother Isaiah. "Let's see what develops before you accuse your mate of sabotage."

When her father referred to Alton as her mate, she stopped breathing. Neither of her parents had flinched at the idea. They seemed to be taking it in stride. Their only concern was for the health of her relationship. Not one judgment had been passed over her choice in mates.

In her heart, however, her parents had never been her biggest concern. It was the rest of the pack that worried her. Several aunts and uncles and cousins were determined to badmouth the Tarbens for the rest of their lives. The feud had gotten so out of hand it was ridiculous.

But Joselyn couldn't do anything about that. She needed to worry about herself from now on. Her happiness. Her sanity.

With or without Alton Tarben at her side, she needed to stop living a lie and face the music. Telling her brother and now her parents was a start. She didn't need to get carried away today of all days. But soon she needed to come out of hiding and out herself. Even if she never saw Alton again in her life, she wouldn't go to her grave with this damn secret. To hell with everyone's stupid quarrel with the Tarbens.

Alton picked up his phone for the tenth time in less than

an hour.

Nothing. No response from Joselyn.

He'd texted her a blank message the first five times, and then he'd said fuck it and typed actual words at least five times also.

Call me.

Are you okay?

That one was a joke.

You're scaring me.

Jos, please.

Jos?

After several hours, he'd also called several times. The phone went to voicemail every single time. It rang four times and then he heard her sweet, gentle voice.

"You've reached Jocelyn Arthur with Glacial Brewing Company. I'm sorry I'm not available to take your call. Please leave your name and number after the tone, and I'll get back to you as soon as possible."

He was close to total panic.

When Austin popped his head in at lunchtime, Alton shot him a glare that would have frozen a mere mortal to stone.

Austin winced. He eased inside, shut the door, and leaned against it. "I take it she isn't happy."

Alton narrowed his gaze. "Worse. She isn't answering my texts or calls."

"Well, what did you expect? I'm sure she's busy

scrambling around trying to come up with a new business model. She's the marketing director, right?"

"Yes."

"Then she's been in meetings all day planning how to repair the damage and what to do in response."

"You're right." Alton took a deep breath. It made sense. Of course, she was busy. And she'd undoubtedly never had a moment alone.

"I wouldn't worry. Not for a while, anyway. Maybe tonight. If she hasn't called by this evening, then you can get concerned. In the meantime, come to the break room. Dad ordered a spread of sandwiches to celebrate."

Alton nodded. "I'll be there in a few." He needed to compose himself. His nerves were wearing on him. He wouldn't be able to fully relax until he spoke to Joselyn and knew for certain she wasn't ready to string him up by the balls and light him on fire.

It was business. That's all it was.

She had to understand that. Right?

It wasn't like this launch was going to put Glacial Brewing Company out of business. Sure, it might hurt their bottom line while they recuperated in the short run, but that was to be expected. They'd bounce back.

Was he kidding himself? What did he know about the dealings at Glacial Brewing Company? For all he knew, they'd been hanging on by a thread, and this product launch would seal their fate. He had no idea what their bottom line looked like.

Granted, if things had been that bad at work, Joselyn would have said something, wouldn't she? Maybe not. But she at least would have been worried. She'd never given him any impression business was anything but status quo.

Alton stuffed his concerns to the back of his mind and stood to join his family now celebrating in the break room.

None of them, except Austin, had the first clue how detrimental this entire thing could be for him and his mate.

It wasn't until later that night that Alton really freaked out.

Several more calls had gone to voicemail and still not a single peep from Jos. Was she that mad?

He sat in the living room of his lonely apartment and flipped the remote around in his hand, not caring that he hadn't turned on the television.

He debated getting in his Explorer and going straight to her parents' house. To hell with what anyone thought. He needed to see her. Touch her.

Instead, he talked himself out of it. Who knew how her parents would ultimately react to them binding on a good day? But today was not the day to throw Joselyn under the bus in front of her family.

Maybe Jos was still at the office. It was possible. However, no matter what, it wasn't reasonable that by now she hadn't seen all his texts and heard his messages.

She might have been extremely busy the entire day. He didn't doubt that. But at this hour, almost nine o'clock, there was no way to avoid admitting she was ignoring him.

He lifted the remote in the air and threw it hard against the far wall.

If this damn launch ruined his relationship with Joselyn, he would never forgive himself.

If he had never agreed to return to Silvertip after university in the first place, this wouldn't have happened. The two of them would be living blissfully happy anywhere but here.

Maybe they wouldn't have their families, but they would have each other, and that was all that mattered in the end.

CHAPTER 13

Joselyn rolled onto her side, hugging her pillow against her chest, staring at her phone. She'd thumbed through the texts from Alton a hundred times. She'd listened to his messages several times also.

Something didn't add up. His voice was strained, but he didn't sound like he expected them to be over because of this.

She wasn't ready to face him yet, not even by phone. She was exhausted and wrung out from stress and crying.

Even though she hadn't come out of her office a single time that day, she'd heard all the news from her family as they scrambled around in meetings, trying to decide what to do. The biggest problem was that someone leaked information to the Tarbens. That wasn't deniable. The question? Did they do it inadvertently or intentionally?

Joselyn certainly didn't intentionally share company secrets. She could have done it accidentally if Alton snooped through her phone at some point while she wasn't paying attention over the last few months, but that idea was so far-fetched that it meant her entire relationship was a farce and had been for years. She couldn't swallow that anymore twelve hours later than she had this morning.

The passage of time had made her see reason. And her parents had talked her down over dinner, rationalizing that Alton wouldn't be texting and calling if he truly meant her family harm.

Joselyn set her phone on the nightstand and tried to get comfortable in her bed. No position provided relief from her mental strain, and no amount of tossing and turning permitted sleep. It wasn't until the early morning hours that she finally slipped into a fitful slumber, and then only to be yanked awake soon after by the same nightmare she always had.

Shaking violently and sweating as if she'd been for a run, she finally gave up and headed for the shower. At the ridiculous hour of eight o'clock, she wandered into the kitchen.

Her mother looked up from the table, shocked. "You're up early."

"Couldn't sleep."

Rosanne sighed. "Did you call him?"

"No." Joselyn grabbed an apple from the counter and tossed it around in her hand, trying to decide if her stomach would tolerate it. Deciding against the plan, she set it back in the basket.

Hands still shaking, she headed for the coffee pot next, poured herself a mug, and added cream and sugar.

Her mother was staring at her when she joined her at the table. "Hon..."

"Don't, Mom. I need to do this my way."

"If he loves you, he didn't do this. There are so many other possibilities. We employ fifty people, Jos. Any one of them could have caused the leak. We may never even know who it was if it wasn't intentional. It happened. I don't want to see you torturing yourself over it."

Joselyn nodded slowly, twisting her mug around on the table and staring at the contents. "I think the key to everything is the big *if*. I'm afraid to ask the questions. I realize there's no way in hell Alton maliciously plotted to destroy our company. But I can't figure out a plausible way he didn't at least know about it. I'm just not ready to face it, so I haven't called him. I'm chicken."

"And you don't think the fact that he's called you several times tells you something?"

"How do I know he isn't trying to grovel? I don't think I could take it if he looked me in the eye and told me he knew his brewery was planning to sabotage mine. It would kill me. I'm putting off the confrontation."

Her mother set her hand on Joselyn's. "How do any of us ever know for sure what's in another person's heart? Faith is all we have. Now, I'm gonna assume you've had a serious relationship with Alton Tarben for a while."

Joselyn's face heated. "Are you mad I didn't tell you?"

"No. Not at all. You're a grown woman. You can make your own decisions. And I know you have a level head and will make the right ones for you. I'm just sorry you didn't trust me as your mother to love you no matter what."

Joselyn sighed. "It wasn't you or Dad I was worried about. It was the entire extended family. I planned on joining the family business my whole life. Alton planned to join his family's brewery too. So, faced with the possibility it might not happen if people knew we were together, we were too scared to out ourselves."

Her mother's face was pained, her eyes watery on her daughter's behalf. "I'm so sorry, hon. I can't imagine what the past few years have been like for you, but I want you to know Dad and I love you very much. We only want you to be happy. And we're reasonable enough to realize this ridiculous feud between the families is just that —ridiculous.

"I'm not saying it won't be hard, for either of you. Some people will freak out and show their true colors. But let them. It's time the Arthurs and the Tarbens put their differences to bed, anyway."

Joselyn smiled. For the first time in twenty-four hours, she felt like she might live. Now she just needed the balls to call Alton.

She vowed to do so later that night. After work. He was undoubtedly already at the office himself, and she had a policy of not contacting him while he was working.

Alton was staring unseeing at his computer and had been for the entire morning when someone tapped on the doorframe and caused him to jerk his gaze toward the entrance. His father leaned into the room. "Austin and I are headed to Glacial. Come with us?"

"Why?" He sat up straighter, knowing his face had gone white.

"Bernard called. He's fit to be tied. I don't want precarious relations between us to go in the wrong direction over this launch."

"And you think they'll permit you to set foot in their building?"

Allister smirked. "I told him we were coming just before he hung up on me."

Alton blew out a long breath and leaned back in his chair, tipping his head to the ceiling.

Allister stepped all the way inside and shut the door.

"What's going on with you? You haven't come out of your office more than a few times in the last twenty-four hours. And now I find you looking like death warmed over. Did you even go home last night? Did you sleep?"

His father continued into the room slowly. "If I didn't know better, I'd say you aren't happy about this launch." He pulled a chair out across from Alton and sat.

Alton looked at his father, not quite sure what he wanted to say. Where to begin.

It was time.

He cleared his throat. "Joselyn Arthur is my mate."

Allister nodded slowly. "Ah. That explains things." He didn't yell or even flinch. "Does she know?"

That made Alton laugh, which felt good in a bizarre way. "Yes."

"Have you spoken to her?"

He shook his head. "Not since the launch. She's not taking my calls."

His father cringed. "I can see how that would be hard. Have you told anyone else?"

"Austin knows. Nuria figured it out."

"You should be the one to tell your mother."

Alton nodded. "I'll do that now. Is she in her office?"

"Yes."

Alton stood, wiping his palms on his pant legs. He felt like a kid, needing to confess to some crime to his parents. Drugs. Stealing. Something.

Allister stood at the same time. "Take a few minutes. Austin and I will meet you in the truck."

Alton left the room first. He headed down the hall toward his mother's office, feeling slightly nauseous. It wasn't from worrying about her reaction. He knew her to be a reasonable woman who wouldn't judge him. What he hated most was how long he'd kept this secret from his parents. From the world, really.

When he rounded the corner, she was standing behind her desk shuffling papers together as if she'd either just stepped into the room or was about to leave. "Mom."

She glanced up, her face falling as she took in his expression. "What's wrong?"

"Nothing's wrong." He shook his head. "I need to tell you something."

She pointed at the entrance. "Shut the door." And then she rounded the desk and sat on the front edge of it. Her expression was hard to read, but if he wasn't mistaken, she looked pleased with herself, not concerned. "Go ahead."

He tipped his head to one side, wondering about her odd behavior. "I'm in love with Joselyn Arthur."

A smile spread across her face as her shoulders lowered. "I know."

"What?" He winced.

She smiled broader and shrugged. "I've known a long time. I didn't want to pry into your business. I figured you'd tell us when you were ready. I imagine this launch has put a strain on your relationship? Is she mad?"

He chuckled sardonically. "Who would know? Judging from her total silence, I'm going to assume so."

Beth scrunched up her face. "I'm so sorry. Go to her."

He nodded. "I'm going to Glacial with Dad and Austin now. Hopefully, she'll talk to me."

His mother pushed off the side of the desk and came to him. She wrapped her arms around him and hugged him. "It'll work out. This will blow over. I'm sure of it."

"How did you know?" he asked the top of his mother's head, returning her hug and absorbing a rare embrace between a mother and grown son.

"When you were a sophomore at U of C, I came to visit you one Saturday early in the year. That would have been the first semester Joselyn was in school. You gave me a tour of your new apartment. As soon as I stepped in, I could scent a woman."

Alton smiled. Of course.

"I didn't say anything, and I must have stayed longer than you expected me to because when I left, on the way down the hallway, I passed her. She kept her head down and didn't make eye contact, rushing briskly to get past me, but I recognized her scent, and I knew who she was."

"Jesus, Mom. Why didn't you ever say anything?"

"It wasn't my business." She released her son and stepped back, patting his arm. "I knew you would do the right thing for you when the timing was right."

"And Dad? You never told him."

"Nope. Never told a soul."

Alton wiped a hand over his face. "Well, the timing is now. I'm not waiting any longer. We've put our family loyalty first for too many years. It's coming between us. I intend to bind her to me at the first opportunity no matter what the consequences are. I just hope it's not too late."

Beth smiled again. "The draw to bind is strong. It makes me sad you've been keeping it at bay for so many years over a sense of family loyalty, but you know I'll always love you no matter what you do. And so will your father."

"Yes. Thanks, Mom." Alton swallowed back emotion as he backed out of the room.

Why the fuck had he waited to claim his woman for so many years?

Oh, right. Because the reception he was about to encounter from the rest of his pack wouldn't be as warm and fuzzy as the response he'd gotten that morning from his mother and father and two nights ago from Austin.

Fuck the weekend. By the end of this day, he intended to convince his mate to bind herself to him. They would just have to deal with the fallout as it came at them.

Now he needed to convince her to even speak to him.

CHAPTER 14

Joselyn was staring out the window of her office when a noise behind her made her flinch. Before she turned her head, she knew he was there. How had she been so preoccupied that she hadn't sensed him?

He was leaning against the doorframe, but he stepped all the way inside when she turned. She shook herself a little, trying to piece her thoughts together. Alton was there. In her office. In her family's brewery. Where he most certainly didn't belong.

She glanced past him, still too confused to speak. His broad frame filled the space though, and she wished that were the only thing she noticed about him. But of course, as usual, when she set her eyes on him, he sucked the air out of her lungs. He was so damn attractive. The way his hair fell over his forehead. The way he licked his full lips. His fingers were tucked in his pockets—just the tips.

His eyes, though. They were narrowed with concern. "Your mother led me to your office." His voice was low. Deep. Sad. And he reached behind himself to shut the door.

The snick made her flinch, and she pulled her cardigan around her shoulders and crossed her arms as if she were cold. Maybe she was. The chill she felt toward him was real, but it was slowly dissipating the longer he stood yards from her.

"You didn't return my calls. Or my texts." He rubbed his forehead with three fingers and his thumb as if trying to solve a mystery.

Her breath hitched.

He stepped closer.

Her body betrayed her by reacting to his proximity the way it always did—knees going weak, desire flooding her system. It would seem that no matter what he did, she would still find herself attracted to him. How much sense did that make? If he were a knife-wielding serial killer, would she still feel the urge to jump into his arms?

He was in her space now. So close she had to tip her head back to meet his gaze. "Did you know about this?" Above all else, the one thing driving her insane was thinking he maliciously set out to hurt her family.

He cocked his head to one side, his gaze narrowing further.

Her voice rose as she took a step backward, pressing into the window. The cold surface was welcoming. Grounding. It seeped through her jeans, making her clench her butt muscles. "Did you know?" she repeated.

He licked his lips. "I'm not sure I understand what you're asking. I'm the head of engineering. Almost nothing happens inside the brewery without my knowledge. Let alone a new product launch. Of course, I knew. And I was worried about how you'd react, but I have to say I wasn't half as concerned as I obviously should have been. It's business, Jos. Nothing else."

"Business? Are you fucking kidding me?" She tried to

keep her voice soft so no one in the hallway would hear her but probably failed.

He winced. "We agreed not to discuss business. Ever. That was our arrangement. What was I supposed to do? Tell my family not to create a new product because it might piss off my secret girlfriend?"

She felt the heat rush up her face. What was happening? How had things gone so wrong between them that he seemed like a total stranger all the sudden?

Alton spun around, running a hand through his hair. With his back to her, he shifted his weight from one foot to the other. Was he nervous? Good.

Suddenly he froze, his head turning to the left toward the small conference table where all her hard work from the last few months lay spread out. The pile of papers and ads and posters that had glistened with hope and excitement two days ago now appeared to mock her as if it was old news. Useless. Trash. Out of style. Not keeping with the times.

Alton lurched forward and grabbed the ad on the top of the pile. He held it up, grasping it with both hands. As he faced to the side, she could read his expression. His eyes were wide. His hands shook. His mouth hung open. The scent of shock and confusion filled her office.

This was the first time since they'd left U of C he'd ever seen her work up close, she realized. Maybe he was stunned by her skills?

The bright yellows and oranges that dripped from glistening clear bottles, bubbling with promise, made her glance away.

He spun back to face her, holding the page in the air and shaking it. "What's this?"

She frowned, glancing at him only fleetingly. And then

she turned back toward the window, putting her back to him, saying nothing.

"Joselyn, did you do this?"

"Of course I did. I'm the marketing manager. It's my job." What the hell was wrong with him? He acted like he didn't expect to find ads lying around in the marketing office of his competitor a week before a launch. Was he insane?

"But…" his voice trailed off. A slight rustling followed by the sound of chair legs scraping across the floor told her he had undoubtedly taken a seat. "Fuck."

The one word made her jump in her skin. Why was he acting so strange?

Papers shuffled against each other on the table. He was riffling through her work. Ordinarily, this would infuriate her. He had no business looking at trade secrets.

But her months of hard work were hardly trade secrets, were they?

"These are dated next Monday," he pointed out as if by chance she was unaware of her own launch—the one so callously ruined by his brewery. After all, to quote him, it was just business.

"You have an excellent grasp of the modern calendar and days of the week. Congrats."

Before the last words dripped sarcastically from her lips, he was up and moving quickly across the floor. She braced herself for the impact his touch would have on her. Because she knew for certain he was about to set his hands on her.

He grabbed her shoulders, spinning her around so quickly she almost lost her balance. But he didn't let her fall. He pinned her to the window, his sad eyes searching hers. "Shit, Jos."

It was at that moment the puzzle pieces fell into place. "You didn't know."

His face jerked back. "No. Of course not. I knew my family was developing a new product. I hated keeping that from you. But I certainly didn't realize your brewery was doing essentially the same thing."

She narrowed her gaze. "Seriously?"

"Jesus, Jos. Is that why you wouldn't take my calls? Because you thought I stole company secrets from you and rushed to slam a baseball bat to the backs of your knees?"

She lifted her face to his. "I didn't know what else to think. It wasn't that I thought *you personally* rummaged through my stuff and emulated it, but someone in your pack did. It's a little hard to believe you didn't know. How is that possible?" Something didn't add up. "Obviously someone in my pack leaked our release to someone in your family. There's no other explanation. The product and all the marketing are nearly identical. It's like someone hacked my computer and shared every detail of our planned launch."

"It would certainly appear that way, but you have to believe it wasn't me. I've never once touched your phone or computer. Ever. I swear." His eyes searched hers. "And, whoever did this never told anyone inside my brewery that the product development was stolen. I didn't know. I'm telling you there's no way my immediate family is aware of this. They aren't that vindictive."

She tried to process everything he said, her face probably going white as all the heat rushed from her cheeks. "Shit."

"Yeah." He closed his eyes. "I'm guilty of keeping the launch from you, yes. That's business. Though it did put a sour taste in my mouth that worried me more every day as we grew closer to the launch. I hated knowing my company was about to do something that would harm the bottom line of yours. Made my skin crawl.

"In fact, I vowed to myself to leave the brewery as soon as this damn launch was over. I thought it was prudent for me to see it through after being in on the development from the beginning, but my plan was to quit this weekend after we told our parents about us."

"My parents know about us. I told them yesterday," she admitted.

He gave her the first half smile of the day. "Yeah, I figured that when your mother met me at the front desk and then wordlessly nodded over her shoulder and led me to your office."

"I was...distraught yesterday. I told them."

"Mine know too."

She winced. "Were they mad?"

"Not at all. That doesn't mean the battle's over. It's just beginning, but we will get through it and come out stronger on the other side. I promise." He kissed her lips gently, the contact making her body come alive. Her breasts tightened. Her breath caught in her throat.

"So there's a mole, but whoever it is didn't tell *you*."

He chuckled, though she thought he should be angry with her for being so suspicious and accusatory. She cocked her head to one side. "I doubted you." There was no reason to deny it. What a bitch.

He nodded. "Yeah, that's gonna get under my skin when I stop to think about it later, but for now I'm just glad we cleared the air. I can understand why you would think I had to have known, but the answer is *no*. I didn't know the entire product launch was stolen from you. I didn't know until I picked up that ad, noticing how eerily similar it was to ours."

She believed him. She had to.

His next words were spoken into her mind. *"I'm so sorry, baby. This royally sucks."*

She continued out loud. "If you didn't know, then I guess there are others who didn't know. How many people knew? Hell, how many people inside my company knew?" She gripped his biceps with both hands and squeezed. "We have to tell my dad."

He nodded, hesitating only a moment to kiss her lips again, more thoroughly than before. Enough to make her remember who he was to her and vice versa. She'd been so stupid.

"My dad's with him now. I've got to assume he's as stunned as I am. Lead the way." He swept out his hand and angled them toward the door.

When Alton stepped into the Glacial boardroom behind his mate, he was shocked to find his father and brother in a shouting match with several of Joselyn's family members.

Bernard Arthur stood at the head of the table, leaning against the surface with both palms. "You expect me to believe you had nothing to do with this, Allister? You had no knowledge that we were in the middle of launching virtually the same malt beverage?"

"That's what I'm saying." Alton's father stood to one side of the table, totally outnumbered with no one by his side except his other son, Austin.

Meanwhile, six other members of the Arthur family sat lounging around the opposite side of the table looking fit to kill.

Alton didn't blame them. Until they got to the bottom of things, tensions were going to run high. But he also didn't want to witness a complete dressing down of his father, either.

"Dad," Joselyn began, "they didn't know."

Bernard jerked his gaze toward his daughter and stared at her. His shoulders slumped as Alton realized her father trusted her, and by default him.

Alton set a hand softly on her lower back, unsure how outed she was willing to be. There was no way to keep their relationship a secret any longer, but it was also possible she didn't intend to draw attention to herself this very moment in the company boardroom.

He, for one, had a rush of emotion running through him that insisted he put the ridiculous farce to bed. But he wouldn't make that choice for her.

Joselyn shocked him to death, however, when she leaned into him for support, turned more fully toward his side, and set her palm on his chest. "They didn't know," she repeated.

A hush fell over the room. Six sets of wide eyes bore into Alton's. He cleared his throat, ignoring the looks of shock and outrage. "Obviously someone must have known. Someone in our brewery knew. But keep in mind that means there's a chance you have a mole." He glanced at his father, seeing the relief on his face.

Allister stepped forward and tapped his fingertips on the table. "I'll get to the bottom of this. You have my word." He held up a hand when Bernard started to interrupt. "Believe me. I know what you're thinking. Perhaps you're right. Maybe one of my pack members broke into your brewery and stole company secrets. I'll grant it's possible. But do me the favor of considering there's a possibility the culpability lies inside these walls." He turned around and nodded toward his sons. "Let's go."

Alton followed behind Austin and his father, but he slid

his hand into Joselyn's at the same time, luring her into the hallway.

When they were out of the boardroom, Allister turned around, his eyes going to Joselyn. He gave her a slow smile and a wink but said nothing.

Alton's heart pounded with relief, and he felt the warmth that spread through Joselyn at the same time, her hand clenching his.

Allister and Austin continued walking, escorted by some member of the Arthur family Alton didn't know.

Alton halted, though, heedless of the fact that the wall to the boardroom was made of glass and everyone inside was watching at a low growl. He took Joselyn's face in his hands. "I have to go. I have work to do. You do too. But tonight you're mine. Got it? My place. Dinner. Seven o'clock." He closed the distance between them and set his lips on her ear. "Don't plan on going home."

She shuddered in his arms. "Seven."

He smiled, a giant weight lifting off his shoulders.

Someone inside the room roared with unintelligible words.

Alton lifted a brow. "On second thought, maybe I should take you with me?"

She shook her head. "I can handle them. My parents are on my side." She gave him a strained smile.

He frowned. Leaving her with her angry pack wasn't something he wanted to do, but his father was probably pacing the lobby waiting for him. There was a lot of work to do. At the very least, someone inside his pack stole or was given trade secrets from the competitor.

"You bitch. You smug bitch." Joselyn winced at the tone

and the words as she stood in the hall, still staring at the spot where Alton had disappeared around the corner. She knew the words were directed at her, just as she also knew her father would lose his marbles over the behavior. With her head held high and her shoulders squared, she reentered the room.

"Not another word, Fletcher," her father said, his booming voice vibrating through the space. "Sit down and close your lips before I kick your ass out of the building."

Fletcher was on his feet—everyone in the room was— and he leaned forward, his face every shade of red. "You threatening me, old man?"

"Damn right, I am." Bernard glanced around the room, meeting the gaze of each person. "I'm the leader of this pack and the CEO of Glacial Brewing Company, and I expect a certain level of respect from my pack members and my employees. If you can't comply, get out of this building now."

Joselyn was proud of her father. Not that he had ever been a pushover. He was born to be the leader of the Arthur pack, but she'd never witnessed such a bold smackdown from him before.

Bernard glanced around the room. "I suggest the rest of you hold your tongues too, or you'll find yourselves standing in the parking lot with a box of belongings from your cleared desks."

Fletcher opened his big mouth again, but her father stopped him with an outstretched palm.

"Instead of focusing your energy on some perceived slight you're feeling over the private relationship between my daughter and her mate, I suggest you remember what Allister Tarben so kindly just pointed out. There's probably a mole inside these walls. So, besides pissing me off and making me doubt your loyalty to the brewery, anyone who spouts a line of bullshit about some ancient family feud moves to the top of the list of possible suspects."

Joselyn had to lean against the glass pane at her back to keep from falling to the floor. Her father wasn't only not angry with her for hooking up with a Tarben, but he was totally sticking up for her. She wanted to smile. She instead kept her gaze to the floor and held her emotions at bay.

Fletcher had the balls to speak again. "Seriously, Bernard? Listen to yourself. There's a mole all right. It's your fucking daughter. She's obviously shacking up with Allister Tarben's goddamn son." His voice rose. "Are you so blind you can't see the writing on the wall?"

She flinched. This was exactly what she'd expected.

Bernard lifted a hand and pointed at the door. "Get out."

Fletcher laughed. "You can't fire me. I'm a member of your own family. It's *your* job that's in jeopardy, old man. You've been colluding with the Tarbens for months now. First when your oldest son went all wackjob and then when your next son got into a bind. Now we find out your daughter is slutting around with Alton Tarben? That's too much, Bernard. It's you who should leave. Obviously, your loyalty to the business has been compromised. And I'm pretty sure if the board took this to a vote, you would lose."

Her father looked fit to kill, and for a man who rarely lost his temper, it was impressive. "Fletcher, get out of this room right now before I make decisions you'll later regret."

Fletcher shoved off the table, rounded it, and shot Joselyn a piercing look of disgust as he left the room.

The hush that fell in his wake was deafening.

Joselyn didn't move or breathe. She thought she might faint. All her worst nightmares coming to life. She'd worried for years that several members of her pack wouldn't take her binding to a Tarben well, but this was so much worse. Could they actually kick her parents and siblings out of the company over her actions?

The answer made her shudder. How many people, when up against the wall, would side with some fucked-up old feud over love?

CHAPTER 15

At seven o'clock Joselyn stood outside the door to Alton's apartment—a place she'd never been to even though he'd lived there two years. She lifted her hand to knock before the door swung open, and she found herself tugged into the warm embrace of the man she loved.

She flinched when he kicked the door shut and plastered her to it, threading his fingers in her hair until the ponytail dislodged. And then he sealed his lips to hers. She dropped her purse to the floor and wrapped her arms around his waist.

This was her lifeline. This man was her story. Nothing else mattered.

His hands were everywhere at once, shoving her cardigan off her shoulders and then worming their way under her shirt without breaking the kiss.

She moaned into his mouth when his huge palms flattened on her back. Her eyes slid closed as her body ceased belonging to her and melded with his. The passion was still steaming hot between them. When they came together, they always seemed to become a third separate entity, unified somehow, though she didn't know how to describe that in words.

"Alton…" she mumbled against his lips.

"Mmm." He nibbled at her top lip and then bit it gently between his teeth, giving it a tug.

She moaned again, loving the pressure, the dominance.

He shoved his hands farther up her shirt and slid it over her head. When he dropped it on the floor without looking, he flattened his palms on the door at the sides of her face. His brow was furrowed as he searched her expression. "You're mine."

"Yes," she breathed…as if there were any doubt.

"I never want you to doubt that again."

She nodded slightly.

He cupped her face with one hand, his thumb stroking over her bottom lip to pull it down. "We're done with this farce. It's over."

"Yes." She kissed his thumb and then licked the tip.

"You willing to take this leap of faith with me?"

"Yes."

"Now. Here. Tonight."

"Yes." Her voice was stronger. A part of her knew they would bind tonight from the first mention of her coming over. If he hadn't suggested it, she would have pushed the issue.

"You're gonna take a lot of flak tomorrow at work."

"So are you."

He shrugged. "I no longer give a single fuck. I asked myself, what's the worst thing that can happen, and I didn't come up with any answer that would give me hesitation."

"You could lose your job."

"Yep." Obviously, that fell in the category that gave him no hesitation.

"I'll probably lose mine. My pack is furious. They

threatened to fire my dad today."

"What?" Alton shouted. "Can they do that?"

"Yes." She nodded. No sense pretending otherwise.

"But he's the leader of your pack. That brewery is more his than anyone's."

She lifted her brows. "I'm not sure he has the numbers to back him on this. More members of my pack are opposed to making amends with yours than in favor. If there were any doubt, their true colors came out today."

"What happened?" Alton stepped back, his hands sliding down her arms until he had a grip on her fingers and was luring her farther into his apartment. He sat on the couch and tugged her onto his lap.

She spun around, preferring to face him head on, lifting one leg to swing it over his so she straddled him.

He grabbed her waist, and then his hands slid up until his thumbs brushed the undersides of her breasts.

She ignored the way her body demanded they stop talking and start fucking. Things needed to be said. "One of my cousins went ballistic after you left. He was spouting stupid shit about you and me, and my dad told him he could pack his stuff and get out of the building. My dad threatened to fire him and anyone else who decided to talk smack."

"That's reasonable."

"Yeah, except I don't think even my father counted on the response he got, which was an indignant counter that if a vote were taken, the board would remove my dad instead of the other way around."

Alton's eye widened. "You think they would do that?"

She sighed. "I'm not sure. If you're asking if they have the numbers, probably. But would they? I don't know."

"This is super fucked up, baby."

"I know." She bit her lip. "And I feel responsible. It's

impossible not to. What if my immediate family is shunned over my choice in a mate?"

He hesitated, prodding into her mind as she tried to give him an honest glimpse of her sincerity. "What will your parents say?"

"They'll have my back. I know I have their blessing. They love me. So does my brother Isaiah. I haven't spoken to Wyatt yet, though perhaps Isaiah has. After today, I wouldn't be surprised. He has a right to know. He wasn't in the meeting this morning."

"Oh, Jos, this is so unfair. Why the hell do our private choices have to affect so many lives?" He held her closer, his grip on her rib cage tighter.

"Except you're looking at it the wrong way. This isn't a choice. It's not that simple. It's not something we can deny and walk away from. It feels like a clock has been ticking at our backs for years, chasing us down. And time has finally caught up with us, overrunning us, getting ahead of us, even. We either keep up…or we die."

He stared at her.

"Not literally of course, but our souls. Our hearts. I wouldn't be able to live without you. A part of me isn't whole without you. Something's always missing.

"I assume for those who have never met their mates, they don't feel this pressure, but anyone I've ever heard of who knew who they were meant to be with couldn't go on without binding."

"And yet we've done exactly that for years. Too many to count," he pointed out.

"Exactly."

He tugged her forward until her pussy pressed against his cock. Even through the two layers of denim, the heat was intense. The pressure made her breath hitch. "Doubts?"

"None." She lowered her face to his and kissed him briefly. "We can't worry about everyone else anymore. I'm done waiting. We have to worry about ourselves now."

He smiled wide and then spread one hand up her back and into her hair. He tugged, hard enough to get her to tip her head back and to one side, exposing her throat. He licked the spot where her neck and shoulder met, his breath sending a shiver down her arms.

She gripped his waist, her heart racing with the anticipation.

He whispered against her skin. "You won't go back to your parents' house after."

"Of course not," she muttered.

"Ever."

"I wouldn't want to."

"You belong in my bed. We won't ever spend a night apart. Not *ever*, Jos."

She swallowed, her arousal growing higher with every word. "Yes."

"I want to finish the binding first. Then I'm going to fuck you."

"Please…" Her voice was shaky with desire.

He nuzzled the spot again, nibbling the area until she shuddered. "Open your mind to me, baby. Let me in."

Her fingers flexed against his lower back where she'd wiggled them under his shirt. She inhaled deeply and then blew out the breath as she let him in. She felt him delving instantly, poking around in her thoughts.

"Oh, baby." He kissed her neck again. "I love you so much."

"I love you too," she told the ceiling. Her head was still wrenched back, his grip firm in her hair. Did he think if he let go she might be able to get her teeth on him and beat him to the punch?

She could. She could have done so at any point over the years. No law said he had to be the one to bind them together, but there was a law that said no one could be bound to another without permission. She bit her lip between her teeth, willing him to bite her. Now.

His cock throbbed against her pussy, driving her so close to orgasm she thought she might come before he finished the binding.

She lowered her walls a little more, knowing how important it was to him for her to let him into her mind. And she reached into his at the same time, feeling the intensity of his love and devotion. He wanted nothing but amazing things for her, as she did him.

When his teeth grazed her skin, she gasped. *"Please, Alton. I've never wanted anything more in my life,"* she communicated.

The second his teeth broke the skin, she arched into him as much as she could in his grip. Her lips parted in anticipation, her breath hitching. Instead of the sharp sting she expected to feel when he broke the skin, she felt nothing but need. Her mind pleaded with him to let his serum enter her bloodstream. That last step was necessary to complete the binding.

A moment later, her wish was granted. The instant he sealed them, a wave washed through her, like an adrenaline rush that took her by surprise and made her entire body tingle. The need to be naked and impaled by him made her skin itch. She moaned, gritting her teeth, wishing they had at least removed their clothes before taking this final step.

Alton released her neck only to lick the bite. His serum would seal the wound, but the small scar would forever mark her as taken. Not that anyone would need to see the scar to know she was bound to another. They would scent it on her. Every single shifter she passed from this moment forward would know she was in a permanent, committed binding with another.

She loved that fact about their species. Pride raced through her bloodstream. She was his, and she never needed to announce it.

She released his waist and fisted his shirt, tugging it over his head.

"In a hurry?" he mumbled against her lips as he lowered her head to kiss her.

She ignored him, flattening her palms on his shoulder blades in an attempt to draw him closer, not that they could get any more plastered together while they both wore jeans.

Alton tucked his hands under her ass and lifted them both off the couch. He took brisk steps to round the couch and headed out of the room. She didn't take her gaze off his. She hadn't seen a single aspect of his apartment yet. She didn't even know the color of the couch they'd just vacated.

In seconds, they were in what she assumed was his bedroom, and she was falling through the air to land on her ass.

"Jeans off, baby. Now."

She scrambled to unbutton and unzip them with shaky hands, lifting her hips to slide the denim and her panties down her legs while she watched him shrug out of his at the same time. His eyes were dark and piercing. And when his cock was finally released, it bobbed between them thicker and harder than she ever remembered.

She popped her bra off next and tossed it aside.

In a flash, he was over her, climbing between her legs. He grabbed her wrists with both hands, lifted them over her head, and pressed them into the mattress. One second later, he thrust into her.

She screamed. The walls of her channel were more sensitive than she'd ever noticed before. Every stroke of his cock made her more aware of her sexuality. Her vision blurred as he claimed her mouth.

She squirmed beneath him, needing to touch him, but he held her hands tighter. Her breasts ached from the need to be touched, but only her nipples received any sort of contact as he pulled partway out and thrust back in deep.

A grunt escaped his mouth.

A sound she didn't recognize left her lips. Every single stroke pushed her to a new cliff. As if she had a new awareness of her body and was more fully alive than before, she came hard around him.

He groaned as she milked his cock, the first orgasm never fully ending as her arousal continued to build to a new height. The fact that he held her arms shot her desire through the roof. His torso pinned her to the bed, not permitting her the opportunity to arch into him or lift.

More importantly, he knew this. He knew how fucking hot she found this binding because she let all her walls down and permitted him to delve into every corner of her mind.

As he plowed into her faster, he set his forehead on the bed next to hers and whispered into her ear. "Love you… So much…" Some of his words were garbled, and she didn't understand them, but the sentiment was there. And the emotion that wafted off of him and into her was palpable in the room.

When he came, stiffening inside her, she was right at the edge of a second orgasm. *"Come with me, Jos,"* he communicated one second before letting go. His body repeatedly spasmed as he leaned more of his weight into her. She followed right behind him, milking his cock with the pulsing of her channel.

"Joselyn..." That one word slid from his mouth, strewn out as if it were a sentence. He finally slid to her side, his cock pulling out, one thigh remaining between her legs. He released her hands and cupped the side of her face, even though she couldn't see his eyes because she didn't have the energy to turn her face toward his.

She nuzzled into his palm instead, speaking into his mind while trying to catch her breath. *"That was amazing. Why did we wait so long?"*

He chuckled into her head. *"Stupidity?"*

She smiled. Sated. Never happier. And sharing that with him without blocking him in any way.

"Love you letting me into your mind. So much." He pressed his palm tighter against her face.

She took deep breaths, trying to find the energy to move. Failing.

"Hope you like my apartment," he whispered, nibbling on her ear.

"No idea what it looks like, but if you plan to be in it, I won't care."

He chuckled out loud this time, seeming to recover enough strength at least for that. "We'll move. Soon. We'll build something or pick something out together."

She giggled. "Stop worrying. I'm sure this will be fine. We don't have to hurry." She finally turned to face him and kissed his lips. "You know it doesn't matter. I only care that you're with me. I wouldn't care if we lived in the back of a car as long as you were there."

"Good, because we might end up fleeing town with nothing more than the SUV."

She sighed. "Let's hope it doesn't come to that."

He lifted onto one elbow. "I haven't shown you the bathroom yet. The shower is an incredibly amazing two-foot-by-two-foot space with fantastic water pressure.

You'll almost be able to turn all the way around if I ever let you use it alone, but not today."

She giggled again as he heaved himself off the bed and scooped her up in his arms to pad across the room. Where he got the strength was a mystery. When he swung her around to let her slide down his body until her feet hit the floor next to the shower, she snuggled against his side, waiting for the water to heat up.

Her first glimpse of his apartment was the bathroom. It was a rental, so the standard off-white paint job was boring. The sink and toilet and shower were crammed into a small space. There was no tub. "How big is this place?"

"About seven hundred square feet." He smiled. "Cozy, right?"

"Why the hell didn't you get someplace you could stretch out in?" He'd been living there two years. She had never realized it was so small.

He kissed her cheek and lured her into the water. "I saved every dime I made in the last two years, Jos."

"Seriously?"

"Yep. So, no matter what happens in the next few days, we have a nest egg. We can leave town if we need and never look back." He angled the showerhead over her hair, tipping her head back.

She closed her eyes as the warmth spread through her body.

"We're educated. We can find work. And we can take our time doing so if need be."

She leaned forward, wrapped her arms around his middle, and plastered her cheek to his chest. "I didn't even have rent to pay. You should see my bank account."

He smoothed his hands up her body and back down to cup her ass. "See? We're fine. No worries at all."

She sighed. "Except for the stress of excommunication."

"Well, there's that."

They had showered together a few times in the past. They almost always did when they were in a hotel, not wanting to waste a moment of their precious time separated by a glass wall. But never had they washed each other in a space this confining.

She reached for the soap and ran it over his chest while he shampooed her hair. Together they easily completed the task in synchronized motions that were innate to them.

By the time they stepped out, she was at least as aroused as she'd been when she set foot in his apartment an hour ago. Perhaps more. She rubbed her sensitive skin with the towel, moaning around the contact of the material against her nipples.

He dropped his towel on the floor before he managed to swipe it over his hair and yanked her against him. "Damn, they were not kidding?"

"Who wasn't kidding about what?" She licked a line of water from between his pecs.

"The increased need to fuck after binding. I'm so hot for you right now, I can't think of anything else but getting you back under me again as fast as possible."

"What if I want *you* to be under *me*?"

"Mmm." He backed them out of the bathroom, steering their combined bodies toward the bed. "We'll see." And then his mouth was on hers again. He devoured her, making it difficult to breathe, which was highly overrated anyway.

When the backs of her knees hit the bed again, she grabbed his arms to keep from tumbling backward. Pulling her mouth away from his, she whispered against his lips. "Let me be on top."

He licked the seam. "Why would I do that? You obviously like a bit of kink. It makes you hotter than ever. I say you climb up on your back, spread your legs, and let me tie you to all four corners and blindfold you." He grinned.

She groaned. There was no way to hide the flood of arousal that leaked from her at the suggestion. Blindfolds? Ropes? Was he planning to amp up the kink now that they were bound together?

He pinched her ass, making her clench her butt cheek, and spoke out loud to the thoughts he read in her head. "I'm going to add to the kink because you enjoyed it so much the first time. And because the mention of it made your pussy wet, your pulse speed up, and your nipples pucker." He looked so proud of himself as he bent his head down to flick his tongue over one nipple and then suck it into his mouth.

She threaded her fingers into his hair and held his head to her breast. Every single thing he did to her was amplified to an entirely new level of pleasure since the binding.

When he slid a hand from her ass to reach between her legs from behind and dragged a finger through her wetness, she bit her lip and lifted onto her tiptoes. "That all sounds amazing. And you're welcome to do whatever you want to me some other time. For now, I want to take care of you the way you just did me. On top."

Alton released her nipple with a pop, pulled his finger away from her pussy, and climbed onto the bed, teasing her by sucking that finger into his mouth.

She shook her head as she followed him, straddling his enormous body with her own and setting her hands on both sides of his face in an absurd display of control she knew he was only humoring her with. She hoped she was at least coherent enough to block her plans and keep him off balance.

He confirmed as much when he narrowed his gaze. "What are you plotting, imp? You blocked me."

She wiggled her eyebrows. "Trust me?"

"Implicitly."

"Then why are you worried?"

"I don't like surprises."

She giggled but ignored him to scoot down his body until her face was level with his once-again erect cock. She licked the length from the base to the tip, eliciting a low groan from deep inside him.

Empowered, she sucked the head into her mouth, wrapping her fingers around the base and stroking up and down in sync with her lips.

"Joselyn," he warned.

"I need to taste you. Don't fight me," she communicated without breaking her suction.

"I'm so aroused I'm gonna come too fast if you do that." He wrapped a hand around a section of her hair.

She'd grown to crave the slight tug. But she had plans and didn't want him to thwart her efforts. The way he made her come after binding them made her want him to have a similar experience. And now was the time.

Releasing the head of his cock, she continued to hold the thick length in her palm while kissing a path down to his balls. She flicked her tongue over one, pleased when he flinched on a moan. When she gently sucked it into her mouth, he nearly shot off the bed.

He outweighed her significantly, so any attempt to control him was fake but still heady.

As she let the sac fall from her mouth, she slid her tongue to his thigh and shoved his knee out farther so she would have more room to maneuver.

"God, that feels so good. Lick my cock again. I want to be in your mouth."

She ignored him, thrusting her hand loosely up and down the shaft faster while she nibbled on his inner thigh.

He didn't balk. If he had any idea what she was about to do, he didn't let on. Although he also didn't share any thoughts at all. Nor did he pull away.

So she took the opportunity, licked a spot high on his thigh, and punctured his skin with her teeth. At the same time, she pumped his cock harder.

He stiffened. His body arched off the bed, but she was aware of his hands dropping to his sides to fist the sheet. His head tipped back. His mouth fell open, but no sound came out.

So heady. She let the binding serum run into the small puncture wounds to seep into his bloodstream. It wasn't precisely necessary for her to bite him as he'd done to her. In fact, it made no difference whatsoever. They were fully bound for life. But many couples enjoyed doing it simultaneously or soon after. And she'd felt compelled to participate equally.

A new rush consumed her, like a drug, as her serum entered his blood stream. Amazing. If she'd known how damn good it would feel, she might have pressured him to do this years ago.

He groaned as she licked the small mark on his thigh at the same time as he came. The force of his orgasm shook his body. She lifted her gaze to watch him shudder with every pulse from his cock. Before he was finished, she sucked him back into her mouth, anxious to swallow the rest of his orgasm.

"Jesus, Jos..." he somehow managed to convey.

When he was spent, she released him with a pop and climbed back up his body to straddle his hips. Her pussy rubbed against his still-erect length, and she shocked herself with the amount of sensation that spread through her body. With both hands on his chest, bracing herself, she masturbated against his cock. Her clit was swollen and sensitive, but she wanted more.

"That's it, baby." His hands landed on her sides, gripping her hips, helping her slide back and forth. "Take what you need."

Her head fell forward, her eyes closed, as she concentrated on how incredible it felt. Her orgasm grew at the same time his erection fully returned. The second she was about to come, he lifted her off him, grabbed his cock, and lined it up to thrust into her.

She screamed. It was exactly what she needed. The last second of contact against her clit came from the base of his cock, pushing her over the edge while he filled her.

She didn't raise her body, but she did lift her face to his, blinking around the pulsing grip she had on his length.

"So sexy." His words were gentle.

When she was spent and her arms would no longer hold her up, he eased her to one side and tucked her against his chest.

"That was hot," he said as he rubbed up and down her arm and then cupped her hand against his pecs. "I was a little worried when I realized your intention, but it turned out explosive."

"Mmm, I'm glad. I needed to bite you too. The need was crawling under my skin. I hope you didn't freak out over my location choice." She spoke against his chest.

"It went straight to my cock."

"That was the plan."

He smoothed his hand up and down her body and kissed the top of her head. "You want to rest, or are you hungry?"

"I can't move."

He held her tighter. "Sleep, then."

CHAPTER 16

The sun was coming over the horizon when Alton sat on the edge of the bed and stared down at his mate. She was still asleep, not having moved a muscle as he slid out from under her and tucked the covers around her naked body.

Mornings had never been her friend. She hated to get up. At U of C, she rarely took an early class. He'd teased her about it often. Some days he managed to go for a run, eat breakfast, shower, and study before she got out of bed and would return his calls.

He loved to watch her sleep, though. And today was special. Their first day as mates. The first day they would not be able to hide their relationship from anyone, not even when they weren't together. Any grizzly shifter would be able to scent their status as bound to another.

He cringed, unable to imagine them going their separate ways to tackle the insanity that would fill their day. He'd give anything to stay inside his tiny apartment and fuck her ten more times instead of dragging their asses into the shower and out the door.

A nudge from Austin into his mind had him concentrating on his brother. *"You up?"*

"Yes. Everything okay?" Alton asked.

"I was going to ask you that. We didn't have a chance to speak yesterday. I'm so happy for you and Joselyn. And sad at the same time. Please tell me you aren't going to put this off any longer. I can't imagine the pain. I mean, in a way I can, but at least while I knew Nuria was my mate, for most of my life, she wasn't in town. I can't imagine having her and not finishing the binding."

Alton smiled. *"I'm staring down at her right now. Don't worry about me. It's done."*

Austin let out an audible breath in Alton's head. *"Thank God. You were stressing me out."*

"Can't imagine how anyone's going to take it, but fuck them. I'm not sure now why I ever cared."

"Best feeling in the world, isn't it?"

"Yeah." He cut off the connection abruptly and stared at his sweet mate as she stirred and then blinked her eyes. Austin would understand.

Her smile lit up the room. She reached for him, "Please tell me we don't have to get up."

He leaned over her and kissed her. "We can pack up the SUV and run for the border if you want."

She groaned. "If only it were that easy."

"It can be. Say the word, and we're out of town."

"Maybe we should try to sort this mess out first, yeah?"

"Maybe," he teased.

She inhaled. "You made coffee."

"Of course." He reached for the nightstand and lifted a mug.

She moaned as she pushed herself to sitting, leaning against the headboard. After taking the cup and sipping, she spoke again. "Bless you."

He glanced down at her breasts as the sheet fell to her lap. God he loved her. "You didn't have any nightmares, did you?" Could they possibly enter a new phase of life—one that didn't include bad dreams or any other barriers between them?

She shook her head, her eyes lighting up. "Not one. Thank God. Maybe the stupid curse is broken."

He stroked a finger down her cheek. "Maybe they were a result of the stress of living a lie."

"Let's hope so. Best night of sleep I've had in years." She took another sip of coffee.

"What's the game plan? I'm not inclined to send you to the wolves alone, Jos." He rubbed her thigh, loving that she had no inhibitions that caused her to cover her gorgeous, naked body.

She cocked her head to one side and then the other, working out the kinks. "It's not a bad idea. We could join a pack of wolf shifters and start fresh."

He laughed. "Okay, not my first choice."

"My brothers met a pack of wolves in Montana when they were there helping with the bizarre series of natural disasters."

"I remember when they did that. But I don't think I realized they were working with wolves."

"Yep. Their stories are fascinating."

"I bet." He squeezed her thigh. "Shower?"

"I suppose." She continued sipping her coffee without moving. It seemed her thoughts were deep.

He didn't want to nose around in her head too deeply without her permission, afraid it would be disconcerting. "Let's go by your office together and see what we encounter. And then we'll go from there."

She nodded. "You think that's the best idea? My stupid, ignorant family is going to pounce on you."

"Well, they sure as fuck aren't going to pounce on *you* without me there. I absolutely won't tolerate that. If anyone disrespects you, I'm going to blow fire out of my ears."

She smiled. "My hero."

An hour later, they were showered, dressed, and out the door. He was glad to find out she'd brought a bag of clothes and left it in her car. At least she hadn't planned on leaving. They would need to go by her parents' house later and pack up more of her things, but at least for today, she had what she needed.

It was comical how they headed to her office with her wearing a dark blue Glacial Brewing Company polo and him wearing a black Mountain Peak Brewery polo. Nothing about their attire screamed competition. Nope. Not at all.

The logos themselves weren't extremely different. His was a white-capped mountain peak. Hers was the flat face of a glacier against a lake.

When they pulled into the parking lot, she sighed. "Not looking forward to this." She turned to him. "Let me apologize for my pack members in advance."

He took her hand, lifted it to his lips, and kissed her knuckles. "You aren't your family. Nor your extended pack."

"I know. But I can't stand for people to be so ignorantly rude."

"We're going to get it from both sides, so keep in mind you don't own a monopoly on bigotry in the family."

She closed her eyes and leaned her head against the headrest before finally seeming to muster the energy to face the day.

They stepped from the SUV at the same time and headed for the front of the office building. He inhaled deeply as they approached the front doors, the air giving him a rush with the rich scent of hops he always smelled entering his own brewery. He loved the smell.

He had realized the layout of her brewery was similar to his the day before. Nice office space in front with the plant attached behind.

Any concerns he had about what her packs' bottom line might look like had dissipated the moment he stepped inside the previous morning. At least they gave off the appearance of a thriving business.

Both breweries employed about fifty people. They were undoubtedly neck and neck. There was no reason for this insane need to attempt to hurt their primary competition. If it were up to him, they would come together, support each other, and grow their businesses until they took the lion share of the market in an expanding territory.

Alas, instead the vast majority of both packs were stuck in their ways, trapped in a cycle of maintaining an ancient feud. Exasperating.

When Alton pulled the glass front door open, he set his hand on Joselyn's lower back to guide her inside. He kept his hand there, making a statement that didn't need physical affirmation at all.

The receptionist, a cute girl about Joselyn's age, lifted her gaze with a smile that immediately fell as her mouth dropped open.

"Good morning, Liddie," Joselyn said in a cheery voice as they walked by her. She bee-lined straight for her office, dropped her briefcase and coat on a chair, and turned around as he took off his own coat.

He wasn't going to lie to himself. He was nervous. But they didn't have options. And he wasn't in the mood for ignorant ranting. No one was going to get under his skin, he vowed to himself.

Two seconds later, someone rounded the corner and stepped into the office. "You have a lot of nerve, Joselyn."

Alton recognized him as Fletcher, the asshole who sat steaming in the boardroom yesterday. The vibe coming off him was ominous. It pissed Alton off, but he refused to let it show. Instead, he wiped his palms on his thighs and reached out a hand. "I don't think we've met. Alton Tarben."

The jerk had the gall to glance at Alton's hand, smirk, and ignore him.

Alton in turn, expecting the reaction, simply shrugged him off and put himself halfway between Joselyn and her cousin.

Alton was pretty sure Fletcher was the son of Carroll and Esta Arthur. Carroll was one of Bernard's younger brothers. He put Fletcher at about twenty-eight years old.

The fucker stared hard at Joselyn before finally having the balls to look at Alton when he spoke. "You're not welcome here. No one in your pack is welcome here. I suggest you get the fuck out of our brewery before I have you physically removed."

"Isn't he pleasant," Alton said into Joselyn's mind.

"Always has been. He's four years older than me, and he's behaved like an imbecile for as long as I can remember."

A booming voice from the hallway interrupted. Bernard. "Fletcher. What the fuck are you doing?" He rounded the doorway, having spoken before he was even in sight. "I believe I warned you about your behavior yesterday. Go back to the plant. You're supposed to be supervising first shift today, not pumping your chest out like some sort of rabid animal." He pointed at the door.

Fletcher glared at him for several seconds and then turned and fled the room.

Bernard lifted a hand toward Alton, unable to fully

unfurrow his brow and hide his disdain for his nephew. "Sorry for the shitstorm." His face softened. "Welcome to the family." His grip was firm.

Alton nodded. "Thank you, sir. I promise I'll always put your daughter first. She will never lack for support from me in anything she chooses to do in life."

Joselyn wrapped her fingers around his biceps as he spoke, leaning into him. *"You're gonna make me cry."*

"I know, son," her father confirmed. "Now, how about we head to my office? Several people are waiting for us."

As Alton followed Bernard down the hallway, his hand wrapped over Joselyn's, he decided Bernard had assumed his daughter would arrive this morning bound to her mate. It warmed his heart.

Joselyn's grip on his arm didn't lighten. She was leaning on him for support or out of fear or rage.

"You okay, baby?"

"I'm still standing."

He grabbed her hand and slid it down his arm to hold it. Threading his fingers with hers, he kept her right at his side. *"We'll get through this. You sure you want me so outwardly claiming you?"*

"As if it would make a difference. It's not like they can't sense it from a mile away."

"Of course, but it's so blatant, and tempers are rising. Don't get me wrong. I'd gladly kiss you in front of them. I just want you to be as comfortable as possible."

As they rounded the doorway into Bernard's office, she responded without looking at him. *"If you let go of me, I'll hurt you."*

He chuckled into her mind and squeezed her hand tighter. *"I've got you. Always."*

Alton hadn't personally met everyone in the room, but he knew most of them. There were five—Bernard, his mate, and all three of his brothers. Joselyn's mother stood and came across the room. She hugged her daughter close, whispering in her ear, "I wondered. I'm so proud of you."

Alton thought it was an interesting way to congratulate her, but then he realized what Rosanne was saying. She was proud of her daughter for taking a stand, for putting aside her family and binding to the man she loved, for showing up at the office today in his arms. Rosanne was proud.

Alton was too. He didn't release his mate's hand. He had no intention of doing so for any reason.

Rosanne turned to him next. She lifted up and kissed his cheek. "Welcome. Proud of you too." She smiled warmly, making him wish he had taken this stand years ago. What had he been afraid of?

He was about to find out.

Joselyn slid in front of Alton, bending her elbow so that her hand was still threaded in his at the small of her back. She leaned into him to absorb his strength. She cleared her throat and lifted her head. "I'm sure the rumors have been rampant, but as you can tell, it's true. Alton and I completed the binding."

Her three uncles, who had been sitting when they entered, jumped to their feet.

Her Uncle Marlin's eyes were twinkling. She knew he would not abandon her. However, her other two uncles on her father's side looked fit to kill. Carroll and Jaren were scowling.

It was a mystery why the older two Arthurs, her father included, were more kind and loving while the younger two were hateful and filled with anger. Normally at large family gatherings, the large crew could put their differences aside and get along. However, lately that was only possible if the subject of the century-old feud was taken from the table.

Like a political squabble, the four sons of the late Normand and Odell Arthur had always been at each other's throats in a house divided. When Joselyn's grandfather Normand died five years ago unexpectedly, his mate passed away months after him. It wasn't unusual for their kind. The bond between mates was strong, and after a lifetime of being together, one mate would frequently die of a broken heart soon after the first.

The death of Normand Arthur had somehow caused the rift between the sons to deepen. Or maybe it was really Odell's passing that catapulted the feud into overdrive. After all, she had always been the family glue, the one who tried to keep tempers on an even keel.

Joselyn wished her grandmother was there now. She suspected things were about to get ugly.

Her Uncle Carroll was the first to speak, his face red, his hand shaking in the air. He looked toward his brother Bernard instead of facing his own niece. "I can't believe you're supporting this farce of a union. Do you have no family loyalty, brother?"

Joselyn's mother stepped into the center of the room, her head high. At five eleven, she towered over many human women, but her mate Bernard and his brothers ranged from six-six to six-eight. They were forces to be reckoned with. Or they would be to some other woman. Rosanne Arthur was not the sort of mother who would be intimidated. "All of you need to calm down."

Several grumbles filled the room. Each of the four brothers had a mate. And none of their mates were pushovers. They were used to being put in their place from time to time, but they didn't take kindly to orders coming from Bernard's mate.

Rosanne continued, "Anyone who thinks these two kids have joined together out of some secret desire to piss you off and create upheaval need to get a head exam. You're all fully aware how a binding works. Don't act like a bunch of idiots."

The slight hush lasted only a moment before Bernard's other brother Jaren tossed his two cents in, staring at Bernard. "If your damn daughter wants to bind herself to one of those heathens, fine. But she needs to submit her resignation right now and clear out of the building."

Alton's grip on her hand tightened to the point of pain. A pain she welcomed under the circumstances. It kept her grounded. She wasn't sure if he was trying to hold her back or if he was simply expressing his frustration. And then he spoke into her mind. *"Let them argue, baby. Don't engage yet."*

She nodded slightly in response, even though she had her back to him. Her heart raced from the adrenaline rush.

Her father stiffened beside her. She'd never felt such anger coming from him. He turned toward his brother Carroll. "Do you feel the same as Jaren?"

Carroll nodded. "Of course. It's obvious your daughter's the one who leaked all of our hard work to the enemy in the first place."

Joselyn opened her mouth to defend herself.

Alton gripped her hand tighter and held her closer. *"Let them shout at each other first."*

"You're a damn fool," her father said. "Both of you. Joselyn didn't leak anything to anyone. As far as I'm concerned, one of you is more likely to have undermined this business than Joselyn. She worked hard on this project for six months."

Jaren shook his head. "Work? That's what you call sitting in her office all day coloring?"

Bernard's eyes bulged, and Rosanne's mouth fell open.

Joselyn pursed her lips to keep from screaming. God damn them both. She had a notion to tell them to go fuck themselves and then take her shit and get out of the building. If they thought the marketing position was so useless, let them handle the department all on their own.

Except that would hurt her father too.

Jaren twisted his head to glare at Joselyn. "Look me in the eye and tell me you didn't rat us out to the Tarbens."

Joselyn's spine stiffened. "I did not. Never said a word about our launch, even though Alton is my mate and it felt wrong."

Carroll jerked in his seat. "Doesn't mean your damn mate didn't steal the information from you at some point. He would have had opportunity." He glared at Alton, sending goose bumps up Joselyn's arms.

She shook her head. "He has never once been to my home, nor have I been to his. We've seen each other so infrequently that I want to kick myself for ever caring what any of you would think," she shot back at her uncle. "The only thing I've ever had on me when I've seen my own mate was my damn cell phone."

Spittle shot out of her Uncle Carroll's mouth as he shared his next thought. "Phones are damn smart these days, little girl. They're like computers. Anything you have on there is easy to access. You telling me you always took your phone to the bathroom with you?"

Apparently, Alton had heard enough. The vibe running from him to her was filled with frustration. "I have never once touched Joselyn's phone. I don't even know her password. I do not dig around in my mate's private belongings without her permission."

Joselyn's mother stepped between everyone, holding up her hands and glancing back and forth at every face. "Stop this nonsense before someone says something they regret."

Joselyn was surprised at how calm her mother appeared outwardly while she knew she was fuming inside.

"I say we call a vote," Carroll said. "We call the board in and take a vote. Now. This morning." He pointed at Alton. "And *you* need to get the hell out of this building."

Alton spoke again, releasing Joselyn's hand to wrap one arm around her middle and set his other hand on her shoulder possessively. "You people need to watch your language, and if any of you disrespects my mate again, you'll find my fist in your face."

He didn't address the way her uncles were treating him personally, but her heart rate soared when he instead insisted on supporting her.

"Don't you dare speak to me that way, you son of a bitch," Carroll shot directly at Alton. "You have no business coming here and a lot of gall. You should be ashamed of yourself for even showing your face in the parking lot. You come from a family of thieves."

Joselyn couldn't hold her tongue again. "For God's sake, what the hell are you talking about?"

Carroll turned his hateful gaze toward her. "Stole land that rightfully belonged to our pack, and they know it."

Joselyn couldn't stop herself from rolling her eyes. "You mean over a hundred years ago?"

"Doesn't matter when it happened. What matters is that it happened. It's in their blood. Bunch of damn thieves."

Alton stiffened. "I'm sure if we were having this conversation at my brewery, my uncles would be calling all of you murderers. It's nonsense."

Jaren growled. "We ain't no murderers."

"Really? Because the same legend you're referring to concerning a homestead on the west side of the river includes a little boy stabbed to death by one of your ancestors."

Jaren fumed. "You can't call an entire pack of people murderers because two little boys got in a fight and had an accident, you fool."

Joselyn felt Alton relax at her back. "Nor can you call an entire pack of people thieves because one man set up a homestead on public land a hundred years ago."

She was proud of him. He never lost his temper as he tried to reason with her damn family. She knew it would do no good trying to get them to see the light, but Alton still took the high road.

Jaren wasn't done, however. "If we're going to point fingers, your ancestors are the real murdering sons of bitches since y'all retaliated by killing our boy's mother. Shot her for no reason."

"Enough," Joselyn's mother shouted.

Alton seemed to shake off his frustration and leaned forward, getting in Jaren's face, still holding Joselyn against him. "Like it or not, I'm bound to Joselyn now. We didn't make this choice lightly or flippantly. But we love each other, and I'm going to have to demand your respect. Family feud be damned. It's time to put aside your stupid differences and let bygones be bygones. I'll expect the same from my own family. Holding a century-old grudge is absurd at best. No one's even alive who started this feud."

"Nevertheless," Carroll continued, "you work for the competitor. A competitor, I might add, who stole our idea and took credit for it, launching it as your own." He pointed at the door. "Not going to say it again. Get out."

Bernard put himself between Joselyn and Carroll. "No one's leaving, Carroll. Stop shouting at my daughter and her mate. If you can't calm down and have a reasonable, productive discussion, you need to leave my office."

For a moment, Joselyn thought Carroll might actually shove his older brother. His face was red, his hands fisted at his sides. "Like I said before, let's take a vote. Now."

Bernard shook his head. "Don't be absurd. We aren't taking a vote on anything. Don't forget who's the head of this pack, brother," he warned.

"Oh, trust me, I'm clear on that. And if you don't get this fucking Tarben out of the building in the next two minutes, I'm likely to call a vote on that too and challenge your rank among our people. You aren't fit to be leader."

Joselyn couldn't believe what she was hearing. She'd always known her uncle was foul and ignorant, but this was going too far. This situation was far worse than she ever imagined. She'd known that outing her relationship with Alton would be damaging and perhaps challenged, but she hadn't expected anyone to challenge her father's leadership role within the brewery, and certainly not his role as pack leader.

The air was knocked out of her lungs. She wouldn't let this happen to her parents. *"Dad, I'll leave."* She permitted her communication to be heard by her mother, her father, and her mate.

"Not a chance in hell," her father responded.

"Just for now. For today. Let emotions simmer. Nothing good is going to happen here today. And I'm not splitting up from Alton today."

Bernard spun around to face his daughter. So did Rosanne, tucking her arm into her husbands. His eyes were narrowed in a scowl. *"I don't want anyone in this room to think they got the best of you. Or me, for that matter."*

Jaren groaned behind them. "Can we please get back to

work while you three leave us out of your stupid private chat?"

Bernard spun around. "Hell no. Sit your asses down. We aren't done here. But Joselyn and Alton have other business to take care of, and I'm not inclined to force them to remain while you continue to say things you can't take back. I've told them to go grab something to eat."

It was a white lie, but she recognized what her father was doing. Not admitting defeat, but soothing the tension at the same time.

"I still say we move to the boardroom and call for a vote," Carroll grumbled.

"Well, that's not going to happen, brother," Bernard said. "We don't operate that way in this building. I'm in charge. And I say we're not calling for any vote of any form." He stood taller, puffing out his chest.

Joselyn grabbed Alton's hand at her waist and tugged, luring him out of the room. She could feel anger wafting off him, but he held his tongue while they walked silently down the hall and stepped back into her office. One minute later, coats on, they headed out the front door.

CHAPTER 17

Alton was furious. He held himself in check for his mate's sake, but inside he was fuming with rage. His mate's mind was more open to him today than it had been in all the years he'd known her. And he knew it had little to do with the binding and more to do with the fact that she was permitting him into her thoughts. And he wanted to hug her for trusting him.

Actually, he wanted to fuck the daylights out of her. But unfortunately, they needed to move from one fire to another.

He was proud of her. So proud he couldn't even express himself in words. If he didn't think half the people in her family would freak the fuck out and go postal on him, he would push her against the side of the SUV before opening the door for her and kiss her until neither of them could breathe.

What he was afraid of was that the number of people in favor of maintaining the feud and sending Joselyn camping was more than half. And if that was the truth, their troubles would be exponentially worse. Were they about to encounter the same thing from his own people? He feared so.

Joselyn leaned her weight into Alton's side, slumping against him as they reached the SUV. He could feel her shaking.

"I'm proud of you." He held her close, one arm wrapped around her middle.

She sighed. "Get me out of here before I start crying in the parking lot. I don't want anyone to think they got to me."

He nodded, unlocking the doors with his key fob and then opening the passenger door of his black SUV. With a hand steadying her, he helped her into the Explorer.

Seconds later, he was seated next to her. He started the engine and pulled out of the parking lot before taking her hand and holding it between them on the console. "It's going to be okay."

She nodded, her lips tucked under her teeth as she faced the window. He knew she was seconds from crying.

"I'm so sorry, baby." He wished he could ease her pain, but there was no way. Instead, he decided to let her have a few moments of silence.

Finally, she wiped her eyes with the back of her free hand and sighed. "I knew it would be hard, but I didn't expect my father's loyalty to the pack to be challenged like that. Not just his job as CEO of the company, but his standing as pack leader."

"I know." Alton worried the same thing might happen when they got to his brewery too. "Do you want to go back to the apartment for a while?"

She shook her head. "No. Let's go to my parents' house. I'll pack up some of my things. It'll give me a chance to catch my breath and remain busy at the same time."

"Good idea." He turned at the next light to head for her

parents' cabin. Even though her family had owned the cabin for many years and they lived just a few miles outside of town, he'd only been to the place a handful of times, and never inside.

"I want you to know where I grew up. I want you to see my room. Lie on my bed. I want your scent in my parents' home. Is that weird?" She turned to face him.

He glanced at her and smiled. "No. I felt a similar sense of connection to you the time you came to *my* parents' home a few weeks ago. Even though it was crowded and no one knew we were a couple, I loved knowing your scent would linger over all the others—at least in my mind."

She squeezed his fingers in understanding.

When they pulled up to the cabin, he took in the amazing view of the mountains in the background. Copses of evergreens climbed the sides, their scent prominent.

He jumped down from the SUV and quickly rounded to help her out of the passenger side. As he held her hand to aid her down from the high seat, she giggled. "I'm almost six feet tall, you know. And I've been exiting cars my entire life without help."

He shut the door and then pressed her against the side of the SUV. The bulk of their coats kept him from getting as close to her as he wanted, but it was close enough to take her face and meet her gaze. "You're mine, Jos. I'm just being chivalrous. My mother raised a gentleman. I know it's been a few years since we had the freedom to go anywhere in a car together, but did I ever show you less respect when we were in Calgary?"

"No."

"Do you think just because we're bound together now I'm going to stop being the man you fell in love with and get all lazy?" He tried to lighten her mood with a half grin.

She rolled her eyes. "No."

"Good. Because it won't happen in this lifetime." He closed the distance between them and kissed her gently.

She seemed to calm marginally, and then she led him to her parents' cabin.

She'd always referred to it as a cabin. Everyone in their family did. The sprawling ranch with a rustic log-cabin look was actually an enormous modern home that made him feel every ounce of the love put into it the moment they stepped inside.

The great room was warm and inviting with a state-of-the-art attached kitchen and a view out the back row of windows that would make most people drool with jealousy. "This is beautiful."

She glanced at him as she shut the front door. "Your family's home is not much different."

He shrugged. "Maybe, but I love the design." He wandered in farther, not releasing her fingers because he had no intention of disconnecting from her in the near future. She humored him by following in his wake. The brown leather sectional facing a fireplace was large enough for several adults. He had no doubt all five of her family members had sat there together to talk or watch a movie on the huge flat screen many times over the years.

"Come on," she whispered, tugging his hand. She led him down the hallway to the right side of the house and into a room he knew instantly to be hers. For one thing, it smelled like her. But more importantly, it had her feminine touch. Neither of her brothers would have had a room like this when they lived at home.

Her bed was made, but he smirked, wondering when she'd done that.

She swatted at his arm, obviously catching his drifting

thoughts. "I came by here yesterday before I came to your house. I straightened up." She tugged her hand free of his to take her coat off and drop it on the floor.

He pretended to buckle forward as if she'd hurt him with her soft swat before he removed his coat and dropped it on top of hers. "Hey, messy. Just curious," he teased. She'd never been the tidiest woman he knew. He rounded on her and stalked forward, backing her toward her own bed. When she hit the edge, she fell onto her ass, sitting. He straddled her legs and tipped her head back to take her lips.

It was a bad idea. He knew as soon as he made a move like this they would have trouble packing her stuff and getting on with their day. At the moment, he simply didn't care. No one was home, and he wasn't about to miss the opportunity to ravage her.

Her hands landed on his waist, and she slid them around to his back before easing them under his shirt. *"We should be packing,"* she murmured into his mind.

"This is so much more fun," he responded in kind. He reached for her hips, lifted her up, and dragged her farther across the bed so he could crawl over her and press his body against hers.

Her scent filled the room in a more overpowering way than he'd been exposed to in recent years. Even when she spent time in his apartment in Calgary, her scent had never fully filled his space. But this was her bedroom. The one she'd grown up in.

He broke their kiss and reached over to grab her pillow. Rising onto his knees, he pressed her pillow to his face and inhaled deeply.

Yes. Pure Joselyn. His.

She giggled. "You'd rather make out with my pillow than me?"

He dropped the pillow and lowered over her once again. "We're taking that with us."

"In a few days, everything in your apartment will smell like me, Alton." She ran her hands up and down his biceps.

"Mmm. Maybe, but not as overwhelming as something only you have touched for several years."

Her face flushed as she held his gaze. *"I love you."*

"Eh, it's just the binding. You can't help it now. How will I ever know for sure?" he joked.

She giggled out loud again. "I'll remind you every day."

"Good plan." He looked at the way her hair was panned around her face and thought he'd never seen anything more beautiful in his life.

Just as he was about to act on his need to claim her body, a door opening and slamming in the front of the house grabbed his attention and made him flinch. He groaned at the intrusion.

"Wyatt," she whispered, not pressuring him to get off her.

"He doesn't live here," Alton pointed out unnecessarily.

"True." She smiled. "But he's here now, and he's heading this way. I'm pretty sure he won't hesitate to barge in whether you're on top of me or not. Your call." She grinned wider.

He sighed. Part of him wondered what Wyatt had come to say. That same part of him felt a bit defiant, thinking maybe it would be best to remain right where he was and let Wyatt challenge him. But that would be childish and unnecessary, so he opted to swing his leg over her body and climb off the bed.

He was straightening his shirt while Joselyn scampered to the edge of the mattress and Wyatt rounded the open door.

He didn't look mad. In fact, he grabbed the frame and

closed his eyes before he made a full appearance. He even covered his face with one hand as if shielding his view. "Is it safe to come in? You aren't naked or something, are you?"

"No thanks to you," Joselyn grumbled, as she stood next to Alton and leaned into his side.

Wyatt was grinning when he dropped his hand playfully. "Sorry. I thought you might come here, so I headed this way as soon as you left the office. Dad told me what happened. I was out in the plant." He stepped more fully into the room.

"What made you think we'd be here?" Joselyn asked.

He ignored her and reached out a hand toward Alton. "You bound yourself to my sister, and I didn't hear about it until afterward."

"Sorry, man," Alton responded as he shook her brother's hand in a firm grip. "You weren't the only one."

"Yeah. I heard that too." He turned toward Joselyn and set a hand on her shoulder. "Are you happy?"

"With my decision to bind to Alton? Yes. With the behavior of our pack members? No."

"Fair enough. And to answer your question, I figured you'd come by the house to pack some stuff. Easy deduction."

"Of course."

Alton could tell Wyatt adored his sister. He released her shoulder, but not before toying with a lock of her hair. His voice softened. "Was it as bad as Dad said?"

"Worse," she responded.

He groaned, glancing at Alton. "I'm sorry. That was uncalled for."

Alton shrugged. "We expected something similar. Not shocking, really."

"Have you gone to your family yet?"

"Nope. Heading there next."

"To the brewery?"

"Yeah." That's where everyone was. They would all be at work, same as her family.

"You think that's a good idea?" he asked, his face drawn, skeptical.

Alton sighed. He had no way of knowing. "Honestly, no idea. But we have to face them at some point. Better to see everyone's true colors today while we're on a roll. If a war's going to break out over the two of us binding, it might as well get all the ammunition it needs on the same day. At least we'll know where we stand."

Wyatt turned back to his sister. "And where do you feel like you stand after that powwow in Dad's office?"

She sighed. "Halfway to the Saskatchewan border, to be honest."

"That's what I suspected." He turned back to Alton. "I know things are ugly. And they might get uglier. But I want you to know that not everyone in my pack is a jackass. Could be the majority. Not going to lie. But not everyone. Please do me a favor."

"Sure," Alton said, knowing in his heart that Wyatt would never request something of him he couldn't deliver.

"Don't take my sister away without telling me. It would tear my parents apart if it came to that. I understand it's a possibility, but I'm begging you to keep us informed so we have a chance to work things out, or at least say goodbye."

If Alton wasn't mistaken, Wyatt's eyes glazed over with emotion. He truly adored his sister.

"She's my only sister. The baby. I was eight when she was born. I changed her diaper. I rocked her to sleep. I don't want to lose her unless it's absolutely necessary to ensure her safety. Don't run from this town to avoid hurting her mother and father. They'd rather give up their business and their homes than lose their daughter. Isaiah and I agree."

Joselyn gasped at his side. "Wyatt..." Her voice was soft.

He grabbed her arm again. "I mean it, sis. Don't run from this out of some sense of guilt."

The man was insightful if he'd learned of their binding only an hour ago and already knew what was going through her mind and by extension Alton's.

Joselyn took a deep breath. "You know it could be worse than giving up the brewery or losing me. Dad could be voted out of his role as pack leader."

Wyatt nodded. "I know. But neither Mom nor Dad care about Dad's role within the pack as much as they love you." He reached out and stroked a hand gently over her hair. "None of us do."

Joselyn threw herself into her brother's side and hugged him tight. She didn't say a word.

Alton knew the reason she didn't speak was because she couldn't make the promise he was asking for. Alton knew his mate well enough to realize she would leave the province in a heartbeat if she thought it was for the best to save her family's status in the community and the pack.

Wyatt returned her hug, kissed the top of her head, nodded at Alton, and turned and left the room. Moments later, the front door opened and closed again, and he was gone.

"We should probably get some of your stuff packed, Jos. The sooner we face the Montagues, the sooner we'll know where we stand with them."

She winced. "You really want to compare this to Romeo and Juliet? It makes me cringe."

He lifted a brow. "You see much of a difference?"

She smiled and lifted onto her tiptoes to kiss him briefly. "Well, yes. I for one have no intention of committing suicide over my family's hatred. Do you?"

"Nope. Not gonna happen. But I won't let you be treated badly, either."

CHAPTER 18

"Why do I think this is a horrible idea?" Joselyn asked as they pulled into the parking lot at Mountain Peak Brewery.

Alton gripped her hand but didn't say anything.

"How about if I wait in the SUV. Or better yet, I should probably wait at your apartment. If your family reacts anything like mine, you're about to get ripped to shreds in there."

"And you don't want to witness it?" he joked.

"I don't want to have rotten tomatoes thrown at me." She waited while he rounded the Explorer to open her door and take her hand to help her down. This was not going to be fun. Today would surely go down in the books as the worst day of her life.

At least she hoped so. A worse day than today would break her.

They walked to the front of the building in silence, the tension building with every step. Alton never released her hand. Except for the few times he'd had to round the SUV to get into the driver's seat, she didn't think he'd stopped touching her since last night.

She liked that about him. It was comforting in the face of mayhem.

When they reached the front door, Alton pulled it open, but a broad enormous man stood in the doorway, legs spread wide, arms crossed, brow furrowed. "She's not welcome here."

Joselyn tugged her hand, trying to back up a pace. The man was almost seven feet tall, taller than most men she knew. Grizzly shifters were known for their height and huge frames, but this guy was outrageous. She hadn't seen him before.

Alton didn't let her retreat. He didn't even let her step behind him. He kept her at his side, his equal. "Don't be an ass, Weldon. I work here. She's my mate. Get out of the way."

"She's an Arthur."

"You're so astute. Now, back off." Alton didn't move physically, but there was no denying he projected a sense of power.

Weldon's phone buzzed, and he tugged it out of his pocket. "Yes." He looked fit to kill as he nodded a few times and then backed up two paces. "Your father would like you to join him in the boardroom." He didn't say another word about Joselyn as she and Alton passed the burly man.

"Great," Joselyn communicated to her mate as she followed him into a lobby not much different from her own family's lobby. *"The welcome committee is waiting for us in the boardroom."*

"Do not let them get to you. The ones who matter will understand and welcome you. The others don't mean fuck to me."

Intellectually she knew that to be true. It was the same

in her pack. However, it still hurt to have people screaming in her face as if she had a vile disease.

She could hear raised voices shouting over one another as they rounded the corner in the sterile gray hallway and then stepped into what had to be the boardroom.

A dozen people were sitting around an enormous oval table. The remnants of bagels and Danishes were scattered on the top on small plates. Napkins and half-empty coffee mugs littered the surface also. They'd been in there a while.

The room held eight men and four women. Among the women was Beth, Alton's mother. His father sat next to her at the head of the table. She stood and worked her way around the chairs to reach the entrance. When she reached her son, she cupped his face and then turned toward Joselyn and wrapped her in a warm hug. *"Do not let these fools get to you,"* she communicated silently.

Joselyn calmed, marginally. At least Beth was accepting. Not that she'd doubted his mother would be anything less than kind and loving.

Someone slammed a hand on the table, making Joselyn jump in her skin. She glanced around Beth to see a man who was undoubtedly one of Alton's uncles fuming as he stood. He had the same square jaw and dark eyes as Allister. "You have got to be kidding me. What nerve you have bringing that woman here."

Allister stood at the head of the table. "Good God, Espen. What's the matter with you? Do you not have any manners?"

Joselyn placed Espen Tarben in her head as the father of Jack Tarben who had gone rogue a few months ago and scratched Heather, forcing her to transition into a grizzly shifter against her will. He was now in prison, held by the Arcadian Council in the Northwest Territories.

"We're in the middle of a serious situation here. We don't need the enemy listening in on our conversations."

Alton stiffened. "Joselyn's not the enemy. And as you can tell, we've completed the binding. So, I'll ask you to show her the same level of respect you'd show anyone's mate in this pack. Your implication is insulting. It's obvious someone inside our own offices stole information from Glacial. She's not the guilty party."

Maybe this wouldn't go so badly after all, especially since Alton had a point. At her office, they were investigating the possibility of a leak. At his, they were looking for the thief himself. There still existed the chance that whoever leaked the plans from Glacial was unaware they'd done so.

Someone in the Tarben clan had maliciously and intentionally stolen the information. If anything, they should be treating her far more kindly than her family treated him.

But it didn't seem several of his family members agreed.

Another uncle of his groaned. "You're a fool, Alton. And you need to stop the cocky attitude. You're our primary suspect."

Alton gasped. "Are you insane, Uncle Quint? Why on earth would I steal company secrets from my own mate? Don't you think that might put a bit of a damper on my relationship?"

Espen spoke again. "Who really gives a fuck who managed to weasel the information from some stupid Arthur?" He smirked. "I don't understand why we're even investigating this. The important thing is that we stuck it to the Arthurs good."

Alton stiffened. Maybe she was wrong. Maybe his family was as completely screwed up as hers. It didn't seem like any headway was going to happen here any more than it had at her pack's brewery. He had the same family division—two reasonable uncles and two hard-headed assholes. Split down the center.

"That's not how we run a business, Espen," Allister stated. "I'd prefer we earn our recognition in the community without using nefarious means."

"Then you'd be holding us back, big brother. Don't be such a fool. It's a cutthroat world out there. If some prick over at Glacial leaked information to one of our people, they deserve to lose this round." He glared hard at Joselyn as he spoke.

She shuddered inwardly, keeping her head held high. Finally, she broke her silence. "If you mean to imply that I would undermine my family's business to help yours, you've lost your mind."

Espen flattened his palms on the table and leaned forward. "Watch who you're speaking to, missy. You're on thin ice as it is. I should have Weldon toss your ass out in the street."

Joselyn started to respond, but Alton beat her to it. "You'll do no such thing, you old fool. Get your head out of your ass, and don't speak to my mate again with that tone."

Everyone started shouting at each other, actually discussing the merits of tossing not just Joselyn but Alton out the door.

When someone stepped up behind Joselyn, she tugged on Alton's hand to get his attention. They were still blocking the door.

A gangly young man shoved his way past Joselyn, forcing her to flatten her body against Alton's side. He held a pile of papers in his hand and rounded the table to hand them to Quint. "Found these in Alton's office, sir." Before anyone could respond, he fled the room as if it were on fire.

Joselyn nearly choked when she recognized the colorful photos. They were hers. Her marketing designs. Early mockups from months ago, but definitely hers. *"Alton?"*

He wrapped an arm around her, holding her back to his front. *"I see them. You know they didn't come from my office."*

She nodded subtly. He was right. She knew in her heart he didn't steal anything from her. But who planted those mockups? And why? More importantly, when? Probably in the last hour if she had to guess.

Espen held up one page after another. "Looks like the work of the marketing manager for Glacial." He looked pointedly at Joselyn. "Isn't that you?" He asked unnecessarily.

Alton, still holding her against him, stepped more fully into the room, reached across the table, and snatched the pages from his uncle's hands. He tossed them in the air so they fell spread out all over the table, wafting to the surface like feathers. "Do I look like a damn idiot to you people?" He looked directly at Espen. "Even if I did steal company secrets from my own woman, do you think I would leave them in my office for anyone to find?"

"He's got a point," his Uncle Riddell stated, tapping his chin. "The boy's not stupid, Espen. Besides, what did you do? Get your damn errand boy to riffle through Alton's office without permission? Did you plant these papers yourself, or did you have Tavion plant them first? Hell, did he even go into Alton's office? Or just show up here saying he'd found them in there?"

Espen's face was bright red. "You calling me a liar, brother?"

"I'm saying you had no authority to lure that young man into your web and ask him to do your dirty work. Tavion's only been a member of our pack for a few years.

Don't corrupt him with your shit. Neither you nor anyone else has business going into Alton's office."

"I didn't go into anyone's office. I simply had Tavion take a glance in every corner of this building this morning to get to the bottom of this while we've been in here wasting time."

Voices rose again.

"Every one of you has lost your mind if you think I had anything to do with this. I suggest you dig a little deeper and not waste your time on bullshit if you want to find the culprit." Alton pointed at the scattered papers. "I'm taking the rest of the day off." He turned toward his father. "Call me if you need me."

Allister nodded at his son and switched his gaze to Joselyn, sending her a pained look of sorrow.

Joselyn was crawling out of her skin by the time they left the office. They had only been there half an hour, but it felt like a lifetime.

Alton didn't say a word on the way back to the SUV. He nodded politely at the few people they passed but didn't engage. She could feel the stress wafting off him. It wasn't until he pulled out of the parking lot that he finally blew out an audible breath.

"You know I didn't believe them, right?" she pointed out.

He shot her a glance. "Yes. Of course. I mean, I would hope so. You did doubt me for a while two days ago," he half-teased.

She glanced at her lap. He wasn't wrong. She'd done exactly that.

Without a word, he pulled over to the side of the road and put the SUV in park. When he turned to face her, he took her closest hand and leaned toward her. "Look at me."

She lifted her gaze, but couldn't stop the tear. "I'm sorry

I ever thought anything bad about you for even a second. It was uncalled for. I wasn't in my right mind. I was freaking out, and—"

He cut her off by cupping her face with one hand and drawing her lips to his. "I know," he muttered against her mouth. "Stop beating yourself up. We're connected now. You've let me all the way into your wonderful mind. I can see your thoughts. Don't waste another moment on the other morning. If the tables had been reversed and I'd been in your shoes, I'm sure I would have had similar concerns."

She reached with her free hand to wipe her eyes. "I doubted you."

"And I didn't let you continue to believe that for long, did I?"

She forced a smile. How did she get so lucky? And then she sat up straighter. "Let's go for a run. I need to shift. My skin is crawling from the inside out. My bear needs release."

He smiled back. "Best idea I've heard all day." He put the SUV back in drive and took off.

She didn't even ask where he was going, but he surprised her when he pulled up to Austin's house a few minutes later. "This is my favorite spot to park and run from. My parents' home is pretty awesome too, but ever since Austin built this place, I've loved coming here. The view is spectacular from every angle."

She jumped down from the front seat before he could round to her side of the SUV.

"Hey, that's my job." He grabbed her hand and led her toward the house. "Nuria's home. Let's let her know we're leaving the Explorer here."

Nuria stepped out onto the porch before they made it to the steps. "Hey. You guys okay?" The concern in her voice was expected. She would be in constant contact with

Austin, who would have told her how crazy things were at the brewery.

"As good as can be expected. Just wanted to let you know we're leaving the SUV here to go for a run."

She nodded. "Of course. Take your time. Anything you need, let me know. I'll fix you guys lunch. Stop in and grab it when you get back. You can stay and eat or take it with you."

Joselyn pursed her lips against the kindness of this woman she barely knew. Before she could thank her, Nuria dipped back into the house.

"Come on." Alton tugged her hand, and they rounded the cabin that was a smaller version of the one his parents owned. The view was equally amazing too. The crisp air beckoned her. It was cold, but in her grizzly form in the middle of the day with the sun shining, it would be perfect weather for a run.

When they stepped into the trees at the back of the property, she closed her eyes, took a breath, and let the shift wash over her. Leaning forward, she allowed her bones to lengthen and shorten and transform while fur replaced skin and clothes. In fifteen seconds she stood before her mate in her grizzly form, watching him finish his own transformation.

He was gorgeous. She'd seen him shift a handful of times over the years, but he never failed to take her breath away. He was nearly twice her size, his dark brown hair almost black. His dark eyes bore into her as he pawed at her. *"Come on. I want to show you something."* He tipped his head toward the mountain and bounded up between the trees.

She stayed right on his heels, following him at a rapid pace as they both ran hard to blow off steam. For fifteen minutes they climbed. And then Alton turned to the east and headed along the side of the mountain before coming back down in another spot.

She figured they weren't too far from where they'd started, but also realized he'd intentionally taken a circuitous route in order to exercise and control the buildup of stress they had lingering from visiting their respective breweries.

When he finally slowed and then came to a stop, she lifted her head and stared in the same direction he was looking. *"Wow. Amazing."* Mountains stretched in every direction. The view was stunning. She held her breath to listen to the sounds of nature. Birds. The rustle of branches. The wind itself. She had fantastic hearing in her bear form. It was better than regular people, even in her human form, but in her grizzly form, she could hear at even greater distances.

"Yeah. I love this spot."

"I guess so. Do you come here often?"

"As often as I can. What do you think?"

She cocked her head toward him. *"I said it's gorgeous. What do you mean?"*

He turned around, facing the land behind them. And then he surprised her by shifting. She watched him for a moment before following his lead.

Their feet crunched through the snow as she stuffed her hands in her pockets and leaned against his side, following his line of sight. What was he thinking? She didn't want to interrupt his thoughts.

Finally, he lifted his free arm and pointed at a spot not far away in the clearing. "I always imagined the house would go there with a wide back porch that faced this direction, allowing us to snuggle in a porch swing and stare at the mountains."

She furrowed her brow for a moment until it dawned on her. "This is your land?"

He smiled down at her. "Yes. It's the section my parents set aside for me. We each have our own. Austin obviously built on his. I wanted to wait until you and I were bound together before I did anything."

She glanced back at the clearing. "Wow, Alton. It's so beautiful."

"Yeah." He sighed. "I hope we find a way to stay living in Silvertip, or this land will never see a house."

"Me too," she whispered, knowing she had as many doubts as him.

If the reaction coming from both of their families was any indication, she didn't have high hopes they would even be able to live in Alberta, let alone develop this piece of land.

CHAPTER 19

It was midafternoon before Alton stepped onto his brother's porch and lifted his hand to knock. Nuria opened the door to him and Joselyn before he had a chance.

She gave them a cheery smile and held the door wide. "How was the run?"

Joselyn shut the door behind her. "Perfect. We needed it."

"I'm sure. I made a beef vegetable soup. Why don't you guys stay and eat? It's ready."

Alton set a hand on Joselyn's back to lead her to the kitchen area. "You made soup in the time we went for a run?"

Nuria waved a hand through the air as if his question were preposterous. "No. I already had it going earlier this morning. You just had good timing."

"This is so kind of you, Nuria," Joselyn said as she sat in the chair Alton pulled out. "I'm in no mood to cook today, and there's no way we would have gone into a restaurant in town."

Nuria frowned as she returned to the table to set a

giant steaming pot in the center. "I can't blame you. This entire thing is crazy. How can people be so stupid?"

Alton sat next to his mate. The table was already set, and a loaf of bread resting on a cutting board had recently come from the oven. It, combined with the soup, smelled up the entire house, making his mouth water.

Alton didn't know Nuria well. They'd only met a few weeks ago. He remembered her vaguely from childhood before her family moved away when she was fifteen, but he was five years younger, so nothing stood out in his mind. She was perfect for Austin, with a kind heart and spirit. He was so happy for his brother.

After the last few months of dealing with the fact that their older brother had wreaked havoc on countless members of society, Alton was glad it seemed both he and Austin had been given a gift. They deserved it.

"Austin's on his way here," Nuria said as she filled their bowls and then carved the bread into thick slices.

"He left the office already?"

She grinned. "Said he couldn't stand another moment of the shouting and finger pointing. He also wanted to speak to you."

Alton nodded.

When Joselyn leaned forward to take her first bite, he watched her face soften. "Delicious. Thank you, Nuria."

Sure enough, three minutes later, Austin's truck pulled up outside, and he joined them in the kitchen. His face was grim.

He nodded toward Joselyn to politely acknowledge her, and then he took Nuria in his arms, threaded his fingers in her hair, and kissed her soundly. When he finally took a seat at the table, he sighed. "Shit went from bad to worse after you left," he stated.

Alton lifted a brow. "How the hell is that even possible?"

Austin filled his bowl and reached for a slice of bread while Nuria headed for the fridge. She returned moments later with four beers tucked in her arms. She passed them out without a word.

Alton popped the top on one and handed it to Joselyn. He then opened his own, shooting her a smirk. "You okay with this nasty swivel from Mountain Peak?"

She rolled her eyes and took a long drink. "Considering the day we're having, I'd drink anything."

Alton turned back to his brother but set his hand on his mate's thigh. "Give me ten minutes to enjoy my meal and drink this beer before you add to the shitstorm, would ya?"

Austin chuckled. "Gladly."

They all tore into the food.

Alton lifted his face only long enough to glance at Nuria. "This is delicious. Thank you again."

"You're so welcome. I'm glad I could help."

"Mmm," Joselyn added. "Heavenly."

When the bowls were empty and everyone was on their second bottle of beer, Alton finally leaned back, tucked his arm around Joselyn, and faced his brother again. "Give it to me."

Austin sighed. "In an interesting twist of events that I'm not inclined to think is a coincidence, guess who was not at work today?"

Alton furrowed his brow, trying to think if anyone was missing from the boardroom. "No idea."

"Vinson."

"You're shitting me."

"Who's Vinson?" Joselyn asked.

"My Uncle Quint's son."

She nodded.

Austin continued. "Considering Uncle Quint is an asshole and his son doesn't fall far from the tree, I don't trust him. Never have. He's conniving. I'm thinking he has something to do with the papers that were mysteriously planted in your office."

"We don't even know that part's true. It's possible Tavion never entered my office. He's so scared of Quint, he might have simply brought them straight from Quint's office to the boardroom without ever looking anywhere."

"But where did Quint get them?" Joselyn asked. "That's the real question. I'm so much more curious about who gave them to someone in your family in the first place than anything else. Those were early mockups of my marketing plan. From months ago.

"It's possible they were the first thing stolen. Or, they could have been the *only* thing stolen. There was enough information on the mockups for your brewery to run with it. It's not like you needed a formula for lemon or orange malt beverages. No one cares how the taste compares. What matters is that you knew what we were working on and when we planned to launch. All of that was in the mockups."

Alton nodded. "She has a point. Someone's goal was to beat Glacial to the starting line and make them appear to be a day late and a dollar short."

"Exactly," Austin agreed. "And I'm inclined to believe neither Uncle Quint nor his son Vinson are innocent in all this. I seriously doubt Tavion is involved at all. He's too young and too stupid. He probably never even looked at those mockups. Quint handed them to him and instructed him to interrupt the meeting as if he'd just found them lying around."

Alton agreed. "Not to mention the fact that Tavion wouldn't have had the first clue what he was looking for.

He's eighteen, for Christ's sake. He knows nothing about the business. He's only been working in the brewery for a few months."

Joselyn sat forward, breaking the contact Alton had with her shoulder to set her elbows on the table. "Assuming your uncle and his son had something to do with all this, who gave them my mockups?"

This was the million-dollar question. Alton knew they weren't going to solve it today. He took the last long swig of his beer and pushed off from the table. "We're leaving," he announced, anxious to be alone with Joselyn again, putting this mess in the backs of their minds. "Please let me know if you find out anything else. Is someone looking for Vinson? Anyone know where he was?"

It's not like the man stayed home sick. Shifters didn't suffer from any of the normal maladies humans could catch. They were created with better immune systems, and their bodies could fight off most things that got in the way, often without them ever being aware.

If someone took a day off work, it was for personal reasons. It didn't happen that often, and even rarer was for someone to call in with no notice. Unless the man met his mate the night before and intended to spend the day binding to her, he was probably up to no good.

"Dad has some people snooping around Vinson's place. No one has seen him. He wasn't at home. I'll get ahold of you if I hear anything," Austin stated as everyone stood.

Alton hurried his mate toward the front door, grabbing their coats on the way and nearly rushing her arms into the sleeves. He was done with family squabbles for the day. He was done with arguing and thinking and being accused and having his mate grilled.

What he wanted was to be alone with her. Naked. His hands on every inch of her body. After four months of sneaking around meeting her in caves, cabins, and hotels, he didn't have to do that anymore. For the rest of his life, he would have her anytime he wanted anywhere he wanted. No one would stand in his way. And he no longer gave a single fuck if anyone approved or not.

He couldn't figure out why he *ever* cared what anyone else thought.

Yep. They had an uphill battle that might not end with a house overlooking his favorite spot on earth, but none of that mattered as much as having Joselyn with him every single day.

When he really thought about it, he wasn't sure he wanted things to work out smoothly, resulting in both of them continuing to work for their respective families. It had seemed simple two years ago, but now? Not at all. Now, he didn't see a future that included secrets and an inability to discuss their respective workdays.

Their initial goal had been based on the hope that both families would get over their incessant need to feud. They had wild pipe dreams of being welcomed with open arms into a united unit where both packs dropped the squabble and came together.

That no longer seemed reasonable. After the morning he'd been through, he'd say the divide was wider than he expected. He'd known some members of both packs would grumble. He hadn't expected half or perhaps more than half of both families to actually voice outwardly their sick disdain for the other.

It made his stomach churn remembering the looks on the faces of half her family and then half his. Both of them could take their stupid feud and go to hell for all he cared. He'd be sleeping soundly with his mate tucked in his arms.

∾

Joselyn was fidgety by the time they got back to Alton's apartment. Her skin was crawling with the need to be with him again. It was unthinkable for two grizzlies to bind together and then spend the next day in public at all, let alone getting a verbal undressing from both families.

When bears bound themselves together, they didn't usually come up for air or step out into public for a few days if they could help it. It was their nature. Even if they found themselves in a situation where they entered into a binding unexpectedly, they still didn't leave the house.

The overwhelming need to mate over and over again was insatiable. Once or twice wouldn't put them at ease. Maybe for a few minutes, but not for an entire day.

It didn't matter that she'd had sex with Alton before the binding, their status had changed. Their chemistry had altered. They were one now. And something in their pheromones drew them closer, a mating call of sorts that demanded attention.

Once again, she jumped down from the SUV before Alton could round the hood and help her out. She rolled her eyes and grabbed his hand to tug him toward the front door as if she had the strength to move the man anywhere if he chose not to follow.

She didn't expect him to resist, and naturally, he didn't. After all, they were going to strip down and have sex the second the door shut behind them. No way was Alton feeling less urgency than she was.

He followed her to the building and didn't say a word as she continued to lead him inside and toward the stairs. She had no intention of waiting for the elevator. He lived on the third floor. It wasn't like they needed to climb a mountain.

One minute later, they were inside his apartment, dropping their coats, kicking off shoes, and peeling off clothes without a word. She watched every move he made, his lean body unveiling to her view while he did the same to her, heat in his eyes.

Her skin was on fire as if she had a fever. Maybe she did.

When the last of her clothes hit the floor before him, she reached for his cock and held it in her palm. "Need you."

He covered her hand in his larger one and stroked up and down, moaning. He wrapped his free hand around her neck and tugged her forward. His forehead hit hers. His eyes were closed, his face flushed. "Need your mouth on me."

She swallowed and then licked her lips. She craved the same thing. Now.

As he leaned against the door, she dropped to her knees, grabbed his thighs with both hands, and sucked him as deep into her mouth as she could.

He groaned, his hands flattening on the door. "Jos…"

She drew her mouth almost off and then sucked him back in deeper.

"Jesus, baby… It's never felt like this before."

She knew what he meant. She was as aroused as him. Her nipples tingled, begging for contact. Her pussy was wet and swollen. He hadn't touched her.

As she flicked her tongue over the tip of his cock on the next pass, her clit throbbed. She needed more.

Releasing his thigh with one hand, she reached between her legs to stroke her clit. A soft moan escaped around his cock.

Alton grabbed her biceps with one hand and pulled. "Give me your hand." His voice was gravelly from arousal, but firm.

She moaned, unwilling to stop touching herself. Given thirty seconds, she would come. Why was he stopping her?

He tugged harder. "Jos, your hand."

She pulled her wet fingers from between her legs and set them in his. Her mouth was still wrapped around his cock as he drew her hand over her head, reached for the other from his thigh, and then combined the two, wrapping one strong hand around both wrists and pressing them against his chest.

She froze, releasing his cock to tip her head back. Her legs shook. She was so aroused and so close to coming, it hurt. And the way he now held her wrists above her head didn't make things better. It amped up her desire.

"Spread your knees wider. I don't want you to masturbate while I can't watch. Keep sucking."

She stared at him, her mouth watering. Could a person die from arousal? After blinking several times, she turned her gaze back to his cock bobbing in front of him, glistening with her saliva, and she wrapped her lips around the head again and sucked, tasting his precome.

Salty. Musky. Alton. Hers.

Her nipples brushed against his thighs as she sucked him deeper. The drive to swallow him was strong. The need between her legs was intense. He knew what he was doing. Driving her crazy.

"Payback," she communicated into his head.

"I wouldn't make threats if I were you," he returned.

His tone in her head made her ardor amp higher. She wanted more. This was so hot. The way he held her firmly, her raised arms making her breasts stand at attention.

Sexy as hell.

Suddenly he was grunting incoherently, and he thrust forward one last time, grabbing the back of her head to steady her.

The first pulses of come to hit her throat were shocking. She'd never been in a position like this before. He knew it too. After all, he was her one and only partner. Every experience she had belonged to him.

When she found a few brain cells, she managed to suck him down, swallowing his come until it slowed and subsided. His erection remained intact, but he released the grip on the back of her head and tugged her hair to pull her back until he popped out of her mouth.

Still holding her hands, he helped her to her feet, pressed her wrists to the center of her chest between her breasts, and kissed her lips. "You're so damn sexy. How do you get hotter every day?"

His words warmed her soul. She felt the same about him.

"I want you to let me spank you. I want to take you over my knee and spread your legs and spank your sweet bottom until you squirm and can't keep from coming at the touch of my hand."

She blinked. There was no way to hide how fucking hot she found the idea.

He smiled. "You like the idea."

Did she ever. He'd swatted her ass just the one time before, and she thought she'd orgasm from the one simple spank.

Was he needing to blow off steam, and this was his method? Or was it her that needed to blow off steam, and this was the chosen way to get it out of her? She didn't care. "Do it."

He led her to the couch, sat on the cushion, and bent her over his lap. The sway of her breasts alone was enough to make her moan. When he grabbed her arms, pulled them to her lower back, and clasped her wrists together, renewed wetness leaked between her legs. She squeezed them together.

"Spread your legs," he demanded in that new commanding tone of his that she loved. "Wider," he added when he was apparently unsatisfied with the space she created.

The position was so erotic she made an unrecognizable sound.

He rubbed a hand over her butt cheek. "How did we go so long without me realizing you liked a little kink?"

She had no response. She was sure no response was needed. He could see her thoughts. And she hadn't been aware of her desire for rough sex until recently. It wasn't as if she'd been holding back.

"Keep your legs parted, Jos. I don't want you getting yourself off by squeezing your thighs together." His first swat landed high on her left cheek, making her stiffen for a moment before the heat spread through her body, and she moaned.

She should be embarrassed at her reaction. He could smell her arousal. It wasn't as if she could hide it.

"Oh, baby." His second spank landed on the same place on her other cheek. Matching warmth coursed through her, but she was more prepared and didn't stiffen.

His hand smoothed over the hot spots, caressing her before traveling down her thighs.

She expected him to stroke between her legs, so she was disappointed when he instead lifted his hand to swat her thighs, one at a time.

She was going to come. *Holy shit*. It wouldn't take much more.

"Give me the first one, baby." His next spank landed harder at the junction between her thighs and her cheeks.

She shot off, her orgasm taking over fast and hard. The pulsing of her clit made her gasp. She'd never come like that without contact to her pussy. Her cheeks heated, making her glad they were shielded from his view by her hair hanging around her face and her gaze toward the floor.

Still gripping her wrists at the small of her back, he finally stroked a finger through her lower lips after her orgasm subsided. She was fully aroused instantly. Needing him inside her.

Instead of giving her more of what she wanted, he audibly sucked his finger clean of her juices.

She arched her back, lifting her head, squirming in his grip. But she said nothing. The only thought in her mind was to beg him to fuck her, and she wouldn't do it.

Her butt burned, but she wanted more.

As if he read her thoughts, he swatted her butt cheeks again, several times in rapid succession.

She inhaled a sharp breath, wiggling against his lap.

When he rubbed his hand over the burning sting, he soothed her with his words at the same time. "You okay?"

He knew the answer, but she liked that he was looking for a verbal. "Yes," she breathed.

"More?"

"Yes." How had she found herself wanting her mate to spank her like this? It was so damn hot, though. She didn't want him to stop.

He hit that sweet spot again, the junction of her thighs with her butt. More wetness leaked from her pussy. Several more swats to the same spot had her on the edge, her body tight and throbbing.

Suddenly she found herself on her feet, her hands released, her belly in front of him. He held her up by her hips, or she would have swayed.

His lips grabbed one of her nipples before she could focus on him.

Her hands were in his hair as she tipped her head back, her eyes closing. Damn, it felt fantastic to have him sucking her nipple into his mouth. He didn't simply lick the tip, he sucked hard. A sharp pain that quickly turned into pleasure spread through her body.

He gripped her hips tighter, holding her in that position, a knee situating itself between her legs, forcing them wider.

She must have tugged his hair too hard. His voice rang in her head. *"Put your hands behind your back, baby."*

She released him and did as he asked, forcing her chest to arch more fully toward him.

And then one of his hands slid to her ass and gripped the warm flesh. The other reached around from behind and stroked her pussy.

She lifted onto her toes, afraid she might fall. But he had her.

When he thrust two fingers into her, she cried out. The feelings were so intense. Was it because of the binding or from the dominance? She didn't care. It didn't matter. As long as it felt this good, who cared?

With a few fingers straying to stroke her clit, he continued to fuck into her with his thumb, pressing toward the front of her channel with each pass.

She whimpered, afraid she might shatter into pieces, while her legs threatened to buckle.

But he knew that. His grip on her ass was firm. She wasn't going to fall on his watch. He continued to work her hard. Stars danced behind her closed eyelids. She felt like she might break free as if from a tether and float away if she came. But when her orgasm hit, it hit hard. And she didn't fly off. Instead, he grounded her, fucking her with that thumb and strumming his fingers over her pulsing clit.

She made incomprehensible noises, unable to share specific thoughts with him, but hoping he read her well enough to know how much this meant to her.

Before her orgasm was fully complete, he removed his fingers, lifted her into his arms, and carried her in a cradle position to his room.

Thank God it wasn't far. She landed with a bounce on her back, but before she could focus on him, he dragged her by the thighs to the edge of the bed, spread her open wide, and lowered his face to her pussy.

She collapsed onto the mattress, her arms giving out where her elbows held her up. His lips suckled her clit, his tongue flicking repeatedly over her sensitive bud that had spasmed only moments before with the best orgasm of her life. Now it was growing again.

She wouldn't have thought it possible, but she needed him inside her as if she hadn't been permitted an orgasm for weeks or months. A breathy, hoarse voice she didn't recognize managed to come from her. "Alton... God...inside me."

He ignored her, thrusting his tongue into her channel, his nose nuzzling her clit.

She screamed. Her body trembled, needing release as if it had been denied. Her feet hung limp when he reached under her knees with both hands to hold her thighs open wider. There was no way to command any part of her body to do a thing, so her arms lay at her sides doing nothing.

In a split second, just before she thought she might seriously come for a third time in minutes, his mouth disappeared, his arms reached under hers, and he hauled her body farther across the bed. "Don't come until I tell you to."

She opened her eyes, searching for him in the dim light of dusk. She should have been able to see him fine in any light, but her vision was distorted by lust. Was he serious?

He climbed between her legs, and his cock lodged at her pussy while she was still trying to grasp the meaning of his words.

"I mean it, Jos. Don't come. I'll tell you when." And then his cock was inside her, filling her so full she gasped.

She grabbed his biceps and held on to keep from being pounded across the mattress and flying over the opposite side of the bed. She blinked. *Don't come?* Was he crazy?

She couldn't breathe. It took all her energy to focus on his thrusts in and out of her while she gritted her teeth against the need to come. If she had fully comprehended how it would be to be bound to him, she would have thrown caution to the wind and completed this binding years ago. What the hell had they been missing out on?

Because no way would she believe the binding wasn't the primary reason for the hotter-than-fuck sex that kept getting better by the hour.

His cock felt like it touched her soul. And he was panting with every thrust. When his breath finally hitched, he tipped his head back and shouted into her mind, *"Now, baby. Come with me."*

The moment his semen shot against her cervix, she came with him, her pussy gripping the hardest erection she'd ever known him to have.

The world stopped spinning. All their problems disappeared. They were one being. United. Powerful. At peace with the universe.

CHAPTER 20

Alton's heart was full. He stared down at his sleeping mate, loving the way her hair fell all around her while her mouth was parted just enough to breathe through. She was so out of it, she had no idea the sheet had slid down to expose her fantastic tits to his gaze.

It was early. The sun was just rising, but Alton knew instinctively this day was going to be long and insane. He'd spent all afternoon, evening, and night with his mate, but there was no way for them to play hooky from their respective problems today. They needed to touch base with their families and forge a path for the future.

As if he'd conjured his father unintentionally, Allister popped into his head. *"Alton. You available?"*

"Yes."

"I know this is inconvenient, but you probably need to come into the office today."

"I figured that would be the case. Planning on it."

"And, son..."

"Yeah, you need me to come alone. I get it. I'm sure Joselyn

will also need to head to Glacial. And I'm not any more welcome there than she is at Mountain Peak."

"I'm sorry, Alton. I know this is a mess. And obviously you expected it to be too, or you wouldn't have put off binding to her for all these years."

"That's right. And the timing stinks, but it also forced us to face our fears head on. Nothing's going to come between me and Jos, Dad. You need to realize that. No matter how bad things get, she and I will stick together, even if it means leaving town and not returning."

"Let's hope it doesn't come to that."

Alton jerked his attention back to Joselyn when he realized she was awake and smiling. She reached for his arm and stroked her hand up and down. "Morning." Her smile lit up his world. It made whatever they would encounter today worth it.

He leaned over to kiss her. He was overflowing with love and emotion. He wouldn't have thought it possible to feel more for her than he'd felt for all these years, but he was wrong. The binding made their connection so much stronger.

"I have to go deal with my family this morning," she declared.

"Yeah, me too." He cupped her face. "I don't like it." More than that, he abhorred the idea. Separating from her so they could each go face a bunch of rabid dogs didn't sit well with him. He had a bad feeling in his gut that told him to grab his mate, pack the SUV, and drive straight out of the city.

"We have to try," she continued, undoubtedly reading his mind. "Heading into the office is not my first choice of fun activities for today by any stretch of the imagination, but we need to know we did everything we could to smooth things over between our families."

He nodded, wondering how it was that she was the voice of reason this morning.

"I need to nose around a little. I'm not buying the idea that someone in your pack broke into my office and stole those mockups. I believe there's got to be a leak in my pack. Someone who could easily walk into my office, take a few pages they knew I wouldn't miss, and meet up with someone from your office to hand them off."

"But why? Who would sabotage their own pack like that?"

She shrugged, running her sweet hand up to cup his face. "Money?"

He smirked. "More likely sex."

She giggled. And then her face grew more serious. "Actually, that might not be a joke. What if it is sex?"

He frowned. "I was kidding. Who would trade company secrets for sex?"

She lifted a brow. "Someone who thinks they're in love."

He pulled himself to sitting and swung his legs over the side of the bed as Joselyn did the same next to him. "I'm in love, and even though there's nothing I wouldn't do for you, no way would I share company secrets."

"Obviously neither of us would, or we wouldn't have found ourselves so shell-shocked Monday morning."

He stood and turned around to straddle her knees, bury his hands in her thick hair, and tip her head back. He needed to see her expression, read her eyes.

She flashed him another of her amazing smiles. "Whoever stole those pages from my office was desperate. And even though I realize we're half joking, I'm not going to rule out the possibility that sex is involved, which means at least one of us might be looking for a woman."

He nodded. She was right. His uncles and even male cousins weren't the only ones who could have pulled this stunt. And although it seemed simple that one of the grouchy, older generation would do anything to sabotage the work of their fierce competitor and long-time rival, maybe he needed to focus on someone younger. Possibly female.

When he got to the brewery, he would open his mind to the possibilities. Everyone needed to be considered a suspect.

He kissed her again. "I think we need to get out of town for a few days." He hoped she would agree.

She smiled. "Best idea I've heard in weeks."

"Good. So we'll each head into our respective breweries, tidy up as best we can, and bail."

She nodded. "Let's take both cars, just in case our few days turns into longer."

He hated to admit she was right. If things continued on the current path, they might need to let the masses simmer for a while.

"I'll meet you back here later this morning. We can head out together. Follow each other."

Except for the part about driving separately, he liked this plan. His mood perked up considerably at the thought of going someplace where no one knew them and no one would bother them. They wouldn't have to jump up tomorrow morning and separate. "Perfect. Let me know when you're done at the brewery."

Joselyn had every intention of heading straight to the office, but as soon as she got in her car, her mother reached out to her. *"Honey, where are you? Are you safe?"*

"Of course. I'm just leaving Alton's apartment. Heading to the brewery."

"Glad I caught you. Come to the house first."

"Okay. Everything all right?"

Her mother sighed into her head. *"Nothing we didn't expect."*

Joselyn decided not to push her mother. It would be easier to head to her parents' house and deal with whatever was happening when she got there.

When she pulled up to the house, she noticed two extra cars parked out front. Apparently, the gathering included both her parents and her Uncle Marlin and his mate Josephine. Marlin was her father's closest brother, in age and temperament.

For a moment she sat in her car, enjoying the silence. She stared at her childhood home, wondering when the world had turned upside down. The log-cabin feel of the enormous ranch house was deceptive from the outside. It blended in with nature, the only color being dark green trim that matched the evergreens. She had always loved the way it sat nestled among the trees, inconspicuously placed as if one with nature.

It looked too peaceful, incongruent with the war waging among the occupants. Easing from the car, she braced herself for a fight.

As Joselyn stepped onto the porch of her childhood home, she glanced around. The air was so peaceful. The universe had no idea there was a storm brewing among its inhabitants. It was a brisk morning, cold but tolerable. A thin layer of snow blanketed the land from the lazy flakes that had fallen all night long. A gentle breeze gave her favorite rocking chair a little push.

If she could stay in this place forever, she would. But she knew in her soul her days were limited. She wouldn't stay in a town where half the population wanted her gone. And it was time to put her mate first above everyone else.

The front door opened, and her mother stepped out. "You okay, honey?"

"Yeah, just catching my breath." Joselyn pulled her coat tighter around her and stuffed her hands in her pockets as if that would ward off the coming storm.

Rosanne smiled, cupping her daughter's head and pulling her in for a hug. "I'm so sorry, sweetie. I can't imagine what you're going through, or what you've been through for the last several years. You've made some tough choices, and I feel bad I wasn't able to help you."

"Not your fault, Mom. You didn't know, and there was no way I could tell you. I never told a soul. For good reason."

"I know." Rosanne rubbed a hand down Joselyn's back. "Come inside. We're discussing strategy."

Joselyn followed her mother inside, feeling the warmth from both the heat and the occupants. Everyone in the house was on her side in this battle.

Her favorite aunt, Josephine, rushed over to give her a hug. "We love you, honey."

Joselyn fought against the lump in her throat. She coughed to clear the emotion away and shrugged out of her coat while she joined her family sitting around the living room. It seemed her mother and father had been discussing the situation with her aunt and uncle for a while. Several mugs littered the coffee table.

Bernard lifted his gaze. His expression was serious. He hadn't slept. His eyes were dark and tired.

"I'm sorry, Dad," she said as she took a seat in an open armchair. "I never meant for this to happen."

"I know, Jos. No one blames you."

She lifted a brow, almost laughing.

He smirked. "Okay. No one in this room blames you."

At least there was that.

"Did Uncle Carroll and Uncle Jaren insist on a vote yesterday? They can't really force you to step down as CEO, can they?"

Bernard shook his head. "No votes were taken yesterday, but unfortunately yes. If they get enough support, they could take over the brewery."

She wanted to scream. "And how would this be helpful? Neither of them ever showed an interest in running the brewery. I don't think they're capable. They would run it into the ground within months."

Marlin sighed. "That's what we're afraid of."

His mate looked toward Joselyn. "We're hoping it won't come to that."

"Did you make any headway yesterday figuring out who might have leaked information?"

Her mother shook her head. "No. Nothing but a dead end. And more importantly, we can't even come up with a plausible motive. Why would anyone in the pack intentionally undermine our own brewery?"

Joselyn pinched the bridge of her nose. "I can tell you what they shared was simple. Someone gave Mountain Peak early mockups of our ad. They didn't need more than that. They had dates and pictures of the products. That was more than enough to hurry through the process, come up with a duplicate product, and set a launch date that was a week before ours."

"Why, though?" Marlin asked rhetorically.

"I'll resign," Joselyn suddenly stated, knowing it was the only option at the same moment she spoke the words.

Her father groaned. "I don't want it to come to that."

"It's the only choice. No matter what happens, half the company will always be pissed at me. Besides, I'm the prime suspect. There will be no way to convince anyone I'm not the leak without proving who did this. It's possible you'll never know."

"Honey…" her mother began.

Joselyn sat up straighter. "I need to focus on my relationship now, anyway. Alton and I can't continue this farce. We've wasted too many years. We can't work for competing breweries without someone always being suspicious of what we share with each other. It's understandable. Even if this was a normal human arrangement, one of us would need to resign."

For the first time in days, she knew this was the right decision. It was time to move on. It would soothe relations among her pack and ease tensions.

"I don't like it," Marlin stated. "It's not fair."

Joselyn smiled. She felt like a weight had been lifted.

Why did she ever put so much importance in her job? She could get another one.

If she were honest, however, this never had anything to do with her job. It had to do with her family. Even her immediate family. Outing her relationship had always been something she knew would alter the course of her life.

But it was time to make those changes. Starting immediately.

Two hours later, Joselyn stood at the entrance to her childhood bedroom and let her gaze roam over the space. It would be a while before she saw it again. So many memories.

She thought of all the nights she'd lain awake in her bed talking quietly on her cell phone with Alton. So many nights when she should have been in *his* bed.

Would it have changed the course of events if the two of them had left U of C together and forged a new life somewhere else instead of returning to Silvertip?

There was no way to be certain the exact same rift wouldn't have formed even in her absence. After all, she hadn't been the one to come up with the product launch in the first place. She had simply been the brains behind the scene who planned for publicity and advertisements. Another marketing director could have done the same thing.

The feud between her family and Alton's had divided the entire town for decades. Joselyn couldn't take the blame for perpetuating it.

What she could do now, however, was leave and let her family figure out what to do next without her presence hovering over the entire pack like a dark cloud. There was always the chance that if she left town, tensions would ease, and the angry, bitter half of the pack who blamed her for the leak would cease this incessant need to vote her father out of his position as CEO and even pack leader.

Everyone had left for the office. She was alone in the house. It was a relief to have the chance to wander around and say goodbye in her own way.

She had boxed up her mementos and left a note for her mother to hold them for her. Everything else she hadn't already moved to Alton's, she loaded in her car.

She was ready. She was a stronger woman than she had been two years ago. She would leave Silvertip knowing her parents loved her and supported her. Same thing for Alton. His parents had also welcomed them with open arms. To hell with the rest of their packs. They could stuff their hatred where the sun didn't shine.

As she left the house and got in her car, she reached out to Alton. *"How's it going at Mountain Peak?"*

"About what you would expect. I need to stick around here a bit longer. I don't like the vibe I'm getting. I might be useful in some way. My damn cousin Vinson is MIA again today, which puts a bad taste in my mouth. I know in my gut he's involved in this. As well as his father."

Joselyn started the engine and headed down the long driveway, aiming for the main road. "I'll swing by the apartment and pack a few things. Load up my car. Clean out your fridge."

"Thanks, babe. Appreciate that. I'll get there as soon as possible."

She broke the connection and focused on driving. It didn't take too long to get to Alton's apartment, and an hour later she had the kitchen clean and her belongings back in the car. She hadn't even unpacked the stuff she'd brought yesterday, so it wasn't difficult to load it back up.

Her skin crawled with the need to get out of Silvertip. Why did it have to be like this?

She dropped onto his couch and stared at the ceiling when she ran out of things to do. She would let him pack up his own clothes and toiletries. Besides, her Honda Accord was stuffed full. They needed his SUV for anything else they wanted to take.

She glanced around. He didn't have much. The place was small, and she doubted he was particularly attached to the furniture or knickknacks. The idea they might not return at all was never far from her mind. She wondered if he was having the same thoughts.

She didn't want to interrupt him. Most likely he was in an extremely stressful environment having to defend himself to his pack and searching for answers. She was relieved she never made it to her own family's brewery. It might have pushed her over the edge.

Her leg bounced up and down as she glanced at her

watch for the millionth time. It was three o'clock. It had also been a while since she heard from Alton. She considered her options and decided she would get a head start and leave town without him.

"Alton? Do you have sec?"

"Yeah, baby. I'm so sorry. Time keeps getting away from me. I feel like police in an interrogation room."

"I'm sure. Sorry you have to deal with that. Do you mind if I start driving? I'll head toward Calgary and find someplace between here and there to stop for the night."

He chuckled into her mind. "Is my apartment lonely without me?"

"This entire town is giving me the heebie-jeebies. I feel like I'm suffocating."

"Go ahead, then. I'll catch up. I'm trying to wrap things up now. But it might take me a few more hours."

"Okay. I'll let you know where I decide to stop and get us a room."

"Love you."

"Love you too." Relieved, she stood and headed for the door. The idea of getting on the road and putting some distance between herself and the insanity that was her family's rivalry helped her breathe easier. As soon as she was totally out of town, she would relax her shoulders and inhale fully.

CHAPTER 21

Joselyn drove two hours before she decided to stop. She was exhausted from not getting enough sleep for the past several days. She hadn't heard from Alton yet, but she didn't want to bother him again. If he hadn't contacted her, then he most likely also hadn't left the office yet.

She chose a hotel she was familiar with. They'd met at this one once a few months ago.

She smiled to herself as thoughts of the two of them catching fleeting nights together flitted through her mind.

Never again.

Never again would she spend the night without him.

Never again would she huddle under the covers in a different house, calming herself to sleep over the phone instead of by his side.

Never again would she have to masturbate to thoughts of the next time she would see him in person.

Never again would she experience the rushed desire to fuck as many times as possible without speaking because she needed to get back home before anyone questioned her absence.

Never again.

She felt lighter, her heart freer as she headed for the front desk. Five minutes later she was in the room, dropping her overnight bag on the bed and shrugging out of her coat.

When a knock sounded at the door, she spun around confused. A smile spread across her face. Alton must have been right on her heels. Inhaling deeply, she furrowed her brow. It wasn't Alton.

She whipped open the door and then took a step back in shock. "Liddie?" Joselyn opened the door wider. "What are you doing here?"

Liddie stepped inside before Joselyn had enough time to question how the hell her brewery's receptionist was in this hotel two hours from Silvertip.

Liddie smiled too broadly. "I followed you."

"Why?" Joselyn shut the door but remained standing near it as Liddie wandered farther into the room.

When Liddie turned around and took a seat in the only chair in the room, she looked nervous. "I need your help."

"With what?" Joselyn's hair stood on end. Something was not right about this situation. She took a few steps forward before stopping again. It seemed prudent to keep her distance.

"You and your mate have messed up my plans. I need you to fix things."

Oh, yeah. This was not good. She considered reaching out to Alton but then thought better of it. Something told her it would be best if he didn't know what was happening yet.

Joselyn played along, pretending to be curious as she padded across the room and sat on the edge of the bed. "What did Alton and I do?"

Liddie cackled.

Joselyn had never heard that tone from her.

"Bad timing. I know you didn't mean to interfere in my relationship, but your binding commitment to Alton Tarben this week was inconvenient. And now I need your mate to help me reunite with mine."

Joselyn nodded as if in agreement. "And who is your mate?"

"Vinson Tarben." Liddie beamed. "You're not the only one in a relationship with a Tarben." She giggled next. "Doesn't it make you feel exhilarated sneaking around?"

Joselyn realized the girl thought they had something in common. Was that why she came to Joselyn for help? Joselyn was glad she hadn't reached out to Alton yet because she had no intention of involving him in this if things went south. He didn't need that kind of added stress when he was still two hours away or on the road driving. "What can I do to help?"

"I don't know where Vinson is. He left town two days ago right after the launch. And he hasn't contacted me."

Joselyn nodded again, trying to seem eager. *Vinson.* Interesting. Alton's not-so-mysteriously-missing cousin. "That sucks. He didn't tell you where he was going?"

Liddie shook her head. "No. He was supposed to take me with him. We had planned to bind and start a new life somewhere else where our packs weren't feuding, but I imagine he had to leave abruptly. I assume the Tarbens are hiding him."

Joselyn narrowed her gaze, trying to follow Liddie's line of thinking. "You think the Tarbens are hiding Vinson?"

"Yes. Of course." She looked confused, as if the idea weren't preposterous.

On second thought, what did Joselyn know? Maybe the Tarbens *were* hiding Vinson. If their pack was anywhere as close to imploding as the Arthur pack, anything was possible. "Why would they do that?" She needed to get deeper into Liddie's head.

She shrugged. "How should I know? Probably because the Arthurs got all upset with the release and thought they needed to blame someone."

"You don't think the Tarbens are responsible?" This was truly weird.

Liddie shook her head. "Just a coincidence is all. So what if they developed a similar product? It happens." She shrugged.

Joselyn licked her lips. "When did you meet Vinson?"

Liddie rambled on. "We've been together for months. We were going to bind as soon as this damn launch fiasco was over. Vinson's been working long hours to see the project to completion. I hardly ever get to see him anymore. He said as soon as this was over we would leave town."

"I see. That's exciting." Joselyn felt anything but excited. What she felt was concern over the mental stability of Liddie. She'd known Liddie for ten years, ever since the preteen had been taken into the pack when her parents died. She'd had no other family, and they'd been living in the area. As far as Joselyn knew, no one had ever had a single problem with Liddie.

But sometimes people made strange choices, especially if they thought they were in love.

Joselyn began to piece things together. "When exactly did you start seeing Vinson?" she asked, hoping she sounded genuinely curious.

Liddie glanced up and to the left, tapping her lips. "It was the day the first batch of Glacial Lemon was tested. I ran into him in town. He was so sexy. I had seen him before, but every time I saw him, I stammered over my words." She giggled at the memory.

Joselyn gave her a fake smile. "Where did you run into him?"

"Tipsy's. I was in line for the bathroom in the back hallway when he ran into me, causing me to stumble. He was so sweet, grabbing my shoulders to keep me from falling. I was a little tipsy myself." She sighed.

Joselyn said nothing, hoping Liddie would keep talking, lost in her story if Joselyn didn't interrupt her. Tipsy's was the only bar in town, aptly named not just for the drunken implications but because the owner thought it was a silly play on the name of the town, Silvertip.

Luckily, Liddie continued. "I took the chance to speak to him since I'd had enough to drink that my tongue was looser."

Joselyn could see where this was going. Somehow she was certain Liddie's loose tongue was the cause of all the commotion. "Were you drinking Glacial Lemon before you went to the bar?"

"Yes." Liddie's eyes danced. "And I loved it." She leaned forward, seeming almost as drunk now as she must have that night. "I might have mentioned it to Vinson." She scrunched up her nose. "I didn't think it would cause all this craziness just telling him the Arthurs were developing a new drink. Who cares?"

Just everyone in the pack, that's all. Joselyn fought the urge to strangle the stupid girl.

"For the first time in my life, a man was interested in me. And not just any man. A sexy god of a man."

"So you started dating?"

Liddie nodded. "In secret, of course. Though I think it's ridiculous how ingrained this weird feud is between the two packs."

259

At least they could agree on that point.

"Did you give him the mockup pictures for the launch ad?" Joselyn decided it was time to get blunt.

"Yeah. I probably shouldn't have done that, but it didn't matter. His brewery was already working on the same product. He told me so. He just wanted to see if our art looked as good as theirs."

I'll bet he did. How could any one person be so stupid as to fall for all this shit? Did Liddie honestly believe she could share trade secrets with her lover and Vinson wouldn't rush back to his pack to develop the same product at warp speed to beat Glacial to the finish line?

"Now everyone is acting like it's some big deal, screaming and yelling about a leak inside Glacial that helped Mountain Peak copy our drink." She laughed sardonically. "Lemon Peak. It's also delicious, by the way." She licked her lips and moaned around the imagined beverage.

Joselyn struggled to keep a straight face.

Liddie refocused. "Doesn't anyone see it was all just a coincidence? Mountain Peak was already making a similar lemon malt beverage. They just got lucky and released first." She snorted. "Who cares?"

Yes. This woman was indeed certifiable. But Joselyn didn't think she was dangerous. She considered asking her to leave but decided to point out the obvious. "Have you considered the possibility that Vinson was using you to get information?"

Liddie's face fell. "What? No. Of course not. Don't tell me you believe all this nonsense too."

Joselyn stared at her. How was she supposed to reason with this girl?

"Have you made contact with Alton yet? When is he supposed to get here?"

Joselyn had made no contact with Alton for over two hours. She couldn't imagine how Alton could help. And the last thing Joselyn wanted to do when he arrived was entertain this strange girl who had single-handedly caused so much turmoil, especially since she was so flaky she didn't even recognize her role in the disaster.

Liddie looked nervous.

"I don't know for sure when Alton's getting here. I haven't connected with him in a while. He was at work." *He might still be at work.*

She sat up straighter, looking alarmed. "But you're going to help me, right? You realize this is your fault, right?"

"I'm not sure how any of this is my fault. But I'm also not sure how Alton can help. He doesn't have any idea where Vinson is." It was possible Quint knew where his son was, but Joselyn doubted many other people knew. Undoubtedly Vinson was smarter than Liddie and fled town the moment the new product launched. He'd probably planned his escape for months. Since the beginning—the first time he spoke to Liddie.

At first, it seemed unlikely because it wasn't until Vinson disappeared that he became a suspect, but now that Joselyn had Liddie's story, she realized Vinson probably always intended to vanish after the launch, knowing this half-witted girl would rat him out eventually.

He was probably halfway to Europe by now. She was certain if there was a paper trace, she would find a stash of money had been set aside months ago for this exact date.

Joselyn needed to get rid of Liddie. She stood. "Listen, do you have a room at the hotel? If not, we can get you one. It's hard to know how long Alton will be, and I'm really tired. I was planning on napping until he got here. Let's get you a room, and I'll call you when he arrives."

Liddie was shaking her head. "No. You're just trying to trick me. You don't want to help me, do you?" She looked like she might cry.

"Of course not." Joselyn pasted a confused look on her face. "Why would I do that?" She took a step toward the door.

Liddie's face changed. Before Joselyn could react, Liddie reached into her purse and pulled out a gun. She lifted it toward Joselyn, her finger on the trigger.

Joselyn froze. *Dammit*. Was Liddie stable enough to avoid accidentally firing the damn gun?

"This is all your fault, you know. It didn't have to come to this. If you had just helped me out, I never would have had to use this."

Joselyn lifted her hands slightly. "Put the gun away, Liddie. You don't want anyone to get hurt."

Liddie shook her head. "No. I don't. So sit back down on the bed and make contact with Alton so he can tell me where Vinson is."

Joselyn backed up slowly. Her heart raced. *Fuck.* "Liddie, I'm telling you, Alton doesn't know where Vinson is. No one does. If they did, they would have spoken to him."

"Stop saying that," she shouted, her hand shaking. "The Tarbens have to know. I'm certain they've hidden him somewhere. He wouldn't leave me behind like this." Her voice rose higher.

Joselyn didn't want the gun to go off. The last thing they needed was for Liddie to shoot a hole in the wall and draw attention to them, possibly hurting someone in another room. She figured if she needed to, she could lurch forward and knock the gun out of Liddie's hand, but only as a last resort.

"Do it. Get Alton here. Now."

Joselyn nodded, lifting up a hand as she lowered herself onto the bed. "Okay. I'll get him." She considered her options. The last thing she wanted was to add her mate to this situation. He was two hours away. There was nothing he could do but worry and drive erratically. She didn't want to put his life in danger.

As if she'd conjured him, however, he was suddenly in her head. *"Hey, Jos."*

"Hey." She tried to sound as normal as possible in his head. She wouldn't tell him. She could easily reach out to her father for help. As pack leader, he could communicate with the Arcadian Council and get help faster than Alton, anyway.

"I'm so sorry. I'm just leaving the apartment now. You would not believe the day I've had. Where did you end up stopping?"

"That hotel with the Denny's outside of Calgary."

"Got it. The one we met at for your birthday." She could hear the smile in his communication.

"Yep."

"You sound tired."

Good. That's exactly what she wanted him to think. *"Exhausted. I just got here. I'm going to lie down for a while."*

"You should do that. It will take me two hours to get there. Sleep. I'll think of ways to wake you up when I arrive."

"Mmm. Sounds good."

"Okay, baby. See you in a while." The second she broke the connection, she knew Liddie was staring at her intently.

"What did he say? Is he almost here? Does he know where Vinson is?"

Joselyn shook her head. Alton was totally going to kill her, but at least he would be alive when he arrived, and she wouldn't have to add his funeral from a horrible car accident to her list of events for the week. "He's just leaving Silvertip. It will be a few hours. He doesn't know where Vinson is, but he'll ask around."

It occurred to Joselyn that Liddie was even more unstable if she thought it would be a good idea for Joselyn to tell someone two hours away that she was being held at gunpoint. Did she not realize Alton would send someone closer to get his mate out of this bind if she mentioned the hostage situation?

"Put the gun down, Liddie," she tried again. "You're not going to be able to hold it up like that for two hours, anyway." She slowly swung her legs onto the bed. "Like I said, I'm exhausted. I'm going to lie down and take a nap while we wait."

Liddie cocked her head. "Are you trying to trick me?"

"Why would I do that? I just completed the binding myself. I totally understand how frustrating it is to be separated from your mate. I was out of my mind before we finally took this step."

Liddie's face softened. "Then you understand." She nodded at the bed. "Fine. You nap. But if you hear anything new from Alton, you tell me immediately." She finally lowered the gun. Thank God.

"You have my word." Joselyn set her head on the pillow, lying on her side, facing Liddie. She pulled her knees up enough to appear to be comfortable, and then closed her eyes.

The entire nap was a ruse so that Joselyn could keep her eyes closed and it wouldn't be obvious to Liddie she was chatting with any number of people over the next two hours. None of them would be Alton, but that didn't mean she wasn't going to try to get some help.

Joselyn forced her body to relax to give Liddie the impression she was asleep, and then she reached out to her father. *Dad.*

"I'm here. You okay, honey? Did you leave town?"

"Yes. Listen, I have a problem."

"What is it?" He sounded alarmed in her head.

"Liddie followed me."

"Liddie? Our receptionist?"

"Yes. She's totally not in her right mind, Dad. She followed me all the way to my hotel outside of Calgary. She's the leak, Dad. She doesn't even realize how serious this is. She thinks the launch from Mountain Peak is a coincidence. She's the one who shared the details of our product with their brewery."

"Are you serious? She's always been such a sweet girl."

"Well, she's not."

"Who did she tell?"

"Vinson Tarben. He's Quint's son. Alton's cousin. And he's been missing since the launch, supposedly."

"What are you saying, Jos? Is Liddie there with you now?"

"Yes."

"What does she want?"

"Vinson. She's convinced he's her mate and that Alton can reunite them."

"Jos."

"Yes."

"What aren't you telling me?"

Joselyn tried to remain as still as possible. The hardest part was to keep her breathing slow and even. If she appeared to be stressed, Liddie would sense it in a heartbeat. *"She has a gun, Dad."*

Her father sighed. He wasn't the sort of man to go ballistic. That's why she'd chosen him. And it wasn't as if her family hadn't been through more than their fair share of drama lately. *"Is she in your room?"*

"Yes."

"How are you able to communicate with me so blatantly?"

"She thinks I'm napping."

"While she holds a gun to your head?" His voice rose in her mind. He was stressed. Concerned. As she'd known he would be.

"It was the easiest way to cover myself."

"Good point."

"Where's Alton?"

"On his way now. I didn't tell him."

"Okay, give me a second. Stay open to me." He broke his side of the connection.

She knew what he was doing, reaching out to someone from the Arcadian Council who might be closer to her.

He could also communicate with the leaders of other local packs, including Allister Tarben. Though she hoped everyone had the sense to keep Alton uninformed for a while. The last thing she wanted was for him to get in an accident because he was driving too fast.

"Jos?" Her father continued several moments later.

"Still here."

"The Council is checking to see if anyone's in the area. I'm going to get in touch with Allister now."

"Okay, but Dad..."

"Yeah, I know you well, honey. Don't let anyone tell Alton yet."

She smiled into his mind, hoping it didn't show on her face. There was no way for her to even peek at Liddie to see what she was doing without accidentally giving away the fact that Joselyn wasn't asleep.

Time moved so slowly it was painful. It was also impossible to keep track of how many minutes went by under the level of stress Joselyn was experiencing.

Finally, Joselyn decided to play another card. She pretended to awaken by stretching out and yawning. When she opened her eyes, she found Liddie staring at her, her eyes narrowed.

"I need to use the restroom."

Liddie shook her head. "No way."

Joselyn sat slowly. "Seriously, how will it hurt anything for me to pee, Liddie? It's not like I've stashed a weapon in there or can call the front desk. It's a toilet, Liddie."

Liddie looked doubtful, but she finally relented. "Fine. But you better be back in one minute."

Joselyn rose and padded over to the bathroom. As soon as she shut the door, she glanced around frantically, looking for anything that might help and coming up empty. She looked at her watch. It had been almost an hour. She needed a plan, and she needed to tell Alton soon. She didn't want him to walk in blindsided, but she also didn't want him to worry too early.

"*Jos?*" It was her mother.

"*Mom.*"

"*Honey, how are you holding up? What's happening?*"

"*Nothing has changed. I pretended to nap for a while.*"

"*Okay, your dad says two members of the Council are almost at the hotel. What's your room number?*"

"*Twenty-three nineteen.*"

"*Okay. Have you told Alton yet?*"

"*No. I'll do that now. Can you have the Council keep their distance for a bit? I want to try to reason with Liddie again first. Do my best to get the gun away from her without her possibly freaking out and discharging it.*"

"*Okay, honey. Be careful.*"

In reality, the two grizzlies from the Council could be standing right outside the door to the room, and neither Joselyn nor Liddie would be able to sense them. The Arcadian Council could block nearly any detection.

"*Joselyn Arthur.*" Alton's voice sounded in her head, irritated and freaked out. He'd used her full name. That wasn't a good sign.

She winced. *"Alton? What's wrong?"*

"What's wrong is that the mate I just bound myself to two days ago is already keeping shit from me. When I spanked your sweet bottom last night, I did so for sexual reasons. When I spank it tonight, it's going to be to knock some sense into you."

She grinned. And in spite of the dire circumstances she was in, she also got aroused. *"Can't wait. Now, where are you? I assume someone told you about Liddie?"*

"Only because I'm in the lobby downstairs with two council members who made me suspicious."

"Downstairs? How did you get here so fast?"

He sighed. *"Because I lied about how close I was when we last communicated. I wanted to surprise you. We'll discuss that later. What's the situation?"*

She quickly gave him the rundown as Liddie bellowed from the other room. "What the hell is taking so long, Joselyn?"

Joselyn reached over for the handle on the toilet and flushed. She then turned on the water and let it run a few seconds before shutting it off. "I'm coming, Liddie. Hang on," she called out.

Joselyn opened the door while communicating again with Alton. *"Give me a sec."*

"Joselyn..." he warned.

"Jesus, Liddie. I had to use the bathroom."

"Took you long enough," she muttered. "Find out how close Alton is, and see if he's found Vinson."

Joselyn nodded, letting her mind go to the connection Liddie would be able to notice when Joselyn's eyes got glassy. *"Okay. Liddie's asking me to see how far away you are and if you've made contact with your cousin."*

"If I had known for the last hour my mate was being held at gunpoint, maybe I would have been able to answer that question,

baby." He added the last word to soften his frustration. She knew him at least that well.

"*Alton, everyone in both our families has been working on this for an hour. There's nothing more you could have done from the car except crash it and leave me alone in the world. Can we argue about this later?*"

"*Believe me, we will. Now listen, no one knows where Vinson is. Or at least no one's willing to admit it. He might have operated on his own. I can tell you his place is cleared out, and he's probably nowhere nearby. I seriously doubt he ever intended to take your receptionist with him. She's lost a marble.*"

"*That's for sure.*"

"*Okay, I'm coming up.*"

"*You can't do that. She thinks you're still an hour away.*"

"*I drove fast.*"

Joselyn sighed, jerking out of the connection when Liddie interrupted. "What's he saying?"

"He's already here."

Liddie sat up taller, gripping the gun in her lap. "How did he get here so fast?"

"Apparently he missed me. He obviously broke the speed limit."

Liddie smiled. "That's cute. Is he coming to the room?"

"Yes."

Alton broke into her mind again. "*I'm going to knock on the door. Any chance you can let Liddie get it?*"

"*I'll try.*"

"*Okay, at least drop to the floor when I come in. These council members have weapons. They'd rather not use them, but they will if they need to.*"

"*Got it. I'll try to let you know who's opening the door.*"

Joselyn turned to Liddie. "You don't need that gun, Liddie. I suggest you put it away. Alton isn't going to respond well to you waving it around."

Liddie rolled her eyes. "I'm not an idiot, Jos. I know how to use a gun. And I'm also not stupid enough to think your mate will be willing to help me without a little incentive."

Joselyn sighed. "Okay, but I warned you." She backed up to the bed and sat on the side, putting some distance between her and the door.

Liddie stood and glanced at the door at the same time Joselyn scented her mate on the other side. What she didn't scent, and neither could Liddie, was the two other men out there. Now was the perfect time for members of the Arcadian Council to exercise their ability to block their scent from anyone they wanted.

"Get the door," Liddie said. "Let him in."

"You open it, Liddie. You make me nervous swinging that damn gun around."

Liddie rolled her eyes again and stomped the few steps it took to reach the handle. She held the gun in her other hand letting it hang at her side.

"Liddie's opening the door. Gun in her left hand, pointed down," Joselyn rapidly communicated.

The second the door opened, Liddie gasped, undoubtedly shocked to find three men instead of one on the other side. She lifted the gun but never had a chance to use it because Alton leaped forward, swung his arm through the air, and knocked the gun out of her hand. It went flying across the room.

Two seconds after that, he had her in his grip while all three men pushed their way into the room and shut the door. The last thing they wanted was for anyone in the hallway to know what was happening. Most of the people in the vicinity were humans. The Arcadian Council worked hard to ensure grizzly shifters were kept a secret from all other beings.

Alton handed Liddie off to one of the two men with him and hurried across the room toward Joselyn. "You okay?" he asked as he grabbed her by the face to meet her gaze.

"Yeah. Took you long enough," she teased.

He rolled his eyes. "We're going to have a long chat about your decision to keep things from me, Jos. Later."

"Looking forward to it." She grinned and then lifted onto her toes to kiss his lips.

CHAPTER 22

Alton shut the door to the hotel room half an hour later, leaving no one but himself and his mate inside the room. It hadn't taken much to convince Liddie she was in serious trouble and needed to walk out of the hotel into the custody of the Arcadian Council without causing a scene.

He turned around and stalked toward his mate. "You want to switch rooms? Or even hotels?"

"Why would we do that?"

"This place smells like your crazy receptionist."

Joselyn giggled, reaching for him as he closed the distance. "I don't want to take the time to do either one of those things. I need you naked on top of me about two minutes ago. I'm wondering why it's taking you so long. They've been gone for almost thirty seconds."

He smirked. If the scent didn't bother her, he wasn't going to let it bother him. He intended to drown it completely out with their rampant pheromones before they had a chance to take many more breaths.

"I should be mad at you," he stated, unable to put any

oomph behind his words. He was so damn glad she wasn't hurt, it was hard to remain angry.

"Probably, but I was only thinking about your safety, Alton." She grabbed his shirt and tugged him until their torsos were lined up and touching. "I alerted my dad. He contacted your dad and the Council. Everyone was working on it. The only thing you could have contributed was causing more stress for everyone if they had to worry about you too."

"I would have driven faster."

"My point exactly."

"You were here alone with that woman for over an hour." He shuddered. She was right. He would have freaked out and made things worse for her, but he still didn't like his mate keeping him in the dark on something this important. "Don't ever do something like this again, Jos. If you're in danger, I want to know."

"Hey, you lied to me too. You said you were just leaving the apartment when you were already halfway here."

He flattened himself to her front, threaded his hand through the hair at the base of her ponytail, and gave a slight tug. "You can't seriously compare my desire to surprise my mate with candy and roses to a crazed lunatic waving a gun in her face."

"Where's the candy and roses?" She gave him a huge fake smile, ignoring the point entirely.

"Metaphorical."

She switched to a fake pout. "And you promised me a spanking too. You going to renege on that now also?"

He rolled his eyes. "It would seem, based on the scent of your arousal, that a spanking would not be a deterrent to you no matter how hard I swatted your sweet bottom."

"Probably not, but you could try."

"Another time. I have something else in mind for

tonight." He lowered his lips to hers to shut her up and change the tone. He'd been scared out of his mind when he arrived and found those two council members in the lobby. She was right about one thing—he would have freaked the fuck out driving for an hour knowing a lunatic was holding a gun to his mate. He'd never admit it, but she was probably right about not telling him.

Now all that fear needed an outlet, and he intended to expend it by fucking.

She moaned into his mouth, and he swallowed the sweet sound of her voice. Her hands crawled up his back under his shirt, grounding him and reminding him she was his and she was safe.

He'd meant to arrive at the hotel and finally slow things down a bit. They'd been bound together for two days, and every time they'd had sex so far had been in a rush of need that never abated. His plan for the evening, now that they were no longer anywhere near Silvertip and everything happening between their families, had been a slow seduction that ended with soft, gentle lovemaking all night long. Neither of them needed to work tomorrow. They could take their time. They could stay several nights. Whatever they wanted.

But now? Things were different. Now he wanted to fuck her hard to remind himself she was real and alive. His cock was demanding. And her desperate scent equaled his, filling the room with her pheromones. Slow and gentle was no longer on the menu.

She broke the kiss, gasping for air as she trailed kisses down his face, rapid nibbles that sometimes accompanied scrapes of her teeth as she lowered to his neck.

He released her hair and stepped back. "Clothes off. Now."

She held his gaze as she divested herself of every stitch while he did the same.

And then he grabbed her waist and lifted her onto the bed, shoving her back several feet and then climbing between her legs. He inhaled deeply, his eyes fluttering as the feminine scent of her sex was more fully unveiled.

He pressed his cock to her entrance, holding her head with both hands. "You need more preparation, baby?" His voice was hoarse. He wanted to be inside her. Now.

"No. Alton, God. No." She lifted her hips to his.

He thrust forward so hard she gasped, her mouth falling open. Her eyes rolled back in her head, and he searched her mind to find pure bliss. Nothing more. No hesitation. Not an ounce of hesitation.

This new rougher side of her was heady and attractive. He was going to have to come up with creative ways to fulfill her lust for dominance. Wouldn't be a problem. He had a duffle bag full of new toys with him, including the ropes and blindfold he'd threatened her with. Before they left this hotel room, he intended to make use of at least half the items in the bag.

When he pulled halfway out and slammed back into her, all train of thought fled. Nothing felt better than having his mate wrapped around his cock. And it was inconceivable, but the sensation was so much more intense now that she was his in every way.

No matter what happened in the coming weeks and months, he would never regret binding himself permanently to Joselyn Arthur.

The rest of the world could go to hell as far as he was concerned.

All that mattered was being with his woman. Every day. Anytime he wanted. As often as possible.

CHAPTER 23

Three days later…

"Are you nervous?" Alton asked his mate as they pulled up to his parents' home.

She had been chewing on her lip for most of the two-hour drive. "Yes. But only because I don't feel like dealing with this. I would rather have driven the other direction and never returned to Silvertip, to be honest."

He chuckled, squeezing the hand he hadn't released for the entire drive. After days of having her twenty-four seven with almost no moments of separation, he still felt the urge to keep one hand on her at all times. He intended to continue to do so even in his parents' home. Anyone who thought they might split the two of them up was in for a surprise.

A dozen cars out front told him there were a lot of people inside. Half of them were from her family and half from his. He was glad they were all together in one place.

He just hoped they all had good intentions. He wasn't in the mood for a brawl.

He put the SUV in park and turned off the engine, turning toward Joselyn to take her in for another moment before he had to open the door and step into the cold. "If anyone gets on our nerves, or you're done with the shenanigans, say the word and we're out of here."

"You too," she returned.

He released her long enough to exit the SUV and round the front, and then he had her hand again.

With a deep breath, he led her into the house, and they greeted more people than he expected before they made it two steps inside. One by one, members of both families congratulated them on their binding as if they were in a receiving line.

He was glad to see some family he hadn't been previously sure stood by him. But the looks on their faces and their kind words told him he'd either miscalculated, or they'd had a change of heart.

The same was true of Joselyn's pack. He had no way of being sure what side any particular member stood when push came to shove, but judging by her subtle reactions to a few people, he had to guess she was as shocked by some of their appearances as he was.

After about a half an hour of greeting people, his father finally lifted a hand, whistled through his teeth, and created a hush. In his booming voice, he instructed everyone to have a seat.

People lowered themselves onto every imaginable surface, including the floor.

Alton's mother pointed to a loveseat she'd guarded for the two of them, and he led Joselyn to the center of the room to take a seat with her by his side. Her parents were in the chair next to them, her mother obviously so glad to see her daughter that she never stopped smiling.

Allister started talking. "I want to thank everyone for coming here tonight, especially the members of the Arthur pack. Welcome. All of you."

Several people clapped.

When the noise died down, he spoke again, aiming his gaze at Alton and Joselyn. "A lot has happened in the past few days, and we thought it would be easiest to explain everything to the two of you in a group. Besides, not all of us are completely informed, either."

Alton nodded. "Thank you. We appreciate the love and support we feel tonight from all of you. It's been rough making the decision to bind, and knowing those who matter most to us have our backs means the world." He held Joselyn's hand over his thigh, squeezing her fingers as he spoke.

"That was lovely, Alton. Thank you," she said into his head.

"Anyway," Allister continued. "Like I said, this week has been a week of meetings that followed meetings. Some were held inside Mountain Peak. Some behind the closed doors of Glacial. But others were held in this living room and at Bernard's home too. This is a big week for both our families and our extended pack members." Allister turned toward Bernard. "Wouldn't you agree?"

Bernard nodded. "Yes. We've made progress, healed old wounds, and forged new friendships."

Allister spoke again after everyone finished clapping. "Although it seemed insurmountable just a few days ago, believe it or not, many members of both packs have put their differences aside and have decided to let the past remain in the past.

"We recognize that a hundred years ago there were

many disagreements over land and water. But the reality is that most of us own property now, and water is a commodity that can no longer be stolen. We may in the not too distant future have a shortage of water from the melting of the Athabasca Glacier, but that isn't something that can be blamed on either pack. We'll both have to cross that bridge when we come to it."

Alton listened closely, knowing what his father would have to address next.

Allister sighed, his shoulders dropping an inch. "Yes, two little boys fought one morning over a century ago, and one was mortally injured. That's a horror no family should ever have to face from either perspective. The fact that retaliation was sought and achieved is not something anyone is proud of, either. However, if we want to prevent something like that from ever happening again, we have a responsibility to our offspring to be good role models. The bickering has to stop."

Alton was a little surprised to see a small smile on his father's face that seemed out of place.

But when Allister spoke again, he realized why. "My children are reaching an age where they're binding. That means I hope to have grandchildren filling this house in the near future. They will be raised in homes filled with love and laughter." He sobered. "We can change. We can make a difference. We can raise the next generation to drop this hatred and let the past rest where it belongs."

Someone cheered. Someone else joined. And then there was clapping.

Allister lifted a hand. He wasn't done. "And more importantly, I never again in my lifetime want to hear a tale of two star-crossed lovers denying themselves their right to bind over fear of reprimand from either family."

Allister smiled at his Romeo and Juliet reference. Several members of both families laughed. The cheering resumed.

Alton hoped what his father was saying would henceforth ring true. He glanced around the room, wondering if anyone else was in a secret relationship.

Allister continued, lifting a hand again to quiet the room. "Bernard has a few things to say also."

Joselyn's father stood, keeping his hand on his mate's shoulder as he rounded behind her and spoke to the group. "Early this week I experienced something I never expected to see in my lifetime. Several members of my pack, including two of my brothers, turned on me. Like a mob, they demanded a vote be taken, hoping to overturn my position as both CEO of Glacial but also pack leader."

A hush fell across the room as several people were probably hearing this for the first time.

"After numerous heated meetings, emotions running high, those of us who disagreed managed to convince the majority of the dissenters that this absurd feud was ruining lives and tearing our pack apart from the inside out. Luckily all talk of my removal has died down, and things will return to normal."

Claps resounded once again.

Bernard continued when things quieted down. "In addition, as planned, Glacial Brewing Company will be launching the new Glacial Citrus line, Glacial Lemon and Glacial Orange, Monday. The healthy competition will benefit both breweries."

Another round of claps and some cheers.

Alton smiled. This was going better than he could have expected.

Surprising Alton, his mother stood next to her mate, wrapping an arm around his middle before looking directly at Alton and then speaking. "We feel awful that the two of you were chased from your hometown. And although we realize you might want to forge your own path in another land, we hope you'll consider returning someday, sooner rather than later.

"The land reserved for you that is your birthright won't be touched by anyone else. When you're ready, it belongs to you and your sweet mate, Joselyn." She shot a warm smile at Joselyn who squeezed Alton's fingers so hard it hurt.

He felt her rising emotions from within, knowing it was a struggle to keep from crying.

"Thank you, Beth," she whispered. "That means a lot to us."

Alton addressed his father next. "Has anyone seen Vinson?"

Allister sighed. "Unfortunately, no. And we also have no way of knowing if he was working alone or had inside help. If anyone was aiding him, they covered their tracks well."

Unspoken was Vinson's father's name. Any help Vinson had from within would have come from Quint, who was not present at tonight's gathering. Not surprising. Alton's Uncle Espen was also absent, as were two of Joselyn's uncles. The divide still existed, but at least many people were stepping out of the shadows and rejecting old disagreements.

Allister continued. "Unfortunately, Liddie from the Arthur pack is in the custody of the Council. She might have had innocent intentions and believed Vinson was her mate, but she'll remain under their care, being questioned for the time being. She was in possession of a firearm and using it to threaten others. Also, she held Joselyn hostage for over an hour.

"The Arcadian Council is on the lookout for Vinson,

but stealing company secrets is not high on their radar. I seriously doubt he ever had any honorable intentions toward Liddie. He had saved a great deal of money over the years and wiped out his bank account before he fled Silvertip."

One of Alton's cousins asked a question. "Does anyone know if his father gave him any other money?"

"No. At least Quint isn't willing to admit so. It's still possible."

"Then why go to so much effort to steal company secrets from the competitor if he didn't benefit from it in the long run?" the same cousin followed up with.

Allister nodded. "We may never know. Perhaps he had hoped to never be discovered and reap the benefits of company bonuses for a job well done. In any case, my gut tells me he's long gone and won't return to this part of the country.

"It's unfortunate that things escalated to the point they did over the past week, and I'm still saddened to think how long my son lived in secret, hurting more than most of us can imagine before admitting that Joselyn was his mate.

"I'm glad to know they're together now, and I'm sure everyone in the room will be happy to raise a beer in toast to their future."

The majority of hands lifted into the air when Allister raised his beer.

Someone put a bottle in Alton's hand while someone else slid one into Joselyn's. Alton smiled when he noticed they'd each been given one of their other pack's selection. Apropos.

A collective shout of *cheers* rang throughout the room before Allister declared that the real party should begin.

For the next several hours, Alton—with Joselyn always

plastered to his side—made his rounds, greeting family and meeting new. His heart was full.

He knew by mutual agreement neither he nor his mate was ready to rush back to Silvertip, but maybe someday they could return.

Alton had every intention of claiming his property and building on it one day, but that day was not now.

EPILOGUE

Two weeks later...

"Jos, slow down." Alton looked up from where he sat on the couch in their newly rented home on the outskirts of Calgary. The place was perfect for them. The owners were grizzly shifters from a neighboring pack who were looking for renters while they went on an eight-month sabbatical.

The fact that Alton and Joselyn had been staying in a local hotel suite and met the other couple by coincidence while out getting coffee one morning still gave Alton the chills. Joselyn called it divine intervention.

Stanton and Oleta Osborn had invited Alton and Joselyn to join them at their table. The coffee shop was crowded, and they'd been kind—largely because they recognized fellow grizzly shifters.

Alton had instantly found the older couple to be warm and friendly, and their faces lit up with excitement when Joselyn explained how she and Alton had recently decided to relocate in the area and were looking for housing.

Within hours, a contract was signed, and two days ago Alton and his mate found themselves living in a lovely furnished home. The rent was set ridiculously low in exchange for the two of them agreeing to maintain the place and make sure the walls were still standing when the Osborns returned to the country.

Stanton and Oleta were in their late fifties, and they had a daughter Joselyn's age who lived nearby but had no interest in keeping up her parents' home while they were away.

Joselyn was still bustling around like she was on fire, making Alton chuckle. "Babe, it's your brother, for heaven's sake. I don't think he cares how tidy the house is. I don't think he'll even notice."

She shot him a glare. "This is the first time any member of my family has visited me in my own home. I don't care who it is—we're not leaving dishes in the sink and clothes strewn around the house."

Alton glanced around from his spot on the couch. Not a single thing appeared out of place, but he wasn't going to tease her anymore. He understood.

A car pulled into the driveway, and Joselyn's face lit up. "He's here."

Alton stood to follow his mate to the door. She had it open and was standing in the threshold before Wyatt stepped out of the car.

Alton hadn't spent much time with Wyatt yet, but every time Alton saw him, he was reminded how intimidating the man could appear. With his height, six-seven, and his build, he would stop many people in their tracks—especially non-shifters. But as Wyatt approached the front porch, Alton remembered his stature was only one aspect of Wyatt Arthur.

He had wavy dark hair that he wore slightly longer

than most would. It dipped over his forehead, causing him to run his fingers through it often or shake it away from his face. And his smile. No wonder Joselyn had always adored him. He lit up a room with his warmth.

"Hey, Jos," Wyatt said as he stepped into her space and gave her a big hug. He reached out a hand to Alton next and gave a firm shake. "You gonna have me inside? Or shall we stand in the cold?" he teased.

Joselyn swatted at him and backed into the entrance where Alton had already moved out of the way. "Come in."

Wyatt glanced around as he stepped inside. "Love it. Did you say you're renting it from Stanton and Oleta Osborn?"

"Yes. Do you know them?" Joselyn asked.

Wyatt nodded. "I've met them a few times. They're professors at U of C, right?"

"Yes. Literature and history," Alton confirmed. "Neither Jos nor I ever had them in school."

Wyatt wandered to the mantel and picked up a family photo. He tapped it with one finger. "That's right. They have a son and two daughters. I've met the oldest, Nolan, a few times. He's a few years younger than me. Isaiah's age. I think Isaiah met him at U of C. He has an accounting degree if I remember correctly."

Joselyn headed toward the fridge. "Huh. Small world. I've never heard of them before now, but you're right. Their daughters are Ryann and Paige. Paige is my age. She lives close by. I haven't met Ryann or Nolan yet."

Alton grabbed two of the bottles Joselyn handed him and passed one to Wyatt. "Sit. Tell us what's going on at home." He twisted the lid off his bottle and took a drink.

Wyatt lowered his huge frame onto one end of the couch and took a long drink of his beer, smirking when he glanced at the bottle.

Alton chuckled. "You can switch back and forth. We have a selection from both breweries."

"How's Mom?" Joselyn asked, taking a seat next to Alton on the loveseat when he grabbed her hand. They'd been together for two weeks without leaving each other's sides often, and he still felt the need to have contact with her.

Wyatt swirled his beer around in the bottle. "She's okay. Tries to stay strong. I know she won't admit it when she communicates with you, but she misses you."

Joselyn leaned into Alton. "It's weird. Even though I was gone for five years, living back at home for the last two years brought us closer together."

Wyatt smiled. "Especially since you had so much time on your hands. Now we all know why you were such a homebody and not out scouring the town for a mate."

"At least I had Mom and Dad. Alton was alone in his apartment." She burrowed closer to him.

"Any luck finding jobs?" Wyatt asked.

Alton shrugged. "We weren't in a big hurry. I went on an interview this week, but I'm not sure it's the right fit."

"I'm sure you'll find something," Wyatt said. "This close to Calgary, you have so many options."

"Yes."

"Any chance you'll consider coming back to Silvertip?" Wyatt asked.

Joselyn snorted. "And face Uncle Carroll and Uncle Jaren? I'm gonna need a bit more time and space from them before I'm willing to step into the brewery again. They were very nasty, and our cousins on that side of the family make me cringe."

Wyatt nodded. "I can totally understand. They haven't changed, but fortunately their attitudes aren't shared by the majority. Dad's working with them. He's hoping to get them to see reason. I can see the strain on Dad's face every day. He wants to throttle them for forcing his daughter out of town."

Alton nodded. "My father feels the same way. His two youngest brothers are making him crazy with their incessant need to hold on to this ancient grudge."

Wyatt sighed. "Luckily the nastiness isn't as apparent in the next generation. Time will heal this rift. I'm hopeful. But finding another marketing manager, now that's another thing," he joked, turning his gaze back to his sister.

Joselyn laughed. "Too bad."

Wyatt glanced at his beer and then back at Joselyn. "We want you two to be able to come back to Silvertip. Even if you don't return to the brewery, at least you'd be nearby. Mom will be so sad when you have kids."

"Maybe someday," Alton responded. "But for now, we're enjoying the distance. Less stress."

"I understand."

A car door shut outside, making all three of them glance at the front door. Moments later Alton recognized the new arrival as the Osborn's youngest daughter. He stood and headed for the door as Wyatt lifted an eyebrow.

Joselyn responded to his unasked question. "Paige. The one who's my age. She has her own apartment. She still has some stuff here. Probably forgot something."

"Why isn't *she* living in her parents' home while they're away?" Wyatt asked.

"She already had a lease when her parents found out their sabbatical was approved. She's working on her masters at U of C. She wanted her independence, so she decided not to break her lease. Lucky for us."

Alton opened the front door before Paige was close enough to knock. "Hey. What's up?" He stepped back to let her in.

She was breathless as she spoke rapidly. "Sorry to bother you guys. I can't find a book I need anywhere in my apartment. I'm hoping I left it here. I hope you don't mind. I didn't mean to interrupt your evening." She stepped fully into the house, still speaking. "I don't want you guys to think I'm always going to be over here bugging you or anything." Her gaze landed on Wyatt. "*Oh,* hello."

Alton shut the front door and turned to find Wyatt's eyes a bit wide, his lips parted, and his face a little pale. It only lasted a moment, but it was long enough for Alton to catch the attraction.

Paige licked her lips and glanced away. The twenty-four-year-old woman who rarely stopped talking was suddenly mute. Silence filled the room for several seconds.

Finally, Wyatt pushed to standing and stepped around the coffee table. He reached out with a hand to shake hers. "I don't believe we've met. Wyatt Arthur. Joselyn is my sister."

Paige's voice was low and calm and slow when she responded. "Paige Osborn. My parents own this house." She didn't make eye contact and flinched when Wyatt touched her.

Wyatt nodded, ignoring her reaction. "I've met them a few times, and your older brother Nolan."

Alton glanced at Joselyn in confusion. What was up with Paige? He'd never seen her so flustered. She turned pale and looked like she'd rather be anywhere else in the world.

If Wyatt noticed her discomfort, he didn't let on. Instead, he pointed at the couch he'd vacated. "Please sit. Join us. I just got here myself. I have a meeting tomorrow in Calgary, so I came this evening to visit my sister and see this fabulous place she and Alton have been talking about renting."

Paige backed into the door, grabbed the handle, and pulled it open. She never lifted her gaze as she spoke. "Sorry. I just realized where that book is." She slapped her forehead. "It's in my trunk. I've got a lot of work to do tonight. Sorry to bother you guys." A second later, she was out the door and rushing toward her car. She didn't even realize she'd left it standing open. Alton grabbed the doorframe, watching her reach her car.

"Was it something I said?" Wyatt asked.

Joselyn rushed over to join her mate, leaning around him to watch Paige pull away. "I don't know what that was all about, but I've never seen Paige act so strangely."

Alton glanced again at Wyatt, who was rubbing his forehead with his palm as he lowered himself back onto the couch. He didn't speak as he picked up his beer and chugged the rest of it.

There was definitely a story behind this weird encounter, but Alton didn't think tonight was the night to bring it up with Wyatt. Instead, he closed the door and ushered his mate back to the couch. *"We need to change the subject."*

"Apparently," she said into his mind before addressing her brother out loud. "So, how long did you say you're staying?"

AUTHOR'S NOTE

I hope you've enjoyed this third book in the Arcadian Bears series. Please enjoy the following excerpt from the next book in the series, *Grizzly Promise.*

GRIZZLY PROMISE

ARCADIAN BEARS, BOOK FOUR

Gavin was late. It wasn't like him. He was never late. He was early. Even at fourteen years old, he knew he was more mature than his peers and had high standards for himself. He shared those values and several others with his best friend, Paige, which was why he was pissed with himself for being late to meet her.

He was out of breath as he ran between the trees toward their meeting spot—a tree house of sorts they'd built when they were ten with the help of their fathers. It could only marginally be considered a tree house since it was only a few feet off the ground, and though it did include a large tree trunk, the majority of it was on stilts. It was nestled in the thick grove of trees behind the houses on their quiet street along the Bow River just west of Calgary, Alberta.

It wasn't anything fancy, but it was theirs, and theirs alone.

Voices ahead of him caused him to stop short and lift his gaze. He was still twenty yards from the tree house, evergreens blocking his direct view, but he sucked in a breath when a man jumped to the ground and spun around to shout at the entrance. "You're nothing but a tease, you little cunt. You hear me?"

Gavin's knees nearly buckled, and he couldn't get his legs to move forward. Scared out of his mind, he crouched behind a thick bush so the guy wouldn't see him.

From behind, all he saw was thick brown hair on the largest human he'd ever seen. He had to be at least six and a half feet tall and built. He lifted an arm, pointed a finger at the entrance, and shouted again. "You tell anyone about this, and I'll kill both your parents. You wanted to be grown up. We'll see how well you do on your own."

Gavin couldn't breathe. He needed to run forward. Do something. Anything. Go for help?

No, he couldn't leave Paige, and he knew she was inside the tree house. No way in hell would he leave her there alone.

A loud roar focused his attention again on the man as the unimaginable happened right before his eyes. The behemoth tipped his head back, shouted unintelligibly at the sky, and then fell forward onto all fours in slow motion. As his body angled toward the ground, he freaking transformed into an enormous bear.

Gavin fell backward onto his ass, his eyes wide, his skin clammy, sweat beading on his forehead even though it was cold outside. He had to be mistaken.

Where once a tall man had stood, there was now an equally gigantic bear. A bear who spun back to the tree house and approached on all fours. He lifted both front paws and roared again, leaning toward the entrance. And then, just as fast, he dropped to the ground and spun around. Gavin could swear he looked right at him before he loped off into the trees.

Gavin blinked several times. He had to have imagined

the entire thing. There were no bears in this part of the province. And there certainly weren't humans who could become bears.

Jerking himself back to reality, he scrambled to right himself and push to standing. And then he ran full-out the rest of the way to the tree house, chest pounding, his entire body on high alert.

Leaping onto the platform that served as a porch, he nearly tripped and fell into the single room that made up their hideaway.

What met his eyes made him freeze in the doorway.

Paige—his best friend in the world and the only person who would ever truly know him and understand him—was pressed into the corner of the room. She screamed when he came into view, and then her voice lowered to a whimper when she focused on him. She was in a tight ball, holding her favorite blue cardigan around her shaking body. Her face was covered with tears, and her hair was a mess of long blonde locks hanging limply along her cheeks.

She dragged her knees up closer to her chest as Gavin dropped to his knees several feet from her. His heart beat rapidly, but he couldn't seem to speak. *I was late. I was late. I was late.*

He inhaled deeply, trying to calm himself so he could help her, but all that did was drag the scent of sweat and alcohol and...sex into his lungs. He might not have been able to identify the smell of sex before now, but there was no mistaking it.

When Paige lowered her face to set her forehead on her knees, she started to cry. She gulped, sobbing hysterically.

He inched forward on his hands and knees. "Paige?"

She cringed, pulling tighter into the corner, but didn't acknowledge him otherwise. Her knees were scraped and bleeding. Her fingers, wrapped tightly around her legs, were white from the effort, the nail beds dark. From what? Blood? Dirt?

Oh God. Where were her pants? Gavin jerked his gaze to find her pants, torn and dirty, tossed in another corner. He cringed when he noticed her underwear lying ripped next to them.

Fury he'd never felt in his life filled him. He wanted to scream. He wanted to jump to his feet, run from the tree house, and find that man. Man? Someone had hurt Paige.

Instead, he found an inner strength he didn't know he had and hadn't ever needed to tap into in his fourteen years and pulled himself together. "Paige, we need to get help. You need a doctor."

She jerked her face up to meet his gaze, shaking her head. "No." One word. Sharp. Definite.

"Paige…" She was bleeding. Hurt.

Raped.

He swallowed. His head was swimming with so many confusing thoughts. There was a man. He raped Paige. There was a bear…

She shook her head again more violently. "You can't tell anyone. Ever."

"Paige…"

She uncurled from her ball and leaned forward, placing her hand on top of his where he remained on all fours facing her. "Never. Promise me, Gavin. Never. You can never tell anyone about this." Her voice cracked from screaming. From crying. From lost innocence.

He blinked at her. Why wouldn't she want to tell anyone?

Her eyes were wide and wild as she searched his gaze. "Promise me, Gavin."

"Why?"

"Because. Because. Just because. Promise me," she yelled. New tears fell. Her face was red. Her eyes were swollen. How long had she been here with that madman, tortured by him while…? *I was late.*

"Paige," he pleaded. He hated this plan. She was his best friend. Hurting. Physically and emotionally. She needed help from an adult. She couldn't expect him to keep this secret.

She stopped crying abruptly, stiffening. Her entire demeanor changed in an instant, and she crawled across the room to grab her panties.

Gavin glanced away when she stood on wobbly legs to put them on. Bile rose in his throat as he caught her shrugging into her pants in his peripheral vision.

Her hands were shaking, but her tears were dry now. She came back to him as he sat back on his ass and wrapped his hands around his knees, rocking back and forth. For a moment he felt every ounce of pain she should be feeling even though she'd snapped out of her horror to replace it with something unrecognizable.

Cold seeped into his skin. Not from the temperature but from her behavior. He opened his mouth, but she stopped him with an outstretched hand as she lowered to sit facing him and pulled on her shoes. Even her knuckles were bleeding.

She started to ramble. "I fell from a tree. We climbed out too far on the branch behind the tree house, and I fell."

He stared at her.

She didn't meet his gaze as she tied her sneakers. And then she lifted her head again. "Gavin, I fell from a tree."

He nodded, unable to think clearly.

For a long time, they sat there in the cold. Finally, he found words. "Paige, there was a bear… That man… He…"

She turned whiter if that were possible. And then she shook her head. "Forget you saw that."

He nodded again if only to keep her from slipping into a deeper level of despair.

She rambled on. "We'll talk about it later, okay?"

"Sure." He didn't even know what he saw. Surely his mind was playing tricks on him. But her words confirmed the deceitful images. A bear? She wanted him to forget that he saw a bear?

She seemed on the edge of hysteria.

He needed to steer the conversation back to her. "Paige, why can't we tell anyone?"

"I don't want anyone to know. Ever."

"But this is a horrible thing to keep to yourself. It will eat you up inside. You need professional help. Your parents—"

She cut him off with a sharp chortle. "Who are you to decide what secrets should be kept? Huh?"

He swallowed hard.

She leaned toward him. "I keep *your* secret. It's a horrible thing to keep to *yourself*. It's eating *you* up inside. You need professional help too. *Your* parents should know." As she reiterated his own words back to him, he nearly died inside.

She was right.

She was also so very wrong.

"Promise me, Gavin."

"Okay, I promise."

ALSO BY BECCA JAMESON

Open Skies:

Layover

Redeye

Nonstop

Standby

Canyon Springs:

Caleb's Mate

Hunter's Mate

Corked and Tapped:

Volume One: Friday Night

Volume Two: Company Party

Volume Three: The Holidays

Surrender:

Raising Lucy

Teaching Abby

Leaving Roman

Choosing Kellen

Pleasing Josie

Project DEEP:

Reviving Emily

Reviving Trish

Reviving Dade

Reviving Zeke

Reviving Graham

Reviving Bianca

Reviving Olivia

Project DEEP Box Set One

Project DEEP Box Set Two

SEALs in Paradise:

Hot SEAL, Red Wine

Hot SEAL, Australian Nights

Hot SEAL, Cold Feet

Dark Falls:

Dark Nightmares

Club Zodiac:

Training Sasha

Obeying Rowen

Collaring Brooke

Mastering Rayne

Trusting Aaron

Claiming London

Sharing Charlotte

Taming Rex

Tempting Elizabeth

Club Zodiac Box Set One

Club Zodiac Box Set Two

The Art of Kink:

Pose

Paint

Sculpt

Arcadian Bears:

Grizzly Mountain

Grizzly Beginning

Grizzly Secret

Grizzly Promise

Grizzly Survival

Grizzly Perfection

Arcadian Bears Box Set One

Arcadian Bears Box Set Two

Sleeper SEALs:

Saving Zola

Spring Training:

Catching Zia

Catching Lily

Catching Ava

Spring Training Box Set

The Underground series:

Force

Clinch

Guard

Submit

Thrust

Torque

The Underground Box Set One

The Underground Box Set Two

Saving Sofia (Special Forces: Operations Alpha)

Wolf Masters series:

Kara's Wolves

Lindsey's Wolves

Jessica's Wolves

Alyssa's Wolves

Tessa's Wolf

Rebecca's Wolves

Melinda's Wolves

Laurie's Wolves

Amanda's Wolves

Sharon's Wolves

Wolf Masters Box Set One

Wolf Masters Box Set Two

Claiming Her series:

The Rules

The Game

The Prize

Emergence series:

Bound to be Taken

Bound to be Tamed

Bound to be Tested

Bound to be Tempted

Emergence Box Set

The Fight Club series:

Come

Perv

Need

Hers

Want

Lust

The Fight Club Box Set One

The Fight Club Box Set Two

Wolf Gatherings series:

Tarnished

Dominated

Completed

Redeemed

Abandoned

Betrayed

Wolf Gatherings Box Set One

Wolf Gathering Box Set Two

Durham Wolves series:

Rescue in the Smokies

Fire in the Smokies

Freedom in the Smokies

Stand Alone Books:

Blind with Love

Guarding the Truth

Out of the Smoke

Abducting His Mate

Three's a Cruise

Wolf Trinity

Frostbitten

A Princess for Cale/A Princess for Cain

ABOUT THE AUTHOR

Becca Jameson is a USA Today best-selling author of over 100 books. She is well-known for her Wolf Masters series, her Fight Club series, and her Club Zodiac series. She currently lives in Houston, Texas, with her husband and her Goldendoodle. Two grown kids pop in every once in a while too! She is loving this journey and has dabbled in a variety of genres, including paranormal, sports romance, military, and BDSM.

A total night owl, Becca writes late at night, sequestering herself in her office with a glass of red wine and a bar of dark chocolate, her fingers flying across the keyboard as her characters weave their own stories.

During the day--which never starts before ten in the morning!--she can be found jogging, running errands, or reading in her favorite hammock chair!

...where Alphas dominate...

Becca's Newsletter Sign-up

Join my Facebook fan group, Becca's Bibliomaniacs, for the most up-to-date information, random excerpts while I work, giveaways, and fun release parties!

Facebook Fan Group:
Becca's Bibliomaniacs

Contact Becca:

www.beccajameson.com
beccajameson4@aol.com

facebook.com/becca.jameson.18
twitter.com/beccajameson
instagram.com/becca.jameson
bookbub.com/authors/becca-jameson
goodreads.com/beccajameson
amazon.com/author/beccajameson

Printed in Great Britain
by Amazon